Summer's End

OLIVIA MILES

ROSEWOOD PRESS

ISBN: 979-8986262482 (print)
Summer's End

This is a work of fiction. Names, characters, businesses, places, events and incidents are either the products of the author's imagination or used in a fictitious manner. Any resemblance to actual persons, living or dead, or actual events is purely coincidental.

ALSO BY OLIVIA MILES

Blue Harbor Series

A Place for Us

Second Chance Summer

Because of You

Small Town Christmas

Return to Me

Then Comes Love

Finding Christmas

A New Beginning

Summer of Us

A Chance on Me

Evening Island

Meet Me at Sunset

Summer's End

The Lake House

Oyster Bay Series

Feels Like Home

Along Came You

Maybe This Time

This Thing Called Love

Those Summer Nights

Christmas at the Cottage

Still the One

One Fine Day

Had to Be You

Misty Point Series

One Week to the Wedding

The Winter Wedding Plan

The Briar Creek Series

Mistletoe on Main Street

A Match Made on Main Street

Hope Springs on Main Street

Love Blooms on Main Street

Christmas Comes to Main Street

Harlequin Special Edition

'Twas the Week Before Christmas

Recipe for Romance

Summer's End

1

KIM

It was common knowledge to everyone that knew her that Kimberly Taylor had always wanted a big wedding. By big, she didn't mean one hundred fifty guests, a string quartet, and an ice sculpture. No, she meant *big*. Big as in three hundred guests, preferably in black tie. Big as in not one reception, but two, for the late-night crowd who would party until dawn (a girl only got one wedding night, after all, why not make it last?). Big as in a full-page spread in the Sunday society column.

Well, she'd gotten what she wished for, hadn't she?

"I bought six copies," Bran told her as he reached for his coffee cup. His hair was still tousled from his early run—the one he tried to cajole her into joining every morning, even though she loathed running, always had. Wedding preparations were a good excuse lately, even though most of that was already neatly tied up with a big bow to boot.

Kim tried not to gulp as she looked at the article again, spread out on Bran's glass coffee table, because more and more, this was where she stayed. Bran considered her cute walk-up in a less trendy pocket of Chicago to be too "vintage" for his liking, even though she adored the charming touches like the original brass doorknobs and the small wrought-iron balcony with enough room for a bistro table, and the deep window ledges where she could sit and stare out onto the neighborhood below.

Bran preferred something sleeker. More modern. And Kim hadn't quite brought herself to tell him that she didn't.

She looked over at her fiancé now. The catch of the city, she knew. Probably high on the list of several women on Chicago's North Shore, too. Bran's mother had been sure to tell Kim at their first meeting last fall that many of her friends had hoped that Bran would marry one of their daughters.

Instead, he was marrying her. A girl he'd known for less than a year. A girl who preferred her cozy vintage apartment. A girl who was no longer so sure that all that pomp and flair was what she wanted—from her wedding. Or from life.

And she still hadn't told Bran that either.

Branson Croft. Kimberly Croft. It did have a nice ring to it. She had considered that name several times since their first date, when she knew, halfway through her second glass of wine, that Bran was the perfect guy. And he was perfect, with his six-foot, athletic frame, thick brown hair and dark eyes, and a grin that was just mischievous enough to break up his otherwise clean-cut image. He was an attorney, following the footsteps of his father and older brothers. He was smart, successful, and he was sweet, always letting her pick the movie they'd watch on Sunday nights, always letting her choose the restaurant on Saturdays.

They'd met on the tennis court, at the swanky city health club that her sister Andrea had told her she must join when she'd first moved to Chicago after college. Andrea used her membership for networking and burning off her endless stress, but Kim only dabbled in the yoga classes, while taking more advantage of the nail salon and the outdoor pool come summertime. She hadn't picked up a racquet in years, not since her high school days, but last September she'd needed something to get her mind off her troubles, something, if she was being honest with herself, to hit, and so she'd signed up for some lessons, bought some tennis whites, and shown up that summer Saturday morning expecting nothing more than to blow off a bit of steam and maybe enjoy a mimosa in the sun afterward.

She'd done all of that, only not alone. Branson had been asked to sub that day by his best friend Nick, who had indulged in one too many shots of tequila that previous night. Kim had gotten more than just some tips on her backhand during that hour of court time, and by the time the lesson was over and she and Bran were settled on the club's deck, side by side in two lounge chairs overlooking the swimming pool and sipping drinks, and then extending things into lunch, she'd almost forgotten her entire reason for needing a tennis lesson that day at all, which was probably a good thing, even if she did feel a little bit guilty.

Her mother had only been gone a matter of weeks then. The pain was still fresh and raw. She hadn't expected to be able to escape it anytime soon.

But that was what was so great about Bran. He whisked her off her feet, called her the very next day, and invited her out on his boat, and she'd gone, even if she was prone to sea sickness, even on Lake Michigan. They spent every weekend together for a month, and then soon a few weeknights. He'd proposed within five months, presenting her with a family ring that wasn't exactly her style but an honor nonetheless, and she'd said yes. Of course, she'd said yes.

It was very hard to say no to Bran, after all.

Kim skimmed the article that Bran's mother had set up for them through an old sorority friend who worked at the newspaper. The article that Kim had contributed to, answering the reporter's questions, giving details of their storybook whirlwind romance, a hint of the wedding that was planned for September, at the very end of summer. She and Bran had posed for photos on his parents' expansive stone terrace in their tony north suburban neighborhood where the reception would be held, followed by the later reception down by the impressive walled-in pool, with the climbing vines and a sitting area with a fireplace that was nearly as big as her apartment living room, which would only be hers for the next six weeks.

Six weeks. Her stomach did that funny thing again and Kim carefully folded the newspaper, even though Bran had bought six copies and she was sure that the Crofts had stock-piled plenty more. One would be framed, no doubt.

With an internal groan she noted the time on her gold watch—an engagement present from Bran's parents—and, mustering up all the energy she had, stood and gathered up her belongings. She was due at the bridal salon in forty minutes, and now she ran the risk of being late for her fitting. There was a time when she couldn't wait to plan her wedding, but that was before things started to shift in a new direction. One that had started as her vision and very quickly morphed into Branson's mother's vision, like when her dream of yellow roses turned into blush because Bran's mother had never liked the color yellow.

"I should get going," she said with more reluctance than she intended.

Bran's eyes flicked up to her. For a moment, she wondered if he would ask her if something was wrong, if she would find the courage to admit that actually, a lot was wrong, but instead, he flashed that irresistible grin that made her doubt herself and tossed her his keys.

"Have fun!"

Contrary to what she had once hoped, wedding planning was anything but fun, but she didn't have time to get into that right now, not if she needed to get to the suburbs.

She took the elevator down to the condo building's garage, slid into Bran's luxury car, and carefully set her handbag on the passenger seat, not daring to fumble with the radio buttons because last time she'd tried that, she accidentally messed up the heating system instead, and drove to the bridal salon with about as much enthusiasm as she might going to the dentist. The last time she'd come for a fitting, she'd left feeling frustrated and tearful, and she didn't want a repeat experience. She tried to tell herself that Lynette was just excited about the wedding. That she was trying to help.

That maybe she'd feel more excited about the wedding if her mother were still alive.

A sharp pang in her chest made her press her lips together at the thought of her mother. Kim tightened her grip on the steering wheel and focused on the road. On the present. On the future. On her upcoming wedding day. A day she had dreamed of all her life.

Lynette's silver sedan was already parked in front of the shop when Kim arrived. Maybe she should have called her sisters and invited them to come—but the one time they'd met for their bridesmaid dress fitting had been tense and disappointing, with both of them falling silent around Lynette rather than laughing and sipping champagne the way she'd once imagined it. Besides, her sisters still didn't know about the dress, and even though Kim knew that she'd either have to come clean or leave them shocked on her wedding day, she wasn't quite ready for that conversation just yet. Once, her sisters might have understood, but this past year had been strange for all of them.

Last time, her best friend Kate had at least been with her, which had helped, but now Kate was away on vacation with her on again off again boyfriend and so it was just Kim. Kim and Lynette.

Her stomach felt funny again.

Still, she braved a smile as she pushed through the shop door, for a split second enjoying the beauty of her surroundings, from the crystal chandeliers to the soothing music to the gorgeous gowns that were every way she turned.

Then her eyes fell to Lynette, who was coming around from behind a mammoth of a flower display, dressed as she always was, in a shift dress and heels, her frosted blond hair cut in a neat bob that grazed her chin.

Lynette had insisted on this bridal salon, and Kim hadn't argued. Really, it wasn't that there was anything wrong with the shop itself—it would have been one that Kim might have chosen herself under other circumstances, just like the bridal shower that Lynette had given her last month would have probably been perfectly lovely if her sisters had planned it instead.

But then, her sisters would have planned it completely differently. Lynette hosted the event in the conservatory room of her country club where assigned seating and a formal tea was presented, followed by the public unwrapping of gifts—most of which Lynette had taken the liberty of registering her for, even though Kim didn't see the point of formal dinnerware. Kim knew that she should be grateful, because while it was a little uncomfortable to be celebrating her shower with all of Lynette's friends and family and only a few of her own, at least Lynette had been thoughtful enough to plan it, which was more than she could say for either of her sisters.

Refusing to let disappointment ruin this time for her, Kim rallied herself and forced a smile. Maybe today would be better.

"Kimberly, we need to discuss the veil. I know you already had something in mind, but Cynthia and I have been discussing it, and we just don't think it portrays the look we're going for."

Or maybe not.

Kim pulled in a breath to steady herself before she spoke. She glanced at Cynthia, the owner of the salon, who quickly skirted her eyes and kept them fixed on Lynette. Clearly, she knew who was in charge.

"The veil belonged to my mother," Kim reminded

Lynette, in case she had forgotten. And maybe she had. Maybe she would apologize, say that of course, she understood, how thoughtless of her. After all, it was Kim's wedding day. The day she had dreamed of since she was a little girl.

Even if it was turning out to be nothing like she had dreamt of at all.

"Yes." Lynette licked her lower lip. "It's very...sentimental...to want to have something of your mother's with you on your wedding day. Cynthia and I were thinking that she might incorporate a piece of the veil into a handkerchief or—"

Kim gaped. "You want me to cut up my mother's veil?"

She could feel her heart beating loudly, her temper flaring, heating her cheeks. Lynette, as usual, remained cool, her expression impassive. It wasn't on purpose, per se. Her face was frozen from years of plastic surgery, fillers, and Botox. She gave a slight nod to Cynthia, who took the silent direction and disappeared into the back room.

"Are you concerned about passing it to Andrea?" There was a subtle arch to Lynette's perfectly plucked brow.

Andrea, while nearly five years older than Kim, was not in a relationship and hadn't been since college, at least to Kim's knowledge. She was, as she liked to say, married to her career.

"This wedding is a significant event for our family, Kimberly." Lynette's eyes never strayed. "All of my husband's clients will be in attendance, all of our friends from the club, most of whom have seats on the boards."

At the mere mention of the boards (of museums, charities, hospitals), Kim tensed. More and more these boards represented a future that no longer felt so bright.

"These are influential people, Kimberly, and they're expecting a high-profile event. I'm sure they all saw today's full-page spread. You looked beautiful, by the way." Lynette turned and moved toward the display of veils. The implication was that Kim should follow.

Kim wished that Kate could have been here; even if she wouldn't dare to speak up to Lynette any more than Kim did, it would at least be some form of support.

"My mother wanted to pass down the veil," Kim explained when she was once again at Lynette's side. "And the dress," she added, even though that was an argument she had lost. Her mother's gown was a bit old-fashioned, but it was a classic satin dress with a scoop neck and capped sleeves. It was also the dress she'd always envisioned herself wearing when she walked down the aisle.

"Didn't your sister Heather have a chance to wear the dress?"

Kim thought of her mother. She thought of how different it would be if she was here. She had to defend her wishes in her absence. She had to remember that this was *her* wedding, as Kate had whispered to her after the last disastrous fitting. "My mother had hoped all us girls would wear it."

"Well, Heather had a chance," Lynette assured her. "And now she's divorced."

Kim felt like the wind had been knocked out of her. "The veil—" Was Lynette really not going to back down about this? Could she be so cold as to not understand that

Kim wanted—no, *needed*—a piece of her mother with her on her wedding day? Lynette got to be there in person. Her mother would miss it all.

"It's too bad Heather and Andrea couldn't join us today," Lynette said, though her tone suggested otherwise. If her sisters had come, they would have surely spoken up about the dress, the veil, all of it. "I'm so glad they were happy with their bridesmaid gowns. Blush is such a pretty color with red hair."

All three Taylor sisters had inherited their mother's hair, in rich shades of auburn and chestnut. Once again, Kim couldn't help but feel like her future mother-in-law was making a dig—or maybe Kim was just being sensitive. It had been such an emotional year, sometimes she couldn't be sure. And that was just the problem.

"You know my suggestions come from a good place." Lynette stared at her. "I assume Bran told you about the honeymoon?"

About that... Kim pulled in a breath, wondering if she should shelve the topic of the veil for today and move onto other, equally big issues.

"I wanted to thank you for your generous offer." Kim swallowed hard. Just last night Bran had excitedly told Kim that his father was giving him a month off to have a full-European tour. Kim had just stared at Bran in horror. A month-long vacation across Europe was, again, a dream come true. But it was just that: a dream.

"I'm afraid I'm supposed to start my new job two weeks after the wedding," she told Lynette now, as she'd reminded Bran last night.

"It's only a temporary position," Lynette replied.

Kim struggled to find her voice. Going back to school for her teaching certification had been the only thing that helped her get over the loss of her mother—well, that and Bran.

Remember that, she told herself now. *Remember that Branson is the one you are marrying.*

Even if more and more, it felt like by marrying Branson, she was marrying his mother, too. Lynette had their entire future planned: They'd vacation together every summer, along with Bran's two brothers, older sister, and their spouses and kids. And speaking of kids, Lynette hadn't been shy in saying she wanted more grandchildren, and soon. Two would be best, spaced two years apart, preferably one boy and one girl, preferably in that order, and they could use the same *au pair* service that Bran's brother's wife had used. They'd spend every Thanksgiving at the main house, and every Christmas at the ski chalet in Colorado. When they were in town, they expected Sunday night dinners at the club, and of course, there were the committees...

In other words, there was no space for a job, or a career. Or even her own family. There wasn't even room for Kim's mother's veil.

Kim had tried explaining to Branson that she and her family had their own traditions—at least, they had, once. That was before their mother got sick, back when she still hosted holidays. Kim had always been up for it, longed for more, really. She loved the Christmas brunches and the Mother's Day teas, and most of all, she loved their summer trips to Evening Island, to the big Victorian lake house that faced the water, and the carefree nights where she and her sisters would ride bikes and play cards on the front porch and try to catch fireflies in jars. They'd all been so happy once.

Now, thinking that she hadn't even considered calling one of her sisters and asking them to join her today, she wondered if they'd ever be that happy again.

Lynette was now studying a tulle veil. Perfectly lovely, but not the one Kim intended to wear.

"You're going to be too busy to have a job once you're married," Lynette told her, deciding the veil unworthy as she slipped it back on the hook. "Now, enough about that. Let's see you in the dress."

In other words, the dress that Lynette had selected, after nixing every single one that Kim had liked, explaining that, like Kim's mother's dress, her choices were too simple, too understated, that for a wedding of this caliber, Kim needed something memorable, something unique, something that weighed about hundred pounds and was covered in Swarovski crystals, Kim soon came to discover.

Kim dreaded the thought of seeing that dress again but relished the thought of disappearing into the dressing room for a few moments to herself.

As usual, Lynette had other ideas. She followed her right inside, where the dress was already waiting, displayed in all its sparkling glory on a satin hanger.

"Since your friend isn't here today, I'll assist."

Kim blinked in panic. "I can manage."

"With a gown of this size?" Lynette was already starting to remove it from the hanger. She stared at Kim sharply, clearly waiting for her to undress. Finally, when Kim didn't show any sign of movement, because, at this point, she was nearly frozen with fear, Lynette sighed and said, "I can see you're modest. I suppose that's better than the last girl Bran brought home. His father and I made it very clear that she was *not* suitable." She pinched her mouth and opened her eyes wide on that. Finally, she slipped out the door. "I'll be right here if you change your mind."

Kim eyed Lynette's no-nonsense heels under the door and then looked back up at the dress, knowing that she'd never get the row of buttons fastened on her own.

With a sigh, she removed her sundress and stepped into the giant hoop of fabric, telling herself that maybe she would like it better this time, maybe it wouldn't look so ornate or so regal or so...wrong.

If anything, it looked worse. She frowned, leaning into the mirror. Had Cynthia slipped even more rhinestones onto the bodice? She had. She absolutely had, and no doubt it had been Lynette who made sure of it.

"Everything okay in there?" Lynette asked from the other side of the door.

No, everything was not okay, it was actually very far from okay, Kim wanted to cry. But instead, she pulled open the door, holding the loose dress at her chest.

"Oh yes. This is perfect," Lynette said, dragging out the last word in an almost feline way. She led Kim toward the three-way mirror, where Cynthia looked on with approval, and buttoned the long row of satin buttons, the corset becoming tighter with each row.

It had been taken in last time, and now it felt almost too tight, and the air—had the air-conditioning stopped working? Kim felt suffocated, tight in the chest, her stomach turning all funny again when she stared at her reflection, of a girl she didn't even recognize and wasn't sure she wanted to be.

Her heart was racing and she was starting to panic and she couldn't breathe. She needed to undo the buttons. She needed to take off this dress. She needed air. Really, she needed space. Distance. Miles between her and the Crofts and this wedding and all these expectations.

And she knew just the place.

2

HEATHER

Heather stared at the pile of mail that had collected on her coffee table, wondering if today was the day she could muster up the energy to look through it all. She sighed and set the coffee mug on a coaster, which was the most dignified thing she'd done all week. Maybe all month. Truth be told, she wasn't even sure what day it was. They all blended together in a strange passing of hours that were marked by the shift in sunlight.

She was judging from the full sun beaming through her living room windows that it was sometime in the late morning. At least she'd already showered for the day, even if she did slip back into pajamas afterward. But they were fresh pajamas, not the ones she'd worn last night. An improvement from a month ago when she'd lost her job at the home and garden magazine where she'd worked since graduating college. Maybe there was hope for her yet.

Or maybe not, she thought, carrying the stack of bills into the kitchen at the back of the narrow city brownstone she and Daniel had purchased shortly after they'd gotten married. It had been a steal six years ago, only because of the work that was needed. But work they did. Every evening and weekend for months involved stripping wallpaper, rolling out fresh paint, retiling the bathrooms, installing new fixtures, and of course, renovating this kitchen. The kitchen had been a top priority, a place where she imagined baking cookies with their future children, or cooking Christmas dinner.

It was, she'd thought, a place where traditions would be created and memories would be made.

Instead, the kitchen remained quiet and empty, and lately, unused. She didn't even like going in there anymore, and she only did now so she could refill her coffee mug while she went through the bills. Her heart was hammering with dread when she saw the first one on the pile. An invoice from her attorney. Her divorce attorney. Another from the gas company. The electric company. The cable company.

It was endless. She set the stack on the kitchen table and drained the last of the coffee from the pot into her mug, then added a very generous splash of flavored creamer. She stared at the calendar that was held to the fridge by magnets— miniature photos of her and Daniel, not because she couldn't part with them but because she hadn't gotten around to buying any more magnets yet.

Her sisters would have a fit if they saw that she'd kept these up, but then, even though both of her sisters also lived in Chicago, they rarely saw each other, and when they did, it was on neutral territory. A café for a quick coffee or brunch, and the ever occasional sushi dinner, which had trickled down to once or twice a year. Kim had always been more available—until the past year when she met Bran. Not that Heather was completely complaining. She didn't have the energy to put on a happy face any more than she had the energy to rehash all her problems.

It was Monday. The second week of the month. And other than crossing out each day as they passed, her calendar was completely bare for all of August. No interviews. She tried not to let that distract her too much. Soon enough she'd be employed again, rushing around each morning, hopping on the bus or train to get to work in time, exhausted by the end of the day when she finally turned the key in her door. By then, she'd be wishing she had used this time better—to say, master a foreign language or travel. But then, traveling cost money, and learning a foreign language required motivation, both of which she was lacking these days, and had been, she knew, for quite some time.

She sipped her coffee, a small but meaningful perk to the day that she'd once used as a topic in her monthly column (how to start your day in a perfect way!) and sat at the table, deciding to tackle the stack that had matriculated for weeks into three piles: trash, deal, deal with later.

The invoice from the divorce attorney went into the deal with later category, the bills into the deal, which she did, even if it hurt, because there was no way around it unless she wanted to have her lights turned off, and she couldn't live without the internet or cell phone, not if she wanted to keep applying for jobs and actually stand a chance of hearing back from one. The junk pile was adding up quickly at least, one flyer or catalog after another.

She paused on the newest nursery decorating catalog, her

breath stalling in her chest. She thought she'd unsubscribed from all of that, thought she'd finally buried that dream, but now it was staring her in the face, the perfect picture of a light and airy crib, a sweet little mobile hanging over it, sunlight filtering through the ivory linen curtains, a shelf with a row of soft plush animals and books, much like the one she'd planned to set up.

She pressed her lips together and set it in the trash pile, then slid it to the bottom.

Next up: a creamy, thick envelope with her name hand calligraphed across the front in navy ink. She didn't need to open this to know what was inside. An invitation, officially inviting her to her sister's wedding next month. She'd been hearing about it for months, of course, anytime she and Kim talked, which wasn't often lately. She'd tried to be excited for her sister, who had taken their mother's death last summer the hardest of the three of them, but more and more she struggled to set aside her own hurts, her own past and disappointments, and eventually it became easier to make up excuses for why she couldn't meet for that coffee or that sushi dinner or even, much to her shame, to any of Kim's wedding planning appointments even though she'd covered the topic of floral centerpieces at least once a year in her column. Kim had Lynette for that, anyway.

Heather opened the envelope and pulled out the card, skimming it carefully, even though she knew all the details because Kim hadn't been shy in sharing them, and then walked to the calendar on her fridge, where she flipped to the next month. Like August—and July (save for that tense and overly formal bridal shower that Kim's future mother-

in-law had thrown for her at their country club)—
September was bare. A blank slate. The optimist in her
would have said that it represented a fresh start, but Heather
wasn't feeling very optimistic these days. She added the
details of the rehearsal dinner and the wedding reception to
the calendar, pleased to see that at least one thing was
planned.

At least one thing was certain.

The phone rang, making Heather jump, and then laugh
at herself for such a ridiculous reaction. She'd gotten too
used to the quiet, the solitude. Daniel had moved out
months before her mother's passing, and after the funeral,
the calls of concern came from old friends and extended
family members. But eventually, people moved on with their
lives and expected her to as well.

She straightened her shoulders, even though no one
could see her, and hurried to the table, wondering if it could
be a call about a job—she'd applied to at least ten positions
last week, even if half of them she was unqualified for and the
other half she didn't actually want.

But it wasn't an unknown number. It was her sister.
Kim. And it was far too tempting to ignore it, which was just
the reason she knew she shouldn't. Kim was her younger
sister. One of only two other people in this entire world who
understood her loss. But then, Kim couldn't understand all
of it, Heather thought, letting her eyes drift back to the
invitation.

She pressed the button and held the phone to her ear.
"Hey there," she said, trying to sound cheerful, or at least
normal.

"Is this an okay time to talk?" Kim asked. "I waited until I thought it might be your lunch break."

Right. Heather blinked and adjusted her pajama top as she settled back in her kitchen chair. "Perfect time," she said, hoping that Kim wouldn't pick up on the sounds of the television from the other room. If she did, she could say she was working from home, or that she was nursing a headache. Kim wouldn't question it; she had no reason to. For all her family knew, Heather was adjusting just fine to the dissolution of her marriage.

"How are you?" she asked, hoping to deflect the conversation away from herself even though she wasn't sure she could handle another round of Kim's wedding countdown. Maybe that made her a bad person, and an even worse sister, but then she thought of Andrea, who didn't even pretend to make time for either one of them lately and probably didn't feel bad about it either. At least she was a better sister than Andrea, she told herself.

"Oh...fine." Kim didn't exactly sound fine, and now Heather frowned, leaning forward to reach for her mug again. "Lots of wedding planning!"

Heather rolled her eyes. She'd heard all about the cake, the flowers, and the menu. She'd heard all about how helpful Lynette was being, making long lists and scheduling the appointments and being so organized, because Kim was many things, but organized had never been one of them. That was their sister Andrea's territory. Andrea was the achiever, Kim was the dreamer, and Heather, smack in the middle, was....

The failure. That's how it felt recently, at least. No husband. No job.

No child.

She took another sip of coffee to steady her emotions, and said, "I'm sure it's gorgeous!"

She was a bridesmaid, of course, along with Andrea, Kim's best friend from college, Branson's sister, sisters-in-law, and a handful of cousins on Bran's side of the family that Lynette said balanced out the groomsmen. In other words, it was basically going to be a parade. But then, Kim had always wanted a big wedding.

"Yeah..." Kim faded away for a moment, making Heather hold the phone from her ear to check if they still had a connection.

"I just received your invitation," Heather offered. "I'll get it mailed today."

"You're just now receiving it?" Kim sounded surprised.

Heather reached for the envelope, checking the postmark. Ten days ago. "It was tucked in with catalogs," she said, knowing that Kim would be hurt if she knew that Heather hadn't opened it directly upon receiving it, and she would have if she'd seen it earlier. Hoping to avoid that discussion, she said, "It's beautiful, of course."

"Lynette picked it out," Kim replied.

Ah yes, the ever-helpful Lynette. The very woman who had hijacked Kim's bridal shower—though, in fairness, Heather had only started to plan something, and those ideas were admittedly loose and scattered because she couldn't think clearly lately, not even with the aid of caffeine. Kim had told her not to worry, said that it was the thought that counted, that Lynette had already booked a room at the club. Lynette had done more than that. She'd ignored the texts that Heather had sent offering her services, and when Heather arrived as a guest, she was seated at a table at the back of the room along with Andrea, who was checking her phone for half the tea, left to watch from a distance as her baby sister opened her gifts, laughed at Lynette's painfully self-flattering toast, and seemed perfectly content rather than as irritated as Heather felt.

For a moment, Heather felt the same flare of anger she always did when Kim talked about Lynette, her future mother-in-law, who was starting to feel more and more like a replacement mother altogether, but she refrained. It was part of her grief, she knew, feeling sad one moment and angry the next. She didn't want to push her sister away, not when she was running out of people who were left in her life.

Realizing that the reason for Kim's call was probably to check up on the now delayed response to her wedding invitation, Heather said, "Well, my lunch break is almost over—"

She was a *terrible* sister.

"I just wanted to run one thing by you!" Kim said quickly. There was a strange sort of emotion in her voice—one that Heather might have called desperation if she didn't know better. Kim had nothing to feel desperate about; all her dreams were coming true. Unlike Heather, her future was very bright.

"Oh?" She hoped it wasn't about a bachelorette party that Heather could only hope Kate was planning—Andrea wouldn't take it on herself. Kim had only briefly mentioned at the shower that she wanted something small for that. But nothing about any of this was small in scale.

"I know it's short notice, and you could say no, but I figured, well, everything is going to be different once I'm married. I mean, I'm guessing it won't be as easy to meet for our coffees or sushi dinners."

Not that it was a regular thing now, but Kim probably had a point. Heather nodded, even though her sister couldn't see. "It's a whole new stage of life for you." She swallowed hard, thinking that Kim would be busy with Bran most nights and weekends, even more than now, and eventually she'd have children, who would keep her even busier, and that someday Heather might come to regret not taking advantage of this time when they were both free to spend more time together.

But just like her intentions of using this time for a vacation or an art class or to master a foreign language, she'd managed to find an excuse. The truth was that being with Kim hurt her; she didn't know why, but it did.

Maybe because Kim was a reminder of everything Heather once had and now didn't.

"I might be able to meet for coffee this weekend," Heather said, telling herself that, yes, she could do this, she should do this, even if it was just so she wouldn't regret it.

"Actually, I was wondering if you wanted to come to the lake house with me this weekend."

"The lake house?" Once it had been an annual summer getaway, a place where she and her sisters and mother would spend the entire season, their father coming up on the weekends when time away from work permitted. It was a place of sunshine and laughter and freedom, of long days that stretched ahead as if they would never end. It was a time when the entire world felt small and big all at once, when they weren't bogged down by school or routine, where they could get away from all of that.

Where they could escape.

"I know it's short notice and you might not be able to get away from work," Kim said. "But I was thinking of how much Mom used to love it there, how we all did, and we didn't make it back last August...and she wanted to. We promised her we would."

And they hadn't been able to keep that promise. Instead, they'd spent that time saying goodbye. Nearly a year had passed. It was a date that Heather had not circled on her calendar, but she knew it. Tried to forget it sometimes.

It was already August. August was the month when even as adults they would go to Evening Island, for a week, or sometimes only a weekend in Andrea's case, as life's responsibilities took away the carefree days of their youth.

Only now Heather didn't have any responsibilities, and she didn't have an excuse either. Besides, she wanted to go. Not just for the house, or the view of the water and the long days that drifted into longer evenings, with the sweet smell of flowers and the soft hum of crickets, but for the chance to be away from it all, to step outside her life and all its sorrow for a moment. But more than anything, she yearned to return to a time and a place where she was still happy. To once again feel like everything was possible.

"I'm going for two weeks. It's a long time, but I don't know when I'll get back," Kim was saying.

"It would be a nice way to honor Mom," Heather said, realizing with a start that somehow she'd lived an entire year that her mother hadn't; that her mother didn't know anything that had transpired in these past twelve months.

That, perhaps, was the only blessing.

"So...you'll come?" Kim's smile was evident in her voice.

Heather pulled in a breath, hoping she wouldn't live to regret her next words. "I'll come."

"Woohoo!" Kim squealed so loudly that Heather had to hold the phone away from her ear, but she was smiling now, her spirits lifted.

She listened to Kim's excited chatter as she walked over to the calendar and circled this Saturday. Then, surprising even herself, she turned it into a happy face.

She was going back to the lake house. For at least a little while, everything would be okay.

3

ANDREA

There are good days and bad days. That's what Andrea Taylor tried to tell herself as she sat across the desk from her boss of the past ten years, trying to control her facial features while Pamela explained that she had lost the proposal for the Glenwood Lane project.

Andrea pulled in a deep breath and released it slowly, reminding herself that this was just part of business. Nothing personal. But it felt personal because her job, especially this past year, was her life.

"I'm happy to tweak the design to better fit their vision," she said, hoping that she didn't sound too desperate. The Glenwood project was a big one—it would have been her biggest yet. A ground-up project on waterfront property in one of the most coveted Chicago suburbs. It was a dream project for any architect—one that would likely hit all the trade magazines, and probably some local glossies too.

It was also, Andrea thought, the project that was going to guarantee her partnership in the firm.

"Did they list any specific concerns?" she pressed, thinking that surely, this could be remedied. She'd worked within their parameters and added her own creative touches as well, utilizing the landscape and the view, taking into account the lighting and practical everyday living.

"They didn't feel that your design had...heart." Pamela grimaced across the desk, and Andrea knew that this time there was no hiding her shock.

That stung. And that...well, that wasn't an easy fix.

"Obviously the timing is not ideal," Pamela said delicately, and the two women exchanged a glance that spoke a hundred words and then some. Pamela wasn't just a boss, she was a friend, and as a partner of the architecture firm, she'd been Andrea's mentor and advocate for years. It was Pamela who had nominated her for the upcoming seat, but the decision would rest with Arthur, the president of the company.

There was a tap on the door. Nicole, Andrea's assistant, stood in the doorway looking worried. She winced when she saw Andrea's expression. "I suppose now isn't a good time to tell you that your sister is on line two?"

Andrea thought about this for a second. "Which sister?" Her money was on Kim, who had more reason to call and was probably wondering when they could schedule another fitting for those pink—make that *blush*—bridesmaid gowns.

"Kim." Nicole gave a knowing smile.

Kim was prone to calling when Andrea was at work, despite Andrea nearly always waiting until she'd left for the night to call her back (unless she'd stayed past eleven or fell asleep on the sofa across from her desk, which wasn't uncommon these days).

"I'll call her back after work."

Nicole nodded but showed no signs of leaving. She chewed her lower lip, wringing her hands in front of her pencil skirt. "And Arthur wants to see you."

Andrea's gaze flicked to Pamela, who was already standing. "Does he know?"

"I didn't tell him, but news travels fast around here. Especially if they've already nabbed a competitor."

Andrea closed her eyes. Yep, this was definitely turning out to be a bad day.

Already regretting not taking the call from Kim if only to buy time, she took a steadying sip of her coffee and pushed back her chair, walking with Pamela in silence until they reached Pamela's office.

Her boss gave her a smile of encouragement. "Flag me when you're out. Lunch?"

Andrea nodded. She'd need a break from the office after this.

She formulated her plan as she walked to the end of the hallway on shaking legs. She would just tell Arthur that now she'd have more time for rainmaking—the Glenwood project would probably take years to complete. Sure, it was lost prestige, but it wouldn't be lost revenue if she could help it.

Feeling better—almost—she gave a smile she didn't feel to Arthur's assistant who guarded his phone and his door with an air of authority.

"He's expecting you," Trisha said, giving Andrea a long stare over the rim of her glasses.

"Great," Andrea said a little breathlessly. Just great. The

last time Arthur wanted to see her out of the blue was to tell her she was in line for partner, along with Jace, the boy wonder who had started at the firm only two years ago to her ten but had managed to bring in some big clients along the way.

She tried not to think about Jace right now, not his infuriating smirk, not the fact that she had put in the hours, the sweat, and even, sometimes, though she'd never admit it, the tears to get where she was, and she wasn't going to give up that partnership without a fight.

She also tried not to think about the fact that, probably like half the unmarried women in this office, she couldn't deny that there was something about him, something appealing, something charismatic, that made her look at him a little longer than she wanted to in their weekly meetings. She knew even Pamela was nursing a crush even though Jace was several years younger than her; the two women laughed about it regularly.

Arthur was sitting at his desk when she opened the door, a wall of windows behind him, revealing a sweeping view of Millennium Park and Lake Michigan, unlike her view of crowded, neighboring office buildings which she'd tried to convince herself was fascinating from an architectural standpoint.

"You asked to see me?" Maybe he didn't know. Maybe it was about the partnership. Maybe he had a client dinner and he wanted to ask for some restaurant ideas; it wouldn't be the first time.

But from the set of his jaw and his glance up from his paperwork, she knew that it was none of those things.

"Heard you lost the Glenwood project." It wasn't a question, but a fact.

"I'm not giving up on it so easily," she said, settling into the chair opposite his desk. "I'll circle back with the clients tomorrow, see if we can work something out." She could lower her fee, temporarily. It wasn't ideal, but it was something.

But Arthur was shaking his head. "They already went with another architect."

Andrea swallowed hard. That was quick. "Do we know who?"

"Jace," Arthur said.

Andrea felt like she had been kicked in the chest. She cleared her throat, trying to hide her shock. "I didn't even know that Jace was in the running."

"Part of our regular Sunday teeoff," Arthur said casually, referring to his weekly golf game. "I know you don't play."

No, she didn't, but she could have learned. Besides, she'd never been asked.

So this was what it was. A regular boys' club. She'd been set up, positioned all along to take the fall, or maybe, Jace had just been better positioned to slide right in at the first opportunity.

"It's still a win for the firm." Arthur's look told her that she should be happy too.

She wasn't. With Jace now landing Glenwood, her chances of making partner were slipping through her hands. The announcement was set to come next month. End of the quarter.

She licked her bottom lip. She'd just have to work extra hard between now and then to make up for the loss. She could do it if she set her mind to it. She'd get out, network. She'd go back to her desk right after this and start calling everyone on her contacts list. Set up some drinks and dinners. It was all about connections.

Arthur began shuffling papers on his desk to signal that the meeting was over. Andrea inched to the door, but she kept her shoulders back, her chin high as she walked back out into the hall, past the rows of administrative desks, toward Pamela's office, counting down the seconds until she could close the door behind her.

Pamela took one look at her and said, "Wait until we're outside." She stood and lifted her handbag from its hook on her coat rack. Ten minutes later they were seated across a small bistro table at their usual lunch spot, salads ordered, sparkling water served.

"Jace got the project."

Pamela couldn't disguise her surprise. "Jace? I didn't know he was pitching anything."

"Seems like Arthur facilitated that," Andrea said a little bitterly. "Introduced them through a golf game."

Pamela sighed. "There were many architects on the shortlist."

Andrea knew this was true, she just hadn't expected one to be from in-house, and her biggest personal competition, either.

Pamela was tapping around on her phone. "Give me a minute. I want to see what he came up with. I bet I can have —yep. There it is." She went silent for a moment while she studied her screen and then, while Andrea's stomach heaved with dread, turned to show her the design.

It was beautiful. There was no denying that. Every detail had been thought out, making the most of the view while allowing for privacy and tapping into the clients' New England roots.

Andrea now felt like she might cry. But Pamela was still her boss. She sipped her water instead.

"I could have come up with that if I had more time," she insisted, hoping to convince herself. "I have nearly twice as many clients at the moment as Jace."

"And you put in more hours than most people in the firm," Pamela added. "You're a hard worker, Andrea. Probably the hardest in this entire firm."

Andrea sat a little straighter, uncertain if this was a compliment.

"Mistakes happen when you get sloppy and tired. When you're spread too thin." Pamela gave her a pointed look, and Andrea fought back the urge to refute that statement, wanting to say that it didn't apply to her, even if maybe it did. "When was the last time you took time off?"

She didn't need to think about it. It was last August, for her mother's funeral. "About a year ago."

Pamela nodded. She didn't need to think about it either. She'd been supportive, understanding, having lost her own mother a few years earlier.

"It's been a tough year, Andrea."

"That's not why I didn't win the account," Andrea said firmly.

Pamela gave a small sigh and set her phone back in her bag. "Maybe it would do you some good to slow down a bit."

"Right before the partnership is announced?" Andrea almost laughed, but the tenderness in Pamela's eyes made her want to cry again. Damn it.

"Refill your creative well. Get out of town. See new things. Remember why you're doing this. Why you want to make partner." Pamela tipped her head. "Two weeks." And then, before Andrea could protest, she added, "And that's an order."

She couldn't be serious. Two weeks off in August, when the partnership would be announced next month? When Jace had just landed a tony client?

"I'll take two weeks off in October," Andrea said. She might really need it by then. "I still have the Morrison house to pitch in September. If I get that..." She had to get it. It wasn't an option now.

But Pamela shook her head. "Trust me. Everyone needs to recharge once in a while. Even you. Especially you."

There was no sense in arguing, Andrea knew. It was, as Pamela had said, an order.

She nodded, not trusting herself with words. "Okay."

They ate their salads while discussing that project, but Andrea was unnerved, even uncomfortable. Idly, she wondered if she could slip into the office after hours. She knew from all her late nights and weekends that she was usually the only person there—others had families or social lives. But then, Pamela was her boss, and she respected her. And it was an order.

She could work from home, but there were strict rules

about what files were allowed to be removed from the office... By the time she returned to the office and approached Nicole's desk, Andrea couldn't keep the smile up anymore, and Nicole looked at her with understandable trepidation.

"Have you taken lunch yet, Nicole?" she asked her assistant, knowing that the answer. Nicole knew who she worked for. She didn't take a break until the job was complete, just like Andrea.

Nicole shook her head, looking startled.

"You fly, I'll buy," Andrea said, stepping into her office to pull her wallet from her bag. She handed Nicole, who had followed her in, a few bills. "Get yourself whatever you want. All I need is a latte."

"And maybe one of those oatmeal cookies that you like?" Nicole gave her a little smile.

Andrea felt her shoulders sink. Nicole understood, without having to say it. She also knew that they were both still employed. For now. "Grab two. For both of us."

Nicole seemed almost tearful with relief as she took the money and hurried out the door, knowing without being asked to close it behind her.

Andrea sank into her chair, her mind spinning, trying to figure out what she was supposed to tell people, how she was supposed to find a way to make partner, and what on earth she would do with herself for two straight weeks. She didn't do idle well. The evenings were tricky enough, which was why she spent more and more time at the office, or the gym after the office, or sometimes the gym in between a return trip to the office. Here she could be productive. Here she could keep her mind busy. Whereas at home...

There was a sticky note on her computer monitor. A note to call back Kim, today, if possible. Normally, Andrea saved personal calls for those evenings when she was home, and alone, trying to deny her loneliness with the assistance of television, even though she usually just flicked through the channels without ever settling on one.

But now seemed as good a time as any, because until she had stopped shaking, until she had finally processed everything that had occurred this morning, she wasn't going to be productive at all. And wasn't that what Pamela was implying?

She pursed her lips and picked up her cell phone, only half-surprised that Kim answered after the first ring. She loved any opportunity to discuss her wedding these days, even if she had grown a bit quiet about it lately. Or maybe it was that Andrea hadn't taken as many of her calls. But just like Kim couldn't understand why Andrea loved her career, the challenge of being busy, the thrill of working toward a goal, Andrea couldn't understand why Kim was rushing into marriage with a man she hadn't even known for a year.

"You called!" Kim sounded so happy to hear from her that Andrea felt a wash of shame. As the eldest of the sisters, she'd always taken a special shining to Kim, or Kimmy as she'd always called her. She could still picture the round-cheeked little girl who loved dress-up clothes and playing house, while Andrea was content to read a book to pass the time. Playing wedding had always been her favorite.

She'd make a beautiful bride, Andrea knew. She just didn't know why she couldn't wait a bit longer, establish her own life first.

Still, she kept all these thoughts to herself. Now wasn't the time to put Kim on the defense, not when Andrea's life choices hardly made her the poster child of success. Kim seemed happy enough—ecstatic, really—and Bran had been perfectly warm and pleasant the few times she'd met him, which had been brief, and only twice, come to think of it. There had been the time at Christmas, and then later in the spring, to celebrate the engagement.

"What's new?" she asked, hoping for once that Kim would share all her plans for the wedding so that Andrea wouldn't have to talk about her job, because it was the only thing Andrea ever talked about. The only thing in her life to share.

She chewed on that for a moment and picked up her coffee mug, which had now gone cold. She drank it anyway, hoping to push back the panic.

"Well, I wanted to let you know that I'm going to be visiting Dad later this week," Kim said.

Andrea hadn't seen her father since Christmas when he had come to Chicago to take all of his daughters to the theatre and dinner at his hotel. He was in and out in twenty-four hours, then off on another business trip.

"I'm glad he found the time," Andrea said, even though she was guilty of the same. She was her father's daughter—only her father probably wouldn't have lost a major account.

"I'm just stopping by for the night," Kim explained. "And after that, I'm heading to Evening Island. Heather's going to meet me up there."

Her sisters were both going to the lake house? This weekend? Andrea tried to connect what conversation could have led to these plans not only being made but actually put into action. Evening Island was a solid seven-hour drive plus a ferry ride away from Chicago, regardless of which route you took. When they'd grown up in Michigan, they'd gone every summer, but now Andrea hadn't been back in years.

"Heather's going?"

Heather had become very withdrawn lately, and Andrea had never excelled at heart-to-heart chats. That was their mother's territory.

"I'm as surprised as you are, but yes! And I already know what you're going to say, but I figured I would still ask you just in case you wanted to join us."

Andrea tried not to take insult, but it stung anyway. She'd let Kim down, slowly over time, but this past year especially. Kim had rebounded, found someone to lean on, a whole new family, really, but it didn't go unnoticed that somewhere along the way Kim had realized that Andrea was unavailable, maybe even disinterested.

This weekend. The start of her forced two weeks off. She could do it. She could pack her bags and drive up to Blue Harbor, Michigan, and catch the ferry to Evening Island. By this Saturday she could be sleeping in the front bedroom with the window open and the sounds of nature flowing in with the breeze. She could swim in the cool waters of Lake Huron. She could ride her bicycle into town, have a proper drink on the wide stretch of bright green lawn overlooking the harbor.

She could have something to do. Somewhere to be.

An excuse for her sudden departure.

"I'll come."

There was a very long pause. Finally, Kim's small voice said, "Did I just hear you say you're coming?"

She pulled in a breath. "Yes. I'll come."

"Oh my gosh. Oh my gosh. Wait until I tell Heather! Oh my gosh, Andrea! This is going to be so much fun!"

Andrea was still smiling when she hung up the phone. But as for fun...that part was yet to be seen.

4

KIM

It had been fifteen days shy of a year since Kim had last been home—by home, she meant the large Tudor-style house in Michigan and not the walk-up one-bedroom apartment in Chicago. She could blame it on her master's program, which was a year-long commitment, or she could say it was because of Bran, which would be slightly more true. But the real reason she'd stayed away was that there just wasn't any reason to return now that her mother was gone.

Her father would be at the office until seven like usual, giving Kim time to settle in on her own. She eased her foot off the gas pedal as she pulled onto the tree-lined street, the branches of the large, old oaks creating an arch of shadows that led her to the brick-paved driveway that swept the front of the home, dividing it from the lush green lawn that was just another thing their father didn't have time for and never had. She parked the car—a rental because Bran couldn't part with his vehicle for more than a day—leaving most of her luggage in the trunk except for an overnight bag that contained her toiletries and pajamas, and a few changes of clothes. With trepidation, she walked up the stone steps to the door. She didn't know how she would feel when she went inside and was reminded that her mother wasn't home and never would be again. That there would be no lemonades out by the pool, no card games after dinner over gin fizzes. No stories to share, no laughter to have.

It was so much easier to not think about what she was missing when she wasn't faced with it every day.

She knew the security code: her parents' wedding anniversary that they had locked in when the system was first installed. Now she pressed each button firmly then reached for the door, hearing the lock release at the same moment her phone started to ring.

She didn't know if she should be relieved or annoyed. She'd been spared the momentous occasion of walking into her empty home. Maybe she should see it as a sign.

She glanced down at the screen. Or not.

"Hey, babe," she greeted Bran, hoping that the smile she was forcing couldn't be detected in her tone. She stayed outside and set the bag at her feet. Her back ached from the long drive from Chicago to Grosse Pointe, and she did some stretches, hoping to alleviate the tension but suspecting the drive wasn't the only cause of it.

Bran wasn't happy about her trip. It was too close to the wedding, he'd remarked. And of course, there was that charity dinner that he'd promised his mother they'd attend next weekend, without consulting her first.

"Perfect timing. I just stepped out of the car." She

crouched to sit on the steps, feeling the warm sun beat down on her.

"I can call you later if your father is there."

"I won't see him for a few hours," Kim said. "We'll probably have dinner at his club. It will be nice to catch up."

Bran had met her father briefly, when he'd visited Chicago at Christmastime, delaying their trip to Colorado, where they'd spent the remainder of the holiday with the Crofts. Lynette had made sure to point out everything they'd missed every chance she had.

"Listen, I don't like how we left things off," Bran said, and Kim softened. They rarely argued, and when they did, it always seemed to be about some family obligation—and lately, the wedding. She missed the first half of their courtship when it was just the two of them, and every moment they spent together felt carefree and special. "It's just that the timing is so bad. You've said how much work is involved in the planning."

Now Kim's heart was hammering and it had nothing to do with the fact that she was sitting outside her childhood home for the first time since her mother's funeral. "There is a lot of work, but..." *But your mother is taking care of all of it*, she wanted to say. Instead, she closed her eyes and said, "But everything is pretty much taken care of at this point. Now we're just waiting for the RSVPs to come in so we can finalize the seating chart."

"That's not what my mother said," Bran said after a moment.

Of course.

"Look, the last few things can be taken care of when I get

back. It's important for me to spend time with my sisters too," she said, knowing that by doing so, another argument was brewing.

"Your sisters live in Chicago. You could spend time with them here if they wanted to get together."

The words cut the deepest part of her because she knew that there was truth in them. "My sisters have a lot going on in their own lives. This is a chance for us to get away from—" She couldn't finish that part. "My sisters mean a lot to me."

"I'm just saying that your sisters haven't done anything to help plan the wedding."

Again, true, and again, it hurt to hear. "It's been a tough year for all of us."

"I never said it wasn't," Bran said. "But going away for two weeks, with our wedding next month? It just makes me wonder..."

She blinked. "Wonder what?"

"Are you having second thoughts?"

Now it was her turn to pause. He was voicing the very question she refused to ask herself, the one that even her best friend Kate hadn't said, not in so many words, at least, though the look was there, at every fitting at that bridal salon, every trip to the florist, and of course, at that miserable bridal shower.

"You know I love you, Bran," she said. "But I love my family too, and this is the first time I've been home in a year." And from the way Lynette was packing their social schedule, she wasn't sure when the next opportunity would arise. "And you know how hard it is to get my sisters together. This is a special trip for us. And now is a perfect time, before I start my job."

It was something she'd been excited about—a temporary teaching position that she would start in October when the permanent teacher went on maternity leave. She had jumped at the opportunity, feeling like her life was starting to become more complete. But it wasn't just that—her mother had been a teacher before she'd eventually become a stay-at-home mother to her three daughters. Following her path gave Kim a sense of direction for the first time since losing her.

"About that. Have you given any more thought to our honeymoon?"

Kim stifled a sigh. This was an argument that had been going around and around all week, causing her to struggle to sleep, and wake up with neck and shoulder pain. She rubbed a spot on her back now with her free hand.

"I still think it's something we should plan on our own," she said, stressing the point she'd made earlier this week when she'd come back from the bridal salon.

"My parents are giving us this trip as a gift," Bran reiterated. "How am I supposed to tell them thanks but no thanks?"

Kim had thought long and hard about this, knowing that had it been easy to say no to Lynette, she would have done so, months ago. That maybe, Bran would have, too. "Maybe you can tell them that you'd already been planning something, as a surprise to me."

"My mother will be insulted." Bran's voice sounded stressed and agitated, and for the umpteenth time, Kim wanted to ask if his mother's feelings mattered more than her own.

"Then use my job as the excuse. I already told your mom that I couldn't go away for that length of time." Not that Lynette had accepted that as an excuse, either.

"Kim—"

Kim swallowed hard, hating the direction this conversation was taking. It wasn't always like this, not when it was just her and Bran, going out to dinners and shows, enjoying their free time, and getting to know each other. But that was before Kim learned how close Bran was with his family. Before she knew that Bran was not only expected to take over the law firm with his two brothers but also show up for every event the family held.

Maybe, it was before she knew Bran at all. When she just knew the surface.

"I can't talk about this right now." Her hand was shaking as she reached for her bag. "It was a long drive and I need..." A glass of wine. A bath. A long chat with her mother, who would listen intently and know exactly what to tell Kim to do.

But that wasn't possible.

"So there's no chance of you coming back in time for the gala next Saturday night? It's the hospital's biggest fundraiser all year. You know my dad is on the board. I was looking forward to showing you off... And it won't be any fun without you."

He was sweet-talking her, but Kim didn't need time to think about that one. "I'll be back the following weekend."

"My mother won't be happy," was all Bran could say to that, and Kim couldn't hold back any longer.

"And what about my happiness?"

"What's that supposed to mean?" Bran's voice inched up a notch in volume. "What are you saying?"

Kim stood, feeling angry and frustrated and so confused she felt like she might cry. It was difficult enough coming back here, knowing what she wouldn't find behind that door —that her mother wouldn't be at her wedding. That her sisters weren't around to help plan it in her place. That lately, she felt like she had lost more than her mother; that she'd lost her entire family too. And that maybe that's what Bran wanted. Maybe that would make it easier.

"I'm saying that I think some space right now is good."

There was a long pause. Enough to make Kim wonder if they had lost the connection, if he hadn't even heard what she'd said. And she didn't know if she dared to repeat it.

"Maybe you're right," he finally said, his tone clipped.

Kim ended the call with a heavy sigh. All trepidation of walking into the empty house had disappeared, and now, she stood, picked up her bag, and pushed into the hall, into the familiar home with its bridal staircase and family portrait hanging above the sideboard with the vase that her mother had bought on their honeymoon in Italy and always filled with fresh flowers.

The flowers in it were still fresh—orange roses, to brighten up the space, and no doubt tended to by one of the staff who kept this place running, and clean, who ironed her father's clothes and cooked his meals and cut his lawn.

She didn't go to the kitchen at the back of the house,

which would be dark, or the big great room overlooking the expanse of lawn behind it. Instead, she walked right back outside, opened the car door, found her swimsuit buried in a pile of clothing that she'd crammed into her luggage during yet another argument with Bran last night, and carried it back into the house, through the French doors that led to the patio, and changed in the pool house.

The water was glistening when she stood at the edge, waiting before diving in, even though she knew that her father kept it heated to a comfortable yet refreshing eighty degrees. From her heap of clothing on the deck chair, her phone rang again, the sound grating on her aching shoulders, the noise cutting through the birdsong and solitude. This time she didn't need to check the screen to know who it would be, and she didn't want to talk to him. She was home. She was going to the lake house tomorrow. And for the next two weeks, she would be the girl she used to be, do the things she used to do, back when just being herself was enough, not something she had to think about or plan for. When nothing was expected of her.

The phone stopped and then started again. Kim dove effortlessly into the water, feeling it wash over her hair, her back, her toes, drowning out the sound of the phone. Shielding her, for just this moment, from the world above.

* * *

Kim didn't even realize until she was seated opposite her silver-haired father, in the country club where she once swam for the team, learned tennis, and trailed behind her mother in golf, that it was quite possibly the first meal she had ever shared alone with him. Her mother had been the more active parent, and even when Andrea and Heather had gone off to college, leaving her behind in the big house while she finished high school, her mother was ever-present.

Now, Kim shifted against her chair back, feeling stiff and uncomfortable and dodging for a conversation topic that didn't evoke memories of her mother for either one of them.

Her father seemed just as out of place as she did. He'd always been a little overwhelmed by the drama of three daughters, but now he seemed shy, almost, and he kept glancing her way as if hoping she might spare him and take the lead, the way his wife would have once done.

"I'm glad we're doing this, Dad." Kim smiled and sipped her wine. The salad plates were cleared and the breadbasket was still half full. Kim always thought the Parker rolls at the club were the best part of the dinner, and now, not sure when she'd be able to taste them again, she helped herself to another. Good thing Lynette wasn't here to remind her that she'd just had another dress fitting and they wouldn't want to be letting anything out in the final weeks before the big day.

Just thinking about that, she added some warm butter to the hot roll. "It will be nice to get to the island again, too."

"I wish I could get back, but I'm happy to hear you girls are all going. I'm afraid I haven't put much effort into the house since...well."

Kim pushed back a wave of panic. The lake house was her mother's, passed down through the generations, and her father didn't hold the same attachment to it. Would he still keep it if the rental income wasn't steady or the expenses piled up? Old houses of that size on a remote island weren't exactly easy to maintain.

"I'm sure it's fine. You still have the caretaker," she assured him. Even when trusty Edward had retired, his grandson had stepped in to look after the property.

"So long as you girls still want to keep going back, I'll keep it going," he said with a smile that Kim knew was meant to be reassuring and wasn't in the least.

She cleared her throat, desperate to change the topic. "You've been traveling a lot?"

Her father had always traveled for business, but now it would seem that he had thrown himself into work with full force. She didn't blame him. It couldn't be easy to come home to that big, empty house each night. But she also wished he might make a bit more time to stop by Chicago.

"I have, and I wanted to talk to you about that, actually." He cleared his throat, then reached for his wineglass.

Uh-oh. Kim suddenly wished she had filled the silence with endless chatter about her upcoming wedding, trying to convince herself in the process that she was as excited as she sounded. Instead, she'd sat, thinking about all the missed calls from Bran, enjoying the music from the piano player in the club's adjacent bar.

"You're not selling the house, are you?" She couldn't bear the thought of losing her family home any more than the island cottage. As much as it hurt to return, to walk through the rooms, remembering that her mother used to sit in the leather club chair in the den or the wingback in the sitting room, or to stop and gaze at the framed photos of all their happy moments, she also couldn't bear to have those memories banished. Surely, her father felt the same?

"No, nothing like that," he assured her.

She smiled into a sigh. "Good. Because I know I haven't been back often, and I want to start. It's just been so crazy with the wedding and finishing my degree and..." She was getting nervous. There was news to be shared, and she needed to let her father come out with it.

"It is a big house for one person, though," he said, giving her a funny look.

She tipped her head and reached out a hand to squeeze her father's fingers. "I know, Dad. I just...want to see you happy."

His gaze flickered. "That's what your mother wanted too. You two were so alike. You remind me of her, you know."

Kim felt her eyes mist. "We had a special bond. It can never be replaced," she said, thinking of Lynette.

She took a big bite of the roll. The salty butter melting on her tongue helped brighten her spirits.

"No, never. Your mother can never be replaced," her father agreed, nodding his head. "But—"

Kim's body went rigid. She stared at her father, aware that she had stopped chewing, that there was a hunk of bread in her cheeks. In her father's club. That her manners had flown out the window because her father had something to tell her, something that she now had the very real fear that she wouldn't like to hear at all.

She shouldn't have come here. She should have gone straight to Evening Island. Should have driven up with

Heather and Andrea who would be traveling directly there from Chicago tomorrow because of their work schedules.

"The truth is that I've...met someone."

Kim lifted her wineglass and drank it back, nodding her head while she chewed and swallowed, buying time while her mind spun and her heart sank and she silently cursed her sisters and tried to figure out what exactly she was supposed to say to this.

Her parents had been married for thirty-five years. Her mother had only been gone for a year.

"It's a long-distance thing. Keith's wife's friend. We met playing golf in Palm Beach and then we started meeting up every month and now... Well, now, she's going to be staying at the house for a while."

Kim stared at her father until he squirmed. From her periphery, she caught their waiter passing by and flagged him, pointing to her empty wineglass.

"Let me get this straight," she said slowly. "You haven't been traveling for work, but for...fun." She couldn't say *this woman*, but that was what she meant. A woman who would be moving into her family home and sleeping in her mother's bed.

"Her name's—"

Kim held up a hand. "I don't need to know her name."

Her father closed his eyes. He suddenly looked very tired, and very old, and despite her anger, despite the raw hurt that was gathering up inside her, making her hands shake and making it difficult for her to breathe, she couldn't help but feel a tenderness for him.

"I'm sorry, Dad. It's just…a lot to process," she said, softening her tone.

The waiter arrived with her wine and gave her a little smile when he set it down. Kim took a sip, trying to calm herself.

"When you visited at Christmas you didn't say anything." She tried to piece together the timeline. They'd been visiting each other for months, he'd said! Months!

"We didn't meet until January," her father explained.

Kim quickly did the math. January was at least better than October.

"How old is she?" Maybe it was an unfair question, but she couldn't help it.

Her father actually laughed. "She's three years younger than me. She lost her husband two years ago. She has two sons. You'd like her, Kimmy."

Maybe she would. But she just wasn't there yet.

Their entrees arrived and she stared miserably at her roasted chicken and mashed potatoes—her favorite dish on the menu, even if it was August. She didn't know when she'd be back to have it again.

Now she thought she'd probably never be back, and not because of the endless commitments with Bran's family. There would be a new woman living in her house. It wouldn't be home anymore.

Everything just kept on changing.

"You'll meet her at the wedding," he said gently. "I thought it was only fair that you should know now, hear it from me directly."

He was bringing this woman to her wedding! Her mind

was racing at all that implied. That Heather and Andrea would be there, that one of them was bound to make a stink, and that clearly her father hadn't told either one of them about it yet or she certainly would have received a call by now —a rare one. And then there was the fact that invitations had already gone out. That Lynette hadn't even considered that Kim's father would bring a date—a date! And oh, Lynette wouldn't be happy to reconfigure the seating chart; she'd locked in the family seating arrangements weeks ago.

Then Kim remembered how she and Bran had left things. He hadn't left a message after his last call, and she had taken this as a reason not to reach out again. It was too soon and too fresh. They'd just continue the same argument. Or worse.

"She's not going to make a scene if that's what you're worried about," her father said. "With a wedding this big, you won't even notice her. But she's a part of my life now, and...she makes me happy, Kim."

Maybe she didn't need to worry about this strange woman showing up at her wedding at all. Maybe, she'd have bigger concerns when she got back to Chicago.

But all she could think about was that there would be so many people at this wedding, and the one person who should be there wouldn't be. And maybe that was why everything about this entire experience felt so wrong.

Heather pulled the car to a stop at the ferry lot and turned off the ignition. She glanced to her right in annoyance to see that Andrea was still tapping away at her phone, something she had been doing since Heather picked her up this morning—seven and a half hours ago.

She supposed she shouldn't complain. At least Andrea's focus on work meant she didn't have to talk about her personal life or her work, or lack thereof. It also gave her a chance to relax, to listen to the radio, even if Andrea did clear her throat rather loudly the few times that Heather had started to sing along, absentmindedly. Still, Heather couldn't help but feel the strain of the distance that had formed between them. The ease with which they used to laugh and talk seemed to have faded away so gradually that she couldn't pinpoint when it happened, and she couldn't deny some responsibility for it either.

But now they were here, in Blue Harbor, Michigan, and across the calm water of Lake Huron, Heather could see

Evening Island out in the distance, a great green mass, like another world. A better world. A place she didn't even know how much she'd missed until she saw it now. The air was clearer here, filling her lungs in a way that made her feel like she could breathe again, like she was light again. That the heaviness that had rested on her shoulders and filled her heart for so long was finally gone, just when she had almost gotten used to it.

"If we hurry, we can make this ferry," Heather said before closing her door. Already she felt more invigorated than she had in weeks.

Who was she kidding? Months.

She glanced at Andrea through the rear window as she started unloading the trunk. Not that she'd be letting on any more of her troubles. Or that Andrea cared to ask. It was for the best, she told herself, trying not to feel stung. Andrea had a powerful job, she was about to make partner any day now, and Heather still had to find a way to pay her divorce attorney for services rendered.

Finally, Andrea emerged from the car, tucking her phone into her leather handbag, which seemed so out of place for island life. On Evening Island, there were no cars, just good, ol'-fashioned horse and buggies and bicycles, meaning she'd need to pay for extended parking before boarding the ferry. And she wouldn't say no if Andrea offered to cover it, considering Heather had handled all the driving to the very tip of Michigan, feeling more like a chauffeur than a sister.

She laughed to herself, thinking how many times she had been tempted to tell Andrea that she should take the backseat; at least then Heather might have been able to sing along to the radio.

"You're in a good mood," Andrea remarked, and Heather didn't deny it or fight it. The water stretched far into the distance, interrupted only by a slow-passing ferry, and the sun was warm on her face. She hadn't gardened much this year, even though she'd once prided herself on the small plot of land in the city that was all hers. Now she pulled the air into her lungs and tipped her head back.

"It's nice to have a change of scenery, I suppose. The city can wear on you after a while, you know?" But, of course, Andrea didn't know. She loved the pace of city life; thrived on it.

Heather watched as her older sister just lifted an eyebrow and proceeded to unload her belongings. "I'll get the tickets," she said, leaving her luggage near the car while she walked to the ticket stand.

Heather used the time to start transferring her bags to and from the loading dock. Neither one of them had thought this through, she realized. They'd have to flag down a carriage to take them to the house. They could never manage this much on foot, no matter how walkable the island was. Once, packing for the lake house had been done on autopilot, but time away had taken the routine out of it. Now she was certain she'd overpacked when shorts and flip-flops would do.

But then she looked at Andrea, who, in her crisp capris and heeled sandals, looked like she may as well be about to head into the office or a casual business lunch. Andrea was even more out of touch with island life than she was.

Eventually, they managed to board the ferry with minutes to spare, along with groups of tourists, who fought for the prime seats on the top deck.

Andrea had disappeared, no doubt trying desperately to cling to that last bar of cell reception, and Heather, seeing no space left on the sunny deck with the unobstructed view, went down to the lower level, pleased to see there was one last seat near the edge, on the side of the boat that she knew would give her all the feels as they approached the island, so she could see her family's house as it grew closer and closer.

It was vacant, of course—unless Kim had already arrived. In previous years, the house was rented out for the spring and early half of the summer, but that task had been overseen by their mother, who was careful to review applications and communicate with the caretaker about upkeep and issues. This year, there had been no renters. At best, Heather hoped that their father had remembered to ask the caretaker to stop over a few times a month to make sure that disaster hadn't fallen upon the house.

Fortunately, that caretaker lived in the house next door, with their old friend, Gemma Morgan, who was no doubt sure to keep an eye on things—or so she'd promised in the condolence card that she'd sent last August.

Heather held her canvas tote up higher so she could easily move down the narrow aisle of the boat, but a sudden lurch as the motor started thrust the heavy weight of another person against her back, and she only managed not to fall by grabbing one of the bench seatbacks.

"Are you okay, miss?"

She turned, her shock only compounded by the person she saw standing beside her. "Billy?"

He shook his head, looking at her in wonder. "Well, I'll be. Heather Taylor. There's a face I never thought I'd see today."

She couldn't agree with that statement more, yet here he was. Billy Davidson, longtime island friend, another one of the summer people who came and went with the change of the season, even if her heart still thought of him long into winter.

"You here on your own?" he asked when she pulled back, looking up into his hazel eyes that seemed to always grow greener as his skin tanned.

"I'm here with my sisters," she said. She hesitated, seeing the question in his eyes. He'd known she'd gotten married, of course. Their mothers had been friends and kept in touch. But now Heather's mother wasn't here anymore, so Billy probably hadn't heard the latest update. And of course, Heather had ensured that her mother never knew. "I'm not sure if you've heard that Kim is getting married next month?" Surely, his parents had been invited to the wedding, at least. "It's just a girls' trip this time. Like the old days."

He gave her a sad smile. "I was so sorry to hear about your mother. I still feel bad that I couldn't make the service. My parents said it was beautiful."

Heather pulled in a shaky breath and willed herself not to cry. The backs of her eyes prickled nonetheless, and she darted a glance over to the island, fixating on her happy place. Telling herself that for now, for these two weeks, all her problems would be set aside.

When she looked back up at Billy, he was still grinning at her in that friendly but devilish way that had made her and probably half the other women he ever encountered fall in love with him on the spot. And that's what she'd done when she was too young to even know what it was called back then. As a little girl, she'd only known that Billy was fun, but when she'd grown older, she started to notice that he was pretty cute too, and as the years past she'd dared to think that one day...

Well, there were lots of dreams back then.

"What about you?" She was eager to shift the topic from herself. "I didn't realize you still came back to the island."

The last few summers that she had visited, to her disappointment, Billy had not been there, even if by then she was a married woman, who saw him as an old friend, but more than that, as a part of the entire experience of coming back to the island. Without him, there was a void, just like she knew there would be one on this visit, without her mother.

"I've been coming back and forth all summer, actually," he said.

"Oh?" She hadn't heard any updates in a year on Billy. Last she knew, when she saw his parents at the funeral, he was still single, much to his mother's disappointment. The woman had longed for a grandchild as much as Heather's own mother.

And Heather had failed to produce one. And now, it was too late.

She swallowed hard and pushed those bad feelings away before they crept any further. They were almost to Evening Island. Soon, she would be home—to a home that was more of a home than any other she had known, at least. And Billy was standing in front of her, going her way. Today she deserved to be happy.

"I'm living in Pine Falls now," Billy explained, which made sense why he would come and go. With the ferry port just one town away in Blue Harbor, he could pop over to the island for the day if he wanted. "So I usually spend my weekends at the island house. Sometimes a long weekend. Depending on the rotation schedule at the practice, sometimes I come over midweek when I cover a few shifts at the Island Hospital."

There was that grin again.

"Well, you'll have to come for dinner one night, once we get settled."

"Absolutely! And I still owe you that drink from the time you beat me at rummy," he said.

Her cheeks turned pink when she realized that he still remembered. That must have been...nine years ago? Ten? They were still in college then. Still flush with the hope of a bright future, possibly even one together, or so she'd dared to once hope. "I beat you eleven times in a row, actually, but who's keeping score?"

My goodness! She was actually bantering! Flirting, even. And she was smiling, a genuine, real, heartfelt smile. She had forgotten what this felt like, but Billy didn't know that. Billy just knew her as the carefree summer girl, with the house on West End Road.

He didn't know about the tears and the fights, about the way she and Daniel would sometimes blame each other for all their problems and other times sit in silence, only quietly blaming themselves. He didn't know that she had tried and failed, to hold on to her marriage, to hold on to her job. To have a baby that never came.

He didn't know that part of her at all. A part of her past, really, just not so distant of one.

"Well, as a medical professional, I can't advise eleven alcoholic beverages in one night," he said, "but depending on how long you're staying, I may find a way to make it up to you over time."

"I'm here for two weeks, and I'm holding you to it." She grinned, and he did, too. And his eyes, God help her, they downright twinkled.

She didn't recognize this version of herself right now, being witty, confident, and downright fun. Somewhere along the way, she'd lost that part of herself.

But maybe Kim had been right. Maybe this trip would be fun after all.

6

ANDREA

Andrea finally admitted defeat and tucked her phone into her bag as the ferry approached the dock. She had no cell coverage and knew that it wouldn't be easy to find it on the island, but she would. She'd been scrambling all week to set up more meetings, more lunches, so when she returned to Chicago she could step right back in without missing a beat.

So she might be able to sleep a little easier on this trip, instead of worrying about what was going on at the office, what she was missing. Or worse—how far she was falling behind.

She looked up in time to see a man bend down and give Heather a peck on the cheek and then, with a grin, saunter away, while her sister stood and appeared to bask in the glow of that moment. Wait. Andrea darted her eyes to the retracting figure once more. Was it? It couldn't be. But it must.

She stood up from the wooden bench and hurried along

the boat deck, grabbing her sister's elbow as she approached. "Was that Billy Davidson?"

Heather's cheeks were flushed, and her eyes looked a little wild, but she nodded her head calmly and said, "Yep."

Well, this was certainly an interesting twist. Heather had never been shy about her feelings toward Billy—except to maybe Billy himself.

"What's that look for?"

"I didn't say a word," Andrea said, but she knew she was giving Heather the same coy smile she always used to give her when Billy first showed up each summer, usually on his old ten-speed, his hair windblown, his gaze always landing on the middle Taylor sister. "You and Billy always had a special friendship, that's all."

"We did," Heather said. "And a friendship is what it still is."

It was true, Andrea supposed. The summer people kept in touch over the year—but not by much. Still, they knew enough about everyone's whereabouts—like that the Morgan sisters whose family lake house was right beside theirs had also all ended up in Chicago, at least briefly. Years back, when they'd all been younger and newer to the city, they'd met up, but it felt strange and awkward and out of place. The island was what drew them all together, what kept their relationships special.

Besides, up until recently, Heather had been a happily married woman. Or so Andrea had thought.

She knew that her sister didn't like to talk about her marriage ending any more than she liked to talk about the circumstances that led to it. To this day, Andrea wasn't sure of the reason for the split, but she didn't pry. It wasn't her business, and relationships had never been her area of expertise. That was more Kim's territory. And their mother's, she thought sadly.

She adjusted her shoulder bag and moved aside for other passengers. The air was fresh with just the slightest breeze, and she could hear the sound of horse hooves clacking in the distance. She took a few breaths, trying to pull herself away from all that business back in Chicago, knowing that she would have to find a way to stop thinking about it for a couple of weeks at least.

"Any word from Kim?" Heather asked once their luggage had been unloaded.

Andrea hadn't seen anything pop up on her phone, but then, she'd been engrossed in firing off as many emails to her assistant, her boss, and every active client she had so that everything was covered in her absence.

She shook her head. "Maybe she's already there. I know she had hoped that one of us would have gone to Mom and Dad's." She caught herself, and, seeing the widening of her sister's eyes, motioned to the street ahead. They'd need to flag a carriage, and they wouldn't be the only ones hoping to do so on a Saturday evening. Tourism kept this island going— even if some of her happiest memories were those spent in her youth, early in June when school had just let out and the island felt quieter, like it was their own private world.

"I think she knew there was no chance of you taking another day off work Friday to head out early," Heather assured her as they managed to slowly work their luggage to the street opening. The smell of fudge—the island's famed treat—was strong and sweet. Andrea's stomach rumbled loud enough for Heather to hear and they both laughed. It was a relief to ease the tension.

"I don't mean to be hard on Kim, but she sometimes forgets that while she's been busy collecting another degree and playing wedding planner, the rest of us are trying to earn a living."

Heather's look showed Andrea what she already knew. She was being unfair, even if there was truth in that statement. As the youngest, Kim had always been doted upon by everyone in the family including her, and everything fell into stride for Kim in a way that it never had for Andrea. Kim didn't worry too much about grades but did just fine anyway while maintaining an active social life all through high school and college. She'd worked in her twenties, but clocking out at five suited her, and she always used up every vacation day, sometimes dipping into the sick ones, too. When she decided to go back to school for a one-year master's program, she didn't think twice about walking away from her job or starting over again. And now she was marrying into a wealthy family that seemed to have become her preferred people within moments of meeting them.

Andrea suspected that Heather shared her sentiments. The pinched look on her face all through Kim's bridal shower a few weeks ago said as much.

"Sorry. It's been a crazy week at work and there were a lot of loose ends I was hoping to tie up before I get back." She didn't need to meet her sister's eye to know that there was little chance of that happening on this remote island. In town, she might stand a chance, but at the house, she could probably forget it. "I'll feel better once I have a hot shower and a good night's sleep."

They managed to get on the next carriage coming down the street, and for the entire ride to the house sat in companionable silence, listening to the trotting of the horses' hooves on the dirt road, taking in the scenic view of Evening Island in full bloom, from the lush flowering shrubs and picket fences to the dark blue water of Lake Huron that stretched far into the distance.

It had been a long time since she'd been back to the island. Once they were older, her parents chose to rent out the old Victorian on West End Road for the spring and early summer months, always returning in August to close out the summer. When Andrea had first graduated from college, she used to come up for Labor Day weekend, even though Kim always stayed longer, and Heather came up most weekends for August. But then Heather got married and Labor Day became her time, too, along with Daniel, who balanced things out for their father, not that he'd ever complained about being outnumbered. Still, Andrea knew he enjoyed having another guy in the family, and it wasn't like Andrea was ever bringing anyone home. She didn't have time for anything that serious.

She didn't have time for Evening Island most years, either. She'd told herself—and her mother—that she'd come up last year. Set aside the time for it, even. Little did she know how that time would be spent instead.

She forced her eyes on the road ahead, where a row of large homes faced the water, their front porches inviting and stirring up memories of happier days. Though they were called cottages here on the island, their scale said otherwise. Each home was different, with its own family and story, but over time they'd overlapped, the summers blurring together with the same familiar faces.

As they came to a stop in front of the robin's egg blue house with the white front door and the wraparound porch that was always the best spot for taking in the sunset, she couldn't help but think how much she missed being here. But then, if she used up even a fraction of the vacation days she'd accrued over the years, she'd always assumed she could kiss any chance of partnership goodbye for good.

Now she wondered just how much that choice had cost her, in every possible way.

Quickly, they unloaded their bags and paid the driver. The street was otherwise quiet, as this stretch often was. Occasionally a tourist pedaled by on a rented turquoise bicycle, but otherwise, it was kept to the company of the Andersons, Morgans, and Taylors. The summer friends.

"The house looks good," Andrea remarked, staring up at it from the edge of the grass and admiring the colorful flowers that she couldn't even begin to name. The peonies bloomed in July here on Evening Island, but the lilacs were what it was known for. More than once, they'd made the trip in spring to see them bloom and participate in the island's annual festival. "The paint looks fresh."

"Well, there's a new caretaker," Heather said. "You know that Edward retired a while back. Now his grandson keeps an eye on the place, and he's also dating Gemma. They live here now," she said, motioning to the Morgan home, fondly known as Sunset Cottage.

"I thought Ellie was the one living here year-round," Andrea said. At least, that had been the case last time she'd been here, but that had been years ago.

"Ellie's in Europe right now, focusing on her art career."

Andrea didn't know that, because unlike her sisters, who had engaged with guests at their mother's funeral, and later read each and every card before tucking them into a keepsake box, Andrea had stayed in their father's study for most of that hazy weekend, avoiding the hugs and murmurs of sympathy, aching to get back to Chicago, to think about something—anything—other than her situation.

She pinched her lips, wanting to defend herself for not visiting more, or keeping in touch with their island friends more, but knew that it wouldn't help her case. Neither of her sisters understood the importance of her career. The only person who understood was her father, but then, he was just as busy and hard to reach as she was, making their camaraderie a lonely one.

Andrea scanned the porch and large paned windows, thinking of how familiar and foreign it felt all at once. Like no time had passed even though so much had. The house was frozen in time. A better time.

Kim's old yellow bicycle was propped against the side of the porch: a sure-tell sign that she had already arrived.

Now, as Andrea carefully set her luggage on the porch and waited for Heather to open the door, she felt a pang of jealousy over the evening that Kim had shared with their dad last night while she was putting in her final hours at the office, wishing for that kind of freedom that she'd made impossible for herself to ever find.

Until now.

With an intake of breath, she watched as Heather turned the handle at the same time that Kim pulled it open from the inside.

"You're here!" Kim's excitement was contagious as much as it was somewhat out of place. After all, they all lived in the same city, and even if they might not meet up very often, the opportunity was always there.

"It looks exactly the same," Andrea said as she set her luggage down in the large entrance hall and looked around at the scuffed wooden floorboards and lead-paned windows original to the home. There was a ray of light coming from the largest window on the landing, and now Andrea looked up the stairs, which didn't seem so tall anymore, and set her hand on the ornate banister as she eased off her shoes, which were probably not the most appropriate for the dirt roads all over the island. She hadn't known what to pack, it had been so long, and she hadn't been able to think clearly when she was studying her closet last night. She'd been too shaken since departing the office; even though it was only for two weeks, she couldn't shake the strange sensation that it could be for the last time.

Just in case, she'd left her favorite plant on the window ledge, with strict instruction to Nicole for its care.

"Of course it looks the same," Kim said good-naturedly as she closed the door. There was no air-conditioning in the house, but the ceiling fan in the front living room was running on high, and already Andrea could feel the evening breeze filtering in from the back rooms where Kim must have already opened the windows.

They walked back to the kitchen, with its vintage cupboards that had been painted a soft blue about twenty years ago, with the outdated appliances that still functioned, but only with routine maintenance and care. Andrea could see that the house had been well kept in their absence. She made a mental note to thank this new caretaker when she met him.

"I stopped by the Main Street Market after I arrived so there's a bit of food, but not much," Kim said.

Considering it had to be transported via a bicycle basket, Andrea wasn't surprised to find only a few items in the fridge. Heather reached for the pitcher of lemonade and, as was her nature, poured them each a glass.

"How was Dad?" Andrea asked, sipping her drink and letting it cool her skin. Through the kitchen window, she stared at their old playhouse—which had once felt so big and now seemed so small—complete with curtains in the windows. It had been transformed into a gardening shed years back. Probably, that had always been its intended use. She smiled at it now, exhaling a long breath. She'd be okay. She'd find a new routine. She'd stay busy. She'd get a little fresh air. And then she'd get back to the city. To her life.

Kim flicked on the tap and began filling one of the large ceramic vases that their mother had collected over the years from the boutiques in town. "Dad? He's fine."

Andrea fought back a surge of annoyance and leaned against the counter. "Fine? What else?"

Kim shrugged and turned off the water. There was a pile of hydrangea on the counter, and she proceeded to set a few in the vase. "I'm not sure what you want to know. He's fine. You know how Dad is."

"I do know how Dad is," Andrea said. They all did. The man was busy. Always was, and it had only increased since last summer. But then, she supposed the same could be said for herself. "But I'm not the one who had a chance to see him just a few hours ago."

"Hey, I asked. You could have come."

Andrea stared at her sister. It wasn't like Kim to snap, much less use a firm tone. Kim was happy going with the flow, nothing bothered her, and if it did, she wasn't quick to show it.

Now, Andrea wondered just what she was implying, and what she wasn't saying.

"I couldn't take yesterday off to come to Michigan," Andrea reminded her. "If you really felt strongly about all going together, we could have stopped over to see Dad today and then come up to the island tomorrow instead."

But Kim was shaking her head. "Dad's flying out of town tonight. I told you, but you probably don't remember."

No, Andrea didn't remember, but once again, the tone Kim used was what Andrea cared about more.

"You seem mad at me." She flicked her gaze at Heather, who gulped her lemonade, avoiding input and probably still relishing in the fact that Billy was currently within walkable distance from her at this very moment.

"I'm not mad at you!" Kim lifted the vase of hydrangea from the counter and walked out of the room with it.

Andrea—never one to back down from anything— followed her down the hallway with its wood-paneled walls that housed framed prints of the island, collected over time. "You're clearly mad at me. Can you blame me for having to work?"

"I don't blame you for having to work," Kim said, but Andrea suspected this wasn't true. She'd seen the look on Kim's face over the years when she'd shown up late for a coffee or dinner because a client call delayed her. Kim took it personally, and there was absolutely nothing personal about Andrea's work.

And maybe that was half the problem, she thought, pushing back the memory of Pamela's words.

Kim set the vase on the console table near the fireplace in the front room, the one that was lined with framed photos of their past summers going all the way back to when Andrea was just a chubby baby sitting on her mother's lap on one of the wicker chairs on the porch. Andrea looked at the photos, some black and white, others grainy, knowing each one even though she hadn't seen them in so long. Her heart ached when she saw the last one she was in, a portrait of the entire family. She'd only come for a long weekend that year. She'd promised her mother she'd try to stay longer the next time.

That was a promise she hadn't kept.

"So Dad is fine," Andrea reiterated, looking away. She talked to him about once a month, but between his travel schedule and her long hours, their calls were usually brief, but pleasant. "How did he look?" When she'd seen him at Christmas, he'd seemed older than he'd been just a few months before. Maybe a little thinner too. It had hurt her to see. Reminded her of the circumstances she tried to forget.

Kim seemed to think about this for a moment. "He looked really good, actually."

Andrea wondered then why she didn't seem very happy in reporting this. "Okay, well, that's good. And he's still traveling a lot. It's not too much for him?"

Kim fluffed the flowers, not saying anything. Finally, she met her eye. "He seemed better, Andrea. Really, he seemed fine."

Well, that was something. Andrea sighed, deciding not to push the topic. Kim was upset with Andrea for not going with her yesterday and unwilling to communicate it, and Andrea had plenty of things she could say to Kim, but now was hardly the time. Her clothes felt stale from the long drive, and her skin felt dusty from the carriage ride. She needed a long, hot shower or a soak in the claw-foot tub in the bathroom at the top of the stairs. Maybe an evening walk.

Preferably somewhere she could get some cell reception. It might be a Saturday, and she might be on vacation, but that had never stopped her before.

"Well, I'm going to get settled. It's been a long day." And judging from the way things were going, it was going to be an even longer two weeks.

She picked up as much of her luggage as she could carry and began her ascent up the winding stairs, admiring the carved wood banister and the tall window that let the light flow in on the landing. She took in the high ceilings once she reached the second floor and walked to her old bedroom, letting her hand rest on the old brass knob—they didn't make them like this anymore. Inside, her room was just as she remembered it. A wrought-iron bed flanked by two small tables. A window seat with a view of the lake. Someone—probably Kim, but possibly the caretaker—had already thought to crack the window, letting the evening breeze flow. It was so quiet, as if the outside world didn't exist at all, and all that she had to focus on was the beauty of this house and everything surrounding it.

She supposed there was certainly a worse place to be trapped.

7

KIM

Things were not off to a great start. That much was obvious, even if she could almost fool herself into thinking otherwise. Kim sat on the edge of her bed and stared out the open window at the unobstructed view of the shimmering lake. The first morning on the island was always the most exciting in past years, when the pent-up cabin fever from a long Midwestern winter, or later, city life, made her want to toss back the sheet and faded summer quilt and rush outside, still in her pajamas. And she often did that, even if as she got older it was just to sit on the front porch and admire the view with a cup of coffee.

She'd do it today, per tradition. Convince herself that coming here hadn't been a bad idea. That this trip could be just as magical as all those that came before it. That she and her sisters could shed their real-life problems for a couple of weeks and fall into a different rhythm—the one that was slower, and more relaxed, the one that was almost enough to make them dare to think that life across the water didn't exist at all. At least for a little while.

Unlike in years past, Kim dressed before going downstairs—and showered—because she knew from experience that the hot water tank could easily drain before she had a chance to hop in, and while this might not have bothered her so much when she was young, it did now.

By the time she entered the kitchen, she dared to hope that today would be a fresh start. The entire day stretched ahead without obligation, or even the threat of a text or phone call, unless she happened to hit cell coverage, and maybe she wouldn't bother to try. Maybe, when she went out, she would leave her phone back at the house. Fully embrace this vacation for the escape that it was.

Try not to think about the way she and Bran had left things, even if she'd gone to bed last night unsettled about more than her argument with Andrea, who hadn't shown her face again for the rest of the evening.

The coffee had already been brewed when she went into the kitchen, likely by Heather who was thoughtful like that, but possibly by Andrea, who was keen to stress that she always liked an early start. Kim braced herself for who might be awake right now, but her sisters were nowhere in sight. The fruit that she'd purchased at the Main Street Market yesterday looked a little lean, she noticed. Her money was on Andrea, then, who was more in control of her diet than Kim, and Kim was the one who had to fit into that wedding dress (she could only imagine what Lynette would say if she gained an ounce and something had to be altered). Yes, probably

Andrea. She barely slept. Her hours were long, yet she still managed to get to the gym at least once a day.

Kim was surprised, then, to find that it was Heather who was sitting in one of the wicker chairs on the front porch, sipping a coffee, and staring out onto the water. She looked startled to see Kim and quickly smiled when she saw her.

Kim thought she detected some redness in her sister's eyes, but Heather didn't seem to want to focus on that.

No doubt she was thinking about their mother. There was no avoiding that sentiment here in the house she had loved so much. It had almost been as startling to enter this empty house yesterday as it had been in Grosse Pointe. But the distraction of her father's big announcement had kept her mind on other matters.

She couldn't exactly feel grateful for that.

"You're up early," Kim said, dropping onto another chair —her favorite, which Heather had been considerate enough to leave for her. She noticed little things like that, always had. Their mother used to always say that Heather would make a wonderful mother one day, and it was true. She enjoyed small domestic tasks, taking pride in everything from making her bed to baking. She'd even managed to make a career of it, describing the details of her home renovation, her recipe for a perfect birthday cake, or tips on starting a vegetable garden, even in the city. Kim now realized with a wave of guilt that she had been so busy reading wedding magazines lately that she hadn't read one of Heather's articles in months. "Is Andrea awake yet?"

Heather nodded, then gave Kim a little smile. "She's already taken a run. Lapped the island, I think."

"You're kidding me." The island was eight miles around, and it wasn't even nine in the morning yet. Kim's jaw slacked, but then she and Heather started to laugh. It felt good to share a laugh like this with her sister. It reminded her that too much time had passed since they'd last done it.

She sipped her coffee and admired the view. "She's certainly a shining example of a successful woman."

"Oh, now, don't sell yourself short. As I recall, you have a wedding around the corner and a new job lined up too."

Kim felt her lips thin. She was no longer certain that one of those things would happen. If she was being completely honest with herself, some days, she wasn't sure which one it would be.

She glanced over at Heather, knowing that she could tell her about Lynette's reaction to starting a career, but there was a strange, sad look in Heather's eyes as she looked out over the water, and so Kim decided to let it wait. Besides, she didn't want to taint her first morning on the island thinking about Lynette or the job or the honeymoon or any of it.

The first morning on the island was how the tone was set. Today was a fresh start.

"Where's Andrea now?" she asked, thinking of how they'd left things last night. When she didn't come back downstairs for dinner, Heather had made them both grilled cheese sandwiches with sliced tomatoes—somehow managing to turn their small list of provisions into a delicious and comforting meal which they'd eaten in silence, sharing a bottle of wine on the porch and admiring the sunset before turning into bed. They didn't talk about the tension—or about the fact that Andrea hadn't joined them.

Or that it was a little strange being all together like this, and that something had shifted in their relationship over the past year.

Heather was no doubt thinking of that too because she gave Kim a conspiratorial grin and said, "Don't worry. She was in a better mood after her run. It gets her endorphins going."

That was a relief. "Maybe she burned off some of that stress." Andrea was always stressed, and always declaring it too. But then, Andrea did have a big job. Something that Kim couldn't understand. And possibly never would.

"Or maybe she found some cell coverage," Heather said simply, and they both erupted into a fit of giggles again.

"What's so funny?" It was Andrea, coming up from behind them on the porch, looking perfectly put together in her navy linen pants and a white cotton tee, her auburn hair held back in a low ponytail.

"How was your run?" Kim asked, dodging the question.

Andrea's smile came easier now. "Good. I love getting up before the tourists. It makes me feel like I have the entire island to myself. I almost forgot how beautiful it was. The water on one side, the woods and homes on the other."

"I didn't," Kim sighed. "But it still manages to impress me each time I visit."

She fell silent for a moment, thinking of how much she wished her mother could be here. How much she wished that she could tell someone—anyone—about her father's big news. But telling her sisters would just upset them, and seeing how quick to snap Andrea had been last night, Kim wasn't looking forward to being the messenger.

Besides, it was the first morning on the island. She wasn't going to spoil it by even thinking about this woman who, with any luck, might be out of the picture by the time her wedding came around.

If it came around.

She pushed that thought aside, but she couldn't completely shake it. Ever since her dad had told her about his girlfriend, all she could think was that if she called off the wedding, she wouldn't have to meet the woman who would hopefully be gone by the holidays. Her sisters would never have to find out. And everything could just continue, same as it had always been.

Oh, who was she kidding? Nothing would ever be the same again. Even here, in their happy place. Her conversations with even Heather were stilted, Andrea was practically developing lockjaw, and her eyes kept flicking to the cell phone she clutched in one hand, and Kim...Kim wouldn't stop thinking of everything going on across the water, even though that's exactly what she had come here to do.

She stirred at the sound of someone whistling an unrecognizable tune and looked over to see a man—a good-looking one at that—crossing the stretch of lawn to their house.

"You must be the famous Taylor trio!" He grinned broadly as he approached the base of the steps. All three sisters had now stopped to give him their full attention. "I'm Leo Helms. I took over caring for this place from my grandfather Edward?"

So this was Leo! They were all aware of Edward and Leo's assistance from their mother, but it wasn't until Gemma's letter last August that Kim had learned of her newfound love.

She could certainly understand why Gemma had given up her city life to live on the island full-time.

"Is Gemma stopping by?" Kim asked now, as Leo made his way onto the porch.

He shook his head. "She's on a tight deadline, but she promises to stop by tomorrow."

Gemma was a successful romance novelist, and Kim now wondered if the island would be the backdrop of her next novel—and if Leo would be the hero. With his rugged good looks, she suspected as much, but it was his friendly smile that Kim appreciated. The house had been in good hands. With any luck, it would stay that way.

Thinking of her father's comment, she was depending on it.

Leo extended a hand to each of them, and introductions were made.

"You have your grandfather's eyes," Heather told him, giving a wistful smile.

"How is he?" They'd all been so fond of Edward growing up, and Kim made a mental note to seek him out before she left.

Leo gave a good-natured shrug. "Fishing every day the weather cooperates. And some days that it doesn't."

"He's a wonderful man." Kim smiled, knowing that her sisters shared the sentiment. Old Edward had been just as much a fixture to their annual visits as the people who lived on this street.

"And just like your grandfather, you've done a great job

with the place," Andrea told him. "It looks as if we were just here yesterday."

Kim felt a knot rise in her throat. If only. It had been two years since she'd been back here, but Andrea was right, it was as if they'd walked in and picked up right where they'd left off.

"That was the intention. Of course, there's been a little upkeep needed along the way. These big old homes don't age as easily as we do." Leo grinned, but this time Kim struggled to match his lighthearted demeanor.

Her father's words echoed in her mind. He'd keep the house *if*... And that was a big if, wasn't it? Andrea would likely never come back after this trip, and Heather might, but how often? And as for her... Kim pulled in a breath. She couldn't think about all that right now. She had to enjoy the time while she was here.

"How have the renters been treating the house?" Andrea asked. The demand was usually strong and steady, and the income helped pay for the upkeep.

"Your father didn't set any up for this season, but last year we had a good turnout. Mostly families, large family reunions, that type of thing. Everyone is respectful, but it's still good to be careful. Next year I'll be able to keep an eye on things more closely now that I'm just next door."

Next year. Would there be a next year? Kim couldn't even visualize next month anymore, let alone next year!

"Well, I don't want to keep you," Leo said, taking a step back down the steps. "I've got to get into town, but I couldn't pass by without introducing myself. And just to let you know, the fridge light is a little finicky and I'm still planning to clean out the attic soon on one of the cooler days."

"I love that old attic," Andrea remarked.

"Well, mind the dust up there. And the mice." Leo flashed a wicked grin when Andrea and Heather gasped, and Kim couldn't quite discern if he was joking or not. Still, he managed to pull a smile from her.

After he left, Kim turned to her sisters. "I can certainly see his appeal! No wonder Gemma moved to the island permanently."

"It will be good to see her tomorrow," Heather said. "I'm sure we'll hear all the details then."

Yes, Kim was sure they would. And if she wasn't going to be seeing Gemma today, then it was time to think about how she would spend the time.

"I was thinking we could go into town this morning, maybe do some shopping?" Kim looked from one sister to the next. "We'll need more groceries. Maybe we can all have lunch at the Lighthouse Bistro, and then later take a bike ride?"

The Lighthouse Bistro was a local spot that had been a family favorite for years. Set right on the lawn of one of the larger inns in town, its waterfront views made it the perfect spot to relax and enjoy the scenery. They also made an excellent whitefish sandwich, something that seemed to be perfected here on the island and not something she could ever find on a menu back home.

Home. She considered that word for a moment. Was Chicago really her home? Bran's sterile glass and concrete apartment high in the sky? It wasn't what she thought of as home. And since her mother had died, the house in Grosse Pointe no longer held that title either.

She turned eagerly to her sisters. Lunch and shopping in town. It would be the perfect start to their trip.

Surprisingly, it was Heather who looked reluctant. "I'm still a bit tired from all that driving yesterday, but I won't stop you two from going on ahead."

Kim couldn't hide her disappointment even though she was probably expecting too much. They hadn't all been together here in years, and as much as she wanted it to go back to the way it all used to be, it couldn't. Their mother wasn't down on the steps, watering the hydrangea or snipping the best blooms for a colorful centerpiece to brighten their dinner table. And just like all the other little girls who used to chase fireflies at dusk until their mothers called them in, they'd grown up and changed. Drifted apart.

"It was just an idea," Kim said. They could always go to the bistro tomorrow instead. Maybe she'd pop over next door and see if Gemma was free to join them. She and Heather had kept an eye on the neighboring Victorian house last night, and while the lights were on in the far back, they both seemed reluctant to socialize after the long day.

Maybe that's all it was, Kim thought. Maybe everyone was just tired.

"I know why Heather isn't up for it." Andrea gave a little smile and leaned against the porch rail, her back to the view.

Kim looked up at her sister, wondering what she was missing, but one glance at Heather's pink cheeks told her it was certainly something.

"Heather ran into Billy yesterday," Andrea informed her.

Well, this certainly was news! Kim looked at Heather, happy that for once it wouldn't be her own love life they were all discussing. Andrea never seemed to have time to date, and with Heather's divorce, Kim didn't exactly feel comfortable asking for details on that front. But Billy Davidson had been Heather's first love, or at least first crush, and judging from the way she struggled to fight off a smile, she hadn't completely gotten over it.

"He's on the island?" Kim considered this. They had made friends in the years they had come up—other seasonal people, especially all the girls on West End Road. The Morgan family next door was their favorite trio, similar in age, and always reliable, coming summer after summer until they eventually aged out and grew up, much like the Taylors. Then there were the Andersons, who occupied the house on the other side of the Morgans. Some of their happiest memories were those spent playing all day until they caught fireflies at night, splashing in the cool waters across the road, picking flowers and berries by day, and decorating their play-house in the backyard or swinging on the hammock in the Morgans' backyard, telling ghost stories and counting the stars.

Kim knew that the Morgans' grandmother, who owned their summer house, had passed a while back, and that Ellie, the youngest of the Morgans, had lived on the island year-round for some time. As of last summer, though, things had changed, and Ellie had gone abroad while it was Gemma, the middle sister, who stayed behind, after meeting Leo. Kim had read Gemma's card more than once last August, thinking of life here on the island and the visit that they hadn't been able to make happen. How things were changing, even here, just as things were for their family.

She glanced over at Sunset Cottage now, having a yearning for those old times, when West End Road was filled with the laughter of nine barefoot girls, and sometimes, a cute little boy named Billy.

"Billy is a doctor now and he lives in Pine Falls. He spends his weekends here, apparently," Heather said matter-of-factly. "He also covers some shifts at the Island Hospital."

They all knew that Billy had become a doctor, but the rest was news. "Well, isn't that idyllic. I'd love to be able to get back here more often." Kim frowned into her mug. Maybe she could convince Bran to join her some years. Or maybe she couldn't. She realized that she was almost afraid to ask, to have things confirmed and the hope shut down for good.

"He's still handsome," Andrea chided. She glanced at Kim. There was still some underlying tension in her gaze. "He was on the ferry with us."

Heather's look was rueful. "As I told Andrea, Billy and I are just old friends. But, of course, it's nice to see him again."

Kim nodded. "Of course. We'll have to have him over, or meet up in town."

Heather looked noncommittal and Kim wondered if she'd overstepped. One glance at Andrea confirmed her suspicions.

"I didn't mean to tease," Andrea said gently. "I just know that you used to have a thing for him."

Everyone knew. Probably even Billy himself, not that Kim would point that out.

"That's all in the past now," Heather said.

Kim knew that Heather rarely discussed her ex-husband. The divorce was recent; the reasons unknown or, at least, not shared. One day he was at her side at the funeral, and the next time they spoke, Heather announced that Daniel had moved out. But now they were all here, sisters reunited for two full weeks. Kim realized that this was probably more hours together than all the time they'd spent combined since Andrea had first started working full-time or Heather had gotten married.

And it would only become less once she was officially a Croft.

If she became a Croft.

"You're free to date, though," Kim encouraged. That flush in Heather's cheeks when Billy's name was mentioned was the most like her old self that she'd seen her sister in a long time, even before she announced that she and Daniel were ending their marriage—but then, Kim had always chalked that up to worry for their mother's declining health. "We just want to see you happy."

With a jolt, she realized that those were the very same words she'd said to her father just two nights ago, only the difference was that Heather and her husband had mutually decided to end their relationship, whereas their father...

She closed her eyes. She would not think about it. Not this morning. Not today. Preferably not even on this trip.

"I don't think I'll get married again," Heather said tightly, and Kim could only stare at her. At thirty-one, her sister was only three years older than she was. She was young and pretty and funny when she was in a happier state. She was an excellent cook and a shark at cards, and she was a wonderful listener, too. In other words, she was a catch.

"You say that now, but in time—"

But Heather was shaking her head. "No. I…I'm not cut out for marriage, I've learned."

Kim swallowed hard, falling silent. What did that even mean, *not cut out for marriage*? Maybe *she* wasn't cut out for marriage—the obligations and sacrifices were already piling up, and she was already struggling to balance her needs with Bran's, and they were only engaged.

Was she just not cut out for it? Was she unwilling to compromise? Was she incapable of holding up the promises that she'd already made, much less the vows she'd intended to say?

Her stomach felt a little queasy and she set down her coffee. Her diamond ring glittered in the morning sunlight. She felt like it was trying to tell her something.

The women fell silent, the topic of conversation clearly not up for further discussion.

"Well, I think I'll walk into town before the day slips away," Kim said, fighting off the injured feeling that her sisters didn't jump on board. They still had two weeks stretched ahead of them: long and lazy, sun-filled days.

Besides, right now, she almost needed to be alone with her thoughts. And she wasn't sure how much longer she could pretend that everything was okay…with their father or with her sisters. Or with herself.

8

HEATHER

Since losing her job at the magazine, Heather had grown all too used to long days that dragged out before her without much structure or purpose. Here on Evening Island, she at least felt like she had an excuse to be so idle, or passive. There was no mortgage to worry about or bills to open, reminding her of life's responsibilities and the looming stress that she hadn't received a single call back from the numerous magazines and local papers she'd applied to, despite securing a reference from her former boss, who tried to be understanding of Heather's "situation" but not understanding enough to continue to employ her.

She'd loved that job once—loved sharing ideas for the holidays and tips for the new homeowner, loved thinking that maybe she'd helped another woman start a new tradition or find new meaning in her home—until it had started to feel like a sham and a lie. Like she was pretending to be something she wasn't. She wasn't even sure what she was doing anymore. Or who she was.

Once she had been Heather Taylor, of Grosse Pointe. Then she had been Daniels's wife for five years, with hopes and dreams, hosting small dinner parties for friends, and the occasional holiday meal, too, balancing a career that always came second to family life, until it was all that was left, and then, it hadn't been enough. What made her the expert on a happy home, after all?

She'd let everything slip away, one by one, until she had nothing left. No friends had called in a while. Though to be fair, she hadn't reached out, either. And her career... Now it might be all that remained if she could find a way to even salvage it. She'd be like Andrea, who seemed satisfied enough on her own or at least never complained about being lonely or wanting more. She'd throw herself into her next opportunity, meet new people who wouldn't even have to know about her former life. Her first chapter. She'd be the carefree single woman who made it clear that she preferred it that way. She'd be strong and independent.

But it wouldn't come naturally. Nothing did anymore.

Well, other than cooking. Here in the quiet kitchen on the island, it didn't feel so wrong to make a meal again. Her sisters would live off cereal if left to their own devices, she knew, so she took stock of the lean ingredients and made a lunch out of the tomatoes, cheese, and toasted bread, her efforts worthwhile when Andrea deigned to look up from her work files for a few minutes to smile and thank her.

Heather took her sandwich across the street to the shore, eating alone as she'd grown used to doing and watching the sailboats bob in the distance. Eventually, she stood and followed the lakefront path, dipping her toes in the clear, cool water, staring out over the horizon, wondering about where land hit, what it held. Thinking that she used to look so forward to the future, back when it was all mapped out and planned for her, and now she rarely even gave it much thought. She walked along the West Shore, letting the sound of the lapping water soothe her, all the way down to the view of the South Shore Lighthouse, keeping her feet busy and her mind distracted by her surroundings. She and Daniel used to come down here, to watch the ferries passing by. He'd enjoyed coming to the island, but he'd never loved it as she did. Still, he never complained. He'd been good like that, willing to stand at her side. After they'd already ended things, he'd come to her mother's service, and even though they were pretending that they were still a happy couple, she knew that he wasn't faking his emotion when he wiped the tears from his eyes.

She pulled in a sigh. When she was younger, she assumed that people who divorced just stopped loving each other, but now she knew that life was so much more complicated than that. But some things, like the simplicity of this island, made it easier to accept.

She didn't think about Billy until she began to trek in the direction of home, her route meandering so she could take in some of her favorite sites on the island, her gaze drifting down the tree-lined street of smaller homes closer to the shops and inns in town, toward Billy's family's house. He might be inside, or out front on the yard or his porch, or he might have taken the ferry back today, to get ready for the workweek tomorrow.

She decided to check, under the guise of friendship,

because that was all it was, of course. All it ever had been. And now, she was certain, all it ever could be.

The house was painted a happy shade of blue, softer than the color of the water, reminiscent of summer skies and fond memories. She slowed in front, near the overgrown hydrangea bushes that were bursting with pink blooms, but the wraparound porch was empty, and the inside of the house appeared dark; the windows were closed, not open to any fresh air or lake breezes, and the door was firmly closed behind the screen.

She fought back a sigh of disappointment, telling herself she could always look for him next weekend, or take the ferry over to Blue Harbor, hop in her car and drive to Pine Falls if she really wanted to see him, but that would be something the old Heather would have done. Back when she was spunky and confident. Back when she thought that the world was hers for the taking, not one that would knock her down when she wasn't expecting it.

"Looking for me?" a voice behind her said, and she turned, pleased, to see Billy grinning back at her, his arms full of grocery bags.

"I was out for a walk." She reached out to take the closest bag. "Let me help."

"Thanks." He jutted his chin toward his flagstone path, indicating that she should go first. "Door's unlocked," he told her as they approached the porch.

Heather turned the knob, letting herself into the familiar hall, and back around the corner, to the cozy kitchen, where she deposited the bag on the counter. She could still remember ditching her bike on the front lawn beside Billy's ten-speed and coming into this very room in search of a cold glass of lemonade, their cheeks sweaty and flushed, their eyes bright and eager for more. She'd relished every minute of life back then, looked forward to every hour on this island. She hadn't wasted any of it.

Well, other than never telling Billy how she felt about him.

She opened the pantry and neatly stacked the dry goods, unable to resist organizing a few of the items already there by category. Her cheeks flushed when she caught Billy staring at her with a curious grin.

"Sorry," she said, laughing at herself. "Force of habit. My September article four years ago was about pantry organization, and it was a fan favorite."

"After that, I have to insist that you stay for dinner." Billy flashed her one of those adorable smiles that used to make her want to stare at him until she had to go home and began unloading the groceries: a bottle of wine, some fresh fish, an assortment of vegetables.

"You know how to cook!" She couldn't help but be impressed. Daniel hadn't even tried, not that's she'd minded. She used to enjoy cooking for the two of them, or friends and neighbors who regularly stopped by. She used to enjoy the simple pleasures of domestic life, knowing that something she had created had brought happiness to another.

Other than last night and today, she couldn't remember the last time she'd cooked something more advanced than some pasta with jarred sauce—she nearly laughed when she considered how that subject would have gone over for her readership. Nights out were few and far between, and the one time she'd called her favorite take-out place, they'd assumed she wanted the usual order: meaning, an order for two.

"Yes, I can cook. I find it relaxes me after a busy day." He looked out the window. "Or, a not so busy one."

She laughed. "In that case, I can't see how I can resist."

Not that she needed much convincing. She'd always enjoyed Billy's company, the ease of their banter, not to mention the way her heart would flutter every time he smiled her way. She knew that there had been talk amongst the mothers on West End Road that she and Billy would end up together someday, but when she brought Daniel home that summer after college instead, her mother had been gracious and understanding, and not the least disappointed. "Whatever makes you happy makes me happy," her mother had told her.

Now, Heather didn't know what made her happy. But she knew that she was happy at this moment, being with Billy in this sweet cottage under the shade of the tall eaves.

"What can I do to help?"

"Pour the wine?" He gathered up a few ingredients and motioned back to the door. "I thought we could outside. I find myself never wanting to stay indoors for long when I'm here on the island."

"Me either." She followed him onto the porch that extended back to the kitchen. Soon she was settled on a wicker chair, sipping a glass of wine from a local winery in Blue Harbor, watching Billy man the grill at the base of the far steps.

Billy closed the lid and crossed the wood-planked floor,

happily accepting a glass of wine as he settled onto a chair. "Well, this is the way to spend an evening."

Heather felt her cheeks flush, and she rushed to say, "I hope my sisters will survive without me." But then, they'd survived the past year without each other, more or less. Or at least, gotten through it.

"If they give you a hard time, just tell them I made it impossible for you to say no."

That was certainly true. "I can't remember the last time I had someone cook for me."

"Your husband doesn't cook?" Billy asked lightly.

Heather tensed, thrown for a moment. But then, of course, Billy wouldn't know. He'd assume that she was here for a girls' trip. That's what she'd led him to believe. A little pre-wedding celebration that would hopefully be nicer than that awful shower.

"Daniel and I are no longer together," she said. "We're no longer married, I should say."

He frowned. "My mother didn't tell me."

Heather shrugged. "She wouldn't have known, at least, that was the intent. We were already separated before the funeral, but with my mother being so sick, I didn't mention it to anyone. It didn't seem like the right thing to do at the time."

Even her sisters didn't know this, or her father, because they were dealing with their own grief and struggles. And then it eventually became easier not to talk about it at all.

Billy's smile was sad. "That's a lot to hold in."

She nodded. It had been, but eventually, it became a

relief, because the reason they'd split up, the real root of it all, was too painful to discuss. Even now.

"How about you? Is there anyone special in your life?" Judging from his presence here alone, she assumed there wasn't. Maybe even hoped so, too.

"Nah." He shook his head. "No one special."

Was it the wine, or did his gaze seem to linger on her a little longer than she was used to? She felt her cheeks flush and took another sip from her glass, hoping to hide it or at least blame it on the warm summer night.

"I'm married to my work, as my mother is keen to tell me in a deeply disappointed tone."

She laughed. "She just wants what's best for you." Both of their mothers had.

Heather could still recall one of the last conversations she'd had with her mother about her struggles to start a family, how her mother had told her to keep an open mind and trust that everything would work out as it should in time, even if it didn't feel that way.

Oh, how she'd wanted to believe her. Now, with a wave of guilt, she realized that she no longer did.

"You would think having a doctor in the family would be enough to keep my mother happy for a few years at least." He shook his head. "But I'd be lying if I didn't say it got a little lonely sometimes. That's why I like coming out here every chance I have. With surroundings like this, it's hard to feel anything but completely fulfilled."

Heather couldn't agree more, which was why she couldn't explain that space that still seemed to fill her chest, a gap that couldn't be made whole again. A hole that she might just need to live with, somehow.

"No pets?"

"No time." He smiled. "And how's your job? Last I knew, you were writing for a magazine?"

She hesitated, but then decided that there was no sense in hiding the truth. She and Billy went far back, and she could trust him with things that she hadn't even told her sisters yet.

"I'm between jobs at the moment." She sipped her wine, not sure of what reaction to expect, but Billy didn't seem too surprised or even worried. Of course, he didn't know the part about her missing not one deadline, but two, about how she'd been let go, forced to pack up her things and admit that, yet again, she'd failed at something that had been so important to her.

"So you're a free woman in every sense of the world." He grinned. He always had a way of making her feel better, but something in his words stung this time. She was a free woman. And that was not what she'd planned.

She'd intended to be married, happily so, with a kid or two or another on the way. She thought there would be birthday parties to plan, not just dinner parties. She thought there would be more holidays to host, ones that grew bigger with each new family addition. Instead, her world had become smaller.

"I suggest a toast then," Billy said, raising his glass. "To old friendships and...new possibilities."

Heather sucked in a breath before she brought her glass to her lips. New possibilities. Sitting here beside Billy, she almost dared to believe that could happen. Once, she would have let herself.

* * *

Kim and Andrea were still on the patio when Heather arrived home, full of delicious food, her head only slightly fuzzy from the wine. The remnants of dinner were left on the table —a random meal of bread and fruit that had been sourced from their meager options.

"There you are," Kim said, only it came across as more of an accusation.

Andrea, however, gave her the once-over and seemed to approve. "Let me guess. You ran into Billy?"

"I ran into Billy." She tried to keep her tone neutral, but it wasn't easy, and she could tell by the twist of Andrea's mouth that she had more to say. Her sisters were fully aware of how she tried to hide her tears the entire car ride home at the end of every summer, how she'd kept a framed photo of her and Billy on her bedside table until she'd left for college, and only taken it down when she met Daniel. How when they played "house" or "wedding" as young girls, in her mind, Billy was always her groom, and she wasn't shy in saying so.

Heather glanced at Kim, who wasn't looking at her with the same amused expression. If anything, she'd dare to say that Kim looked annoyed.

"You could have invited us to join," Kim said. "If you're only friends."

This was true, Heather considered, and she hadn't

thought to try to reach them. She wouldn't analyze that decision-making process right now. She'd had a nice time. A relaxing time. And now she felt stressed again. Uncertain and defensive.

"It wasn't planned. I ran into him on my way home and he invited me to stay for an early dinner. There are plenty of other nights for us to have dinner together."

"Maybe, but the same could be said for when we go back to Chicago."

No one spoke because there was no argument. They all lived in the same city, and although they inhabited different neighborhoods, they hadn't made it a priority to meet up but instead pushed it off, vaguely, as something they could always do. But didn't.

"We're all here," Heather said gently. "We came."

"I know, but it just feels different," Kim grumbled.

"Because it *is* different," Andrea said, not unkindly. "We're all grown up now, Kim. We all have our own lives."

"And Mom's not here," Kim whispered.

No. She wasn't.

Heather dropped into a chair. "We made the effort to get here. Now we'll make an effort to make the most of it." And she meant that, because being here was so much better than being back in the city, in that lonely house.

Kim was nodding her head. "That's true, and that's why I put together a schedule for us."

Andrea was the one to laugh out loud in surprise. "A schedule? For a vacation? If I didn't know better, Kim, I'd say that you were starting to sound like me."

"I don't want to squander this time," Kim said. She

reached into her straw beach bag and pulled out a sheet of paper, filled with handwritten notes in some form of bar chart.

Andrea skimmed it and then passed it to Heather. Bicycle rides, shopping trips, lunch at a different restaurant each day. As if Heather had the funds for that sort of thing right now. She was perfectly happy with a sandwich here at the house or tucked into her bag for one of her excursions, because like Billy had pointed out, it was difficult to stay indoors when you were here on the island surrounded by so much natural beauty.

"What if it rains on Thursday when you have us scheduled to go to the beach?" Heather shook her head and handed the paper back to Kim. "I appreciate your intentions, Kim, but vacations don't work like this. I think you're getting it confused with your wedding planning."

"I thought your mother-in-law was doing all your wedding planning?" Andrea said.

She'd said it matter-of-factly, and that was the impression, of course, but Kim's mouth pinched and her green eyes blazed as she slammed the paper back into her bag. "Forget it. Do what you want on this trip, but at least I tried. At least I'm the one making time for my sisters, not always wondering if they're actually going to show up."

"Hey," Andrea's voice softened. "I didn't mean to offend you—"

"You never do, and that's just the point. To be honest, I'm not even sure why you came on this trip if you're just going to spend the entire time searching for cell reception."

"I have a career," Andrea said firmly.

"Of course. Like you'd ever let us forget."

"Oh, sort of the way you never let us forget that you're getting married?" Andrea raised an eyebrow.

Kim opened her mouth to say something and then, seeming to think the better of it, closed it again. Moments later, she was running up the stairs, followed by the sound of her door closing.

"Too harsh?" Andrea winced. "But you know it's all she talks about!"

It was true, and Heather was guilty of being a little exhausted by the topic too, but she wouldn't go so far as to point it out the way that Andrea did. That was the difference between them. One of many.

And this was why Heather had a problem with Kim's agenda. It wasn't that she was opposed to spending time with her sisters or going to the beach or into town, or on a bike ride. It was that she'd learned all too well that when plans were made or counted on, it just led to hurt feelings and a whole lot of disappointment.

9

ANDREA

Andrea woke to the sound of her morning alarm, and it wasn't until after she'd turned it off and flung back the light-weight quilt that she remembered that despite it being Monday, she wasn't going into the office today. There would be no normal routine: no coffee brewing while she dressed for the day, poured it into an insulated thermos, and speed-walked to the bus stop. No skimming her emails while she sat in her usual seat on public transit, near the back exit, so she could make an easy departure, even though, at six in the morning, the city streets were still very empty.

Instead, she had flicked on her bedside light and took her phone off the charger, hoping to skim emails until she was reminded that there was no reception to be found in this entire house, and she had searched every corner of it yesterday, even the dusty attic where their mother kept her parents' old treasures.

Frustrated, Andrea flicked off the light and tried to get back to sleep, but it was no use. She could go downstairs, find a book on one of the shelves in the dark-paneled library off the dining room—it had been a long time since she'd read anything other than trade journals. Now the reminder that she wouldn't be appearing in one herself any time soon loomed heavy, and with a burst of panic, she pushed out of the bed and walked to the window. As the eldest daughter, her room had been assigned first, one of only two at the front of the house, the other being her parents' and before that, her grandparents. The water of Lake Huron could be seen through the tree branches that graced the glass. She'd always loved the contrast of colors here on the island, how the blue water mixed with the vibrant green grass, interrupted only by bright bursts of flowers. It would be another beautiful day. She may as well start it now with a run.

She did her usual lap around the island, but she slowed her pace when she rounded the western curve when the rocky cliffs to her left became wooded lots where large homes sat high on the bluff above the water, their views panoramic. These homes had always caught her attention as a child, then causing her to slow her bike speed, take in the gables and the paned windows, and the aura of a story behind the walls, waiting to be explored.

By the time her sisters came downstairs in search of coffee at half past eight, Andrea had already showered, made her bed, made coffee, and then, after consuming three cups, made it again, for her sisters. Still, she couldn't shake her agitation.

It was Monday morning. She should be at work. Everyone else would be in the office, and she didn't like feeling out of the loop.

"I need to get some work done today," she announced, when she had paced the house, the yard, tried to relax on the porch, and found she couldn't. She'd work on the Morrison project—she already had a clear idea for it, but it would keep her busy, and if she could finish it while she was here, she'd be one step ahead when she returned to the office.

Kim looked at her with something close to hurt in her eyes. "It's supposed to be warm today." She didn't mention the schedule. It was a good idea and Andrea appreciated it— she might even refer to it if her anxiety continued. But today was Monday. She needed to check in with her assistant, or at least, try to stay updated.

"Let's meet up for dinner," Andrea offered. She knew she owed Kim an apology, but the sting had gone two ways. She shouldn't have to apologize for her career any more than Kim should have to refrain from discussing her wedding. They each had important things in their lives. "We could go to the Lighthouse Bistro."

She'd hoped that would smooth things over, but Kim only shrugged in response and stretched her legs onto the wicker coffee table as she stared at the lake.

Andrea fought back the urge to check the time on her phone and turned to stare out over the lawn instead. Even the view of the water across the road couldn't calm her. Jace had probably spent the weekend golfing with Arthur while she was traveling up to this remote island. At least if she'd stayed in the city she might have kept things moving toward the promotion: gone out for lunches, networked at the expensive gym where she had met more than one client over the years.

Instead, in a moment of weakness, she'd let herself be talked into coming here.

Her eyes flitted to a ferry that was crossing the water now, her mind starting to form an idea. She could always go over to Blue Harbor for the day. Spend some time at a café there, where she was sure to have a strong signal on the mainland.

But it would be so tempting to climb into Heather's car and drive back to Chicago. She could be there by nightfall. Tomorrow morning she could wake up in her own bed. She could—

"I understand if you don't want to be here," Kim said, cutting into her thoughts. "But all I can think of is that Mom would have given anything to be here with us now. The least we can do is have a good time in her honor."

Shame filled Andrea and she looked away from the water. From the life that existed on the other side of it.

"We could come back here after dinner and play cards. The three of us this time." Andrea gave Kim a small smile. A peace offering, even if last night's dinner had already covered that. They hadn't discussed their father at all. Instead, they'd eaten toast with cheese or jam, and sat in quasi-comfortable silence, mostly wondering aloud about Heather.

Andrea looked at her middle sister now. It was very clear that Heather still had feelings for Billy. But then, Heather had always been an open book.

Until recently, she thought, feeling a little sad at that realization.

Heather set down her coffee mug. "I'll cook tonight. The view from the bistro is better during the daylight anyway.

Maybe we can go into town together today, Kim. We can get sandwiches at the Island Bakery."

For a moment, Andrea was tempted to join them. She could practically taste the large, handmade sandwiches on the fresh crusty bread that could be smelled baking for blocks down the sidewalk.

Heather gave Kim a little smile, clearly trying to repair the damage from last night when her little outburst had been so out of character. She was good at that, keeping things in stride, going with the flow, which was why it was so strange that she was so quick to shift moods these days.

Well, Andrea couldn't think about that now. Her sisters would spend time together, meaning the pressure was off her to be social. She carried her mug back into the kitchen, washed it and set it to dry, and then hurried up the stairs to pack her tote with her laptop, power cord, and her planner. There were several inns and some large hotels on the island, where she knew their internet access would be strong and steady. She'd park herself in a lobby, or maybe even at the bar or restaurant. She'd need something quiet, not too overwhelmed with tourists soaking in the last few weeks of summer.

She decided on the Lakeside Inn—it was a favorite from their childhood, with its sweeping views of the lake and mouth-watering cinnamon rolls that were a summer staple, especially on lazy Sunday mornings, and it was close enough to town that if she needed to move locations, she could easily do so without interruptions.

She hurried out the door and down the steps, feeling better already with the sun warming her skin and reflecting off the water. Her pace was quick, as it usually was, and with each step she felt more like her old self, back in control of her future, capable of getting things back on track.

She was at the inn within fifteen minutes, only mildly perspiring despite the morning breeze, her shoulder starting to cramp from the weight of her bag. She looked up at the front of the hotel, seeing that it had been spruced up since the last time she'd visited, but then, that had been at least four years back and probably even more since she'd paid a visit to this place. She remembered that there was a restaurant at the back of the lobby with big windows that looked out onto the water, and a long porch with tables that might make a perfect place to set up her office.

She checked her phone signal. Still weak. She'd have to ask someone for the hotel guest internet password.

She hurried along the brick path to the front doors, surprised once inside to see that the dark carpet and woodwork had been replaced with lighter, cooler shades of blue and green that gave the entire space a fresh and new feel. Had Joan Kessler done all this? Andrea's mother hadn't mentioned anything about the woman who ran this inn doing a major renovation, and her mother kept up on all the happenings on the island, either through her annual visits or conversations with other summer people or locals that they'd come to know over the years. But then, Andrea remembered her mother hadn't been back to the island in two years.

And, like Kim had pointed out, she never would come back again.

With a stiff upper lip, Andrea comforted herself with the knowledge that she was here on a mission. Work kept her mind from drifting to dark places, and she was eager to get seated. She followed the smell of cinnamon rolls to the back of the inn, pleased that some things about the place hadn't changed, even if she had to admit the changes were a vast improvement. Subtle, but fresh. In place of the dark and fading carpet and furnishings, the space felt light and airy, with shades of blue that drew on the lake view out the floor-to-ceiling windows in the dining room at the end of the lobby.

The back porch was unchanged, the furniture was still the same whitewashed wood but spruced up with some striped pillows and cheerful centerpieces of bright pink hydrangeas. Happy to be drawn back to a time when she would sit here with a cold glass of lemonade, giggling into her straw with her sisters and mother, Andrea decided to push her luck and hope that the internet access reached just beyond the doors.

She settled at a table that was far from children or other distractions, choosing one near the edge of the porch where only a few people sat quietly reading or taking in the view.

"May I help you?"

She didn't need to scan the menu. What she really wanted was a cinnamon roll, but she didn't need to get crumbs all over her work and icing on her keyboard. She'd had enough coffee to feel jittery, and she was warm from her speed walk over here. "A lemonade, please. And do you have internet access here?"

The man motioned to a card on the center of the table, and Andrea sighed deeply with relief.

She had managed to check all her texts (which were

disturbingly sparse) and was just about to fire off a well-drafted message to Nicole when she felt someone staring at her. She looked up to see a man absentmindedly sipping coffee and watching her with amusement.

"Sorry," he said, realizing he'd been caught. He grinned. It was a very nice grin, technically speaking, but she still barely registered it. Her email was loading now, and her eye caught something that pulled her attention, making her frown. A senior staff meeting was scheduled for this Wednesday. And she would miss it.

She licked her lower lip as her heart began to pound. Maybe Nicole could give her the notes. But then, if Andrea wasn't there, why would Nicole have access to the agenda? She could ask Pamela, perhaps. Yes, she would at least want to keep Andrea updated, but she had also been strangely strict about her taking space. Coming back refreshed—as if such a thing were possible. That meant relaxing first, and how could she be expected to relax when she had not only lost the Glenwood project to Jace of all people, but that he was her primary competition for the partnership seat!

No, she would wait a few days at least before contacting Pamela. It seemed that a cooling-off period was in order, but it felt more like she was being pushed out.

She reached for her spiral-bound planner to see if this had been planned and she had just forgotten, when her wrist hit the side of her glass, spilling the lemonade over the table.

Quickly, she pulled back her laptop and reached for the sole napkin that had been used as a coaster and was now soaked through.

"Here, let me." She looked up to see the man smiling at her as he quickly helped sop up the mess.

"Thanks," she said, giving him a tight smile. "I'm usually not so clumsy. I got distracted with work."

"Maybe you should set the work aside for a bit and enjoy this spectacular view."

She gave him a wry look. Unsolicited advice was rarely appreciated, especially when this man didn't have a clue about the stressors in her life.

"I'm afraid that I don't have that luxury," she said. "And I've seen it before, so..."

He raised his eyebrows in surprise. "I live here year-round and it never gets boring." It was a casual comment, one delivered with a quirk of that grin, but Andrea felt her defenses prickle. Her sisters didn't understand her work. Even Pamela didn't seem to understand its importance to her. She didn't need to explain herself to a stranger, especially one who, from the looks of it, couldn't even begin to imagine the pressures of corporate life.

"Year-round?" She looked him up and down, liking what she saw, not that it mattered. She didn't recognize him, and over the years she and her family had come to know not only the summer people but also the locals. Only a few hundred residents lived year-round on Evening Island—the winters were harsh and the ferry stopped crossing in the coldest months, putting tourism at a standstill. Some islanders stayed on the mainland for that time, in Blue Harbor or the neighboring Pine Falls. But this guy lived here year-round.

Yep, he didn't get it.

"Hard for you to imagine?" He grabbed a stack of napkins from a nearby table and finished drying hers.

"Hard to imagine that pace of life, that's for sure." Here the days were long and carefree, and while she was sure this man worked, he couldn't possibly imagine the demands and responsibilities that came with climbing the corporate ladder, shuffling through the city, putting in long days and, some months of the year, only seeing the light of day from her office window. Grabbing dinner on the go, or sometimes, forgoing it altogether.

"There's something to be said for slowing down and enjoying life, especially in a place as beautiful as Evening Island."

Andrea adjusted her laptop on the table and stared properly at the man. He was attractive, probably knew it too, because he certainly didn't lack confidence.

"Well," she said tightly. "Not everyone is in a position to slow down. Maybe I'll consider it in about fifty years." That would make her eighty-three, she realized with a small frown. Would she ever retire? What would she have without her work?

"Shame," he said. "I'm happy to point out some of the best parts of the island. I can guarantee you that they'll be far more interesting than anything you can see on that screen."

Andrea pursed her lips and sat back down. "Thanks, but I've seen the island, and now I have to see to these emails." There weren't many. A few from clients, who had no doubt received her automatic out-of-office reply. She'd reply anyway. Of course, she would. And she'd set up some calls too, now that she knew she could get cell reception here through their wireless connection. It was worth the trouble —even the trouble of this man.

He gave a disappointed shrug. "If you change your mind—"

She glanced up at him, her fingers poised over the keyboard. "I won't."

"Suit yourself," he said with a shrug. He went back to his table where his iced tea was sweating through the glass.

Andrea tried to compose an email to Nicole, but she couldn't even form a sentence clearly, not when her mind was spinning and her excuse seemed lame and that man—she could still feel his eyes on her.

"What is that you do?" he asked when they locked eyes again.

"I'm an architect," she said. Then, she added, "In Chicago."

"Ah." He nodded as if he should have already known this. "Well, that explains it."

Now she was getting annoyed. She bit back a sigh and leaned back in her chair, looking at him directly. "Explains what exactly?"

"Oh, just that here you are, on a beautiful summer day, on one of the most beautiful islands in the country, with a view like this." He swept his hand over the rail to the lakefront that seemed to stretch as far as the eye could see. "And your mind is still on city time. I get it."

"No," she said tersely. "I don't think you do. And if you don't mind, I have important things to do."

"Of course. Don't let me disturb you from your important work." He flagged down a waiter passing by. "Another lemonade for the lady."

"Oh, no. It's fine. You don't need to." Andrea felt her cheeks flush, but he held up a hand.

"It's no trouble." He stood, pausing ever so slightly at her table. "Don't work too hard."

There was a noticeable sheen of amusement in his gaze, and before Andrea could even react to the wink he gave her, he walked away.

She narrowed her eyes. Don't work too hard? She intended to do just that. Her entire future depended on it.

10

KIM

A shopping trip was just what she needed to put her troubles aside for a little while. Kim used to love spending a few hours at the start of each trip poking in all the galleries and boutiques, never tiring of buying a few pieces made by local artisans to bring back to the cottage or sometimes to her apartment in the city. One of her favorite paintings that hung on her bedroom wall was from her friend Ellie Morgan. It was a watercolor of West End Road, showing all three of the Victorian homes in their summer glory, facing the water and the setting sun.

She often liked to lie in bed in the mornings and stare at that painting, imagining that she was sitting on that porch, wondering what all the residents would be doing at that point in time. Her mother was always on the porch in her scenarios, usually with Mrs. Morgan and Mrs. Anderson; the three of them could laugh and talk for hours, watching as the carriages came up West End Road or tourists passed on cruiser bikes. As for the nine girls on the street—Kim usually thought that they were somewhere nearby. Heather might be making a pie in the kitchen, as she was known to do most summer weekends, and Andrea and Hope Morgan would be exploring the island on their bikes. Kim and her friend Ellie and the younger Anderson girl might be across the road at the beach. Gemma was often imagined to be curled up in her house with a book, in the top window, which she claimed was her favorite spot in the house.

It had been a long time since Kim had woken up to that painting, though. She'd been spending more and more nights at Bran's apartment—the soulless new building with its sharp edges and minimal furniture, no cozy soft blankets on the couch, no colorful pillows, no artwork that evoked emotion.

She told herself that once she moved out of her apartment and brought her belongings into Bran's, she would make it her own. Or at least theirs. But now she worried about another argument. Another compromise that was starting to feel more and more like a sacrifice.

She felt the familiar tug in her chest that had started every time she thought of next month, and beyond. Eager to distract herself, she moved on to a display table that was filled with a collection of handcrafted items for the home. Harbor Home Designs had been their mother's favorite shop in recent years, and she could almost pretend for a moment that everything was normal, that her mother was here with her, looking at embroidered tea towels or picture frames that she'd fill with photos from their most recent trip to the island.

"This would look pretty in your living room." Kim

picked up a set of bookends and held them out to Heather.

Heather glanced at the price tag and shook her head. "Maybe next time."

Kim frowned and set them back on the shelf. She knew that Daniel had always earned more than Heather, but she hadn't considered that things might be tight for her sister. Heather had gotten the small brownstone in the divorce, but Kim wasn't sure how that worked. Maybe she had to buy Daniel out. There was surely still a hefty mortgage—city properties were not cheap.

"Then let me buy it for you," Kim said, feeling bad about whatever struggles her sister might be facing. She wondered if she should suggest that Heather call their father—he'd be more than happy to help. Kim opened her mouth to say just that but stopped herself. Heather was clearly still stung over the divorce. It was so recent—maybe it had been a shock. Maybe she wanted to show that she could handle things on her own. Yes, that was probably why she was so vague whenever the mention of it came up.

"I'm actually thinking of downsizing," Heather said. "So I probably shouldn't be adding more things that I'll need to pack."

"But you love that house!" Kim said, thinking of how excited Heather had been when she'd first found it. She'd had a housewarming party, inviting both of her sisters, and hosted Thanksgiving that first year, too.

"It's too big for one person," Heather said. "It has three bedrooms, two of which are empty. I don't need that much space. Besides, it might be good for me to start over."

Kim could see the logic in this, but it still made her sad to see Heather lose one more thing she loved. She had loved Daniel—that had always been clear, which was why everyone was so confused when she announced they were ending their marriage last fall.

"Well, then, I'll buy them for you now and bring them to you once you're settled into your new place," Kim said, picking them up again.

Heather stopped her. "It will be one more thing for you to hold on to and pack. Aren't you moving out of your apartment next month?"

Kim pinched her mouth. Now, as she once again set the bookends back on the shelf, she felt a swell of unease she couldn't push back. This was the longest she and Bran had gone without speaking since they'd met, and their wedding was less than five weeks away, as everyone kept reminding her.

She forced a smile. "You're right. Next year, then."

But next year seemed so far away and it didn't feel like a guarantee either. It felt more like something she didn't like, something that made her uncomfortable. Something she might call denial. She was already giving up her apartment for Bran's, because it was bigger, because it was owned, not rented, and because it was convenient to Bran's work, even though it wasn't in a part of the city that Kim particularly liked, and it wasn't Kim's style either. They'd already agreed that there was no sense in Kim moving her bed or sofa or her dining set into Bran's apartment, not when he already had all of those furnishings. Next, she was expected to give up her job. And then there was the matter of the endless family obligations that left no room for her own.

She didn't know where Evening Island would fit into any

of that.

"Look, they have a wedding registry!" Heather pointed to the sign that was displayed on a circular table complete with an eclectic array of objects from silver-plated serving trays to cake toppers.

Kim picked up a painting of a bride and groom down near the harbor. "Isn't that beautiful?"

Heather looked over her shoulder, looking a little resigned. "It is. I always think that Mom would have loved to see one of us married here on the island."

Kim set the painting down. Just looking at it made her uncomfortable. "I never heard her say that."

"Oh, she didn't have to," Heather said with a sad smile. "She loved this place. I think she would have lived here year-round if she could have. But with Dad's work that obviously wasn't possible."

Just the mention of their father made Kim's heart skip a beat and she was relieved when the shop owner—a woman named Sheila—approached them.

"Is someone getting married?" Sheila tipped her head. "I thought that was you, Kim. And Heather." Sheila, like many others they saw each year, was on friendly terms with them.

Kim braced herself for what came next.

"I'm so sorry to hear about your mother, dears."

Kim swallowed the lump in her throat and nodded. She didn't know which was worse: talking about her mother or talking about her wedding.

She just wanted to leave. She wanted to buy herself a trinket, something that made her think of the island, not all that other stuff that was across the water and miles away.

"When's the big day?" Sheila asked.

"Next month," Kim said. The last Saturday of the summer. It had seemed so fitting at the time. A way of coming full circle with their relationship in a way. But now just thinking about it made her stomach hurt. It wasn't the wedding she had dreamed of. It wasn't even a wedding she wanted to attend.

With a start, she forced a smile. What was she saying? The wedding was weeks away, invitations had gone out, and she had committed.

"It might be nice to register for a few things from the island," she told Heather.

Pleased, Sheila handed her a clipboard and pen and left them to it. Kim filled in the information with a shaking hand. Suddenly everything in the shop felt inconsequential and even confusing. She didn't know what to write down on the list. She didn't know what she wanted, from this store, or her life.

* * *

The line at Island Bakery was long, as Kim knew it would be, but it was worth it to savor the taste of the island. Besides, the day stretched out ahead of them without much of a plan other than to stop by the Main Street Market before heading home.

Heather, however, looked impatient. "We could go to Trillium Café instead?"

Kim considered this. It was an institution on this island, nearly as cherished as the big hotel up on the hill where a movie had once been filmed. She could order some pancakes because Marge made them best and maybe that was because the Trillium Café was the only place she ever ate pancakes. But a sit-down meal with Heather, where more discussion of her wedding might take place? She shook her head.

"No, let's stay. These sandwiches are worth the wait, and we can go sit on a bench near the harbor." Maybe they'd run into Edward, even if it was now probably a little late in the day for fishing.

A woman in front of them turned around and grinned broadly. "I thought I recognized that voice! Why Kimmy Taylor! And Heather! Oh, it's so wonderful to see you girls."

"Mrs. Hayworth!" Kim grinned and let her mother's old friend hug her.

"Oh, Sally, please. You two aren't little girls anymore. Heather's a married woman!"

Heather gave Kim a brief glance and then, with a tight smile, said, "I'm single now."

Sally's eyes popped and Kim feared that before five today every other local would know. Sally Hayworth may have run the island newspaper for most of her life, but she ran the gossip mill full-time.

"Kim is the one who will soon be married," Heather rushed to say with a smile.

Kim felt her back teeth graze as Sally looked at her in surprise. "Imagine that! Little Kimmy Taylor getting married. Oh, your mother would have done anything to see that day. We were all so sad to hear the news."

Kim's throat felt dry and she struggled to swallow. Luckily, Heather intervened.

"Thank you, Sally. Your friendship meant a great deal to her. This entire island did."

"How long are you staying?" Sally asked as they scooted up a spot in line.

"Two weeks," Kim said, finding her voice. "We just got in this weekend so we haven't had a chance to see everyone yet."

"Well, you know Gemma's living here year-round now," Sally began. "Started dating that handsome caretaker of yours. An attorney, very successful, but he's also starting up a stable and Gemma's helping him, of course, when she's not writing. He apparently has a ton of experience with horses from living on a ranch before moving back here, or at least that's what Edward told me. And Ellie's still in Europe, but we think she'll be back by next summer. No one can leave this island for too long!" Her eyes homed in on Heather. "Oh! And you know that Billy Davidson has been spending a lot of time at his parents' house, fixing it up, and coming over on the ferry once, sometimes twice a week now that he's living in Pine Falls. I keep waiting to see if a young lady will ever accompany him, but so far that hasn't happened."

Kim couldn't look at Heather for fear of laughing, and she could see from her periphery that Heather was smiling and nodding politely, and no doubt biting back a few words of her own.

"Are you still writing for that magazine?" Sally inquired.

Heather opened her mouth and then closed it, but before she could answer, Sally said, "You know, one of my feature columnists moved to the mainland to be closer to her grandchildren. I don't suppose...well, I hate to ask...but you'd be doing me a huge favor if you might fill her spot for next month. Just one lifestyle piece, a thousand words or so..."

Heather's expression turned regretful, and Kim now saw it as her turn to step in and help. "Oh, but we're not here for long."

"Long enough!" Sally wasn't to be deterred. "I just need something in my hands by next Friday. It would really help me out, Heather, and I'll pay, of course. The locals would probably get a kick of seeing your byline too."

Heather glanced at Kim. They both knew that their mother would have, too. They loved reading the island newspaper, which was full of local news and, of course, thanks to Sally's personal touch, just enough gossip to keep things interesting.

"Sure," Heather said, letting her shoulders fall.

"Oh! Thank you!"

Sally looked up at the counter, where the line in front of her had already disappeared, leaving a large space. "Oh! And that's me."

"What are you going to write about?" Kim whispered to Heather as they waited for their turn in line. Sally's no-nonsense ordering style could be heard loud and clear, but the staff all knew her, of course. That was the thing about this island—you could come here to hide, but you couldn't hide anything at all.

"I don't know," Heather said, looking a little worried.

"Well, you'll figure it out," Kim said, knowing that she would. Her sisters always figured things out, even when times were tough.

It was just too bad that the same couldn't be said for her.

11

HEATHER

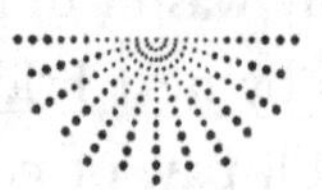

As they came up West End Road, Heather was relieved to see a familiar figure standing on the lawn that divided their home from Sunset Cottage. It took her mind off the nagging anxiety that had filled her ever since she'd reluctantly agreed to Sally's surprising request. A lifestyle piece on any topic? The word count wasn't an issue, and the deadline normally wouldn't be either, but she hadn't written anything in months and, of course, her final articles had fallen short with her readership. She supposed it would at least fill the gap in her resume.

"Gemma!" She waved her hand excitedly and Kim did the same. They quickened their pace up the road as Gemma came to meet them.

"You're really here!" Gemma pulled each of them in for a long hug, and Heather dropped the grocery bag to let her. It had been so long, she realized with a wave of something close to self-pity, that she had been truly, properly hugged. Oh, Billy had hugged her, but briefly, and she and her sisters had never been the type to bother with that sort of affection. No, that had been left to their mother.

And maybe, once, so long ago that it almost didn't seem possible, to Daniel.

She swallowed hard, grateful that she had her sunglasses to shield the hurt that no doubt shone in her eyes.

"We were just about to get started on dinner." Heather picked up the bulging bag of groceries. "Please join us. And Leo too, of course."

"Leo's doing some work on his grandfather's place tonight, but I'd love to!" They walked toward the house and climbed the stairs. Gemma sighed when she reached the last step and looked around the porch. "It's been ages since I've been over here."

It had been. Their visits hadn't overlapped for years, but somehow, as Heather held the door open for her friend, it felt like no time had passed at all. That was what made this island so special. They could stay away for a year, or multiple years, and pick right back up as if they'd never left. Standing here with Gemma, it was like they were the same preteen girls who would curl up together on a rainy afternoon on the wicker sofa, watching the rain, scribbling stories in their notebooks.

"Can I bring a bottle of wine from my place?"

"We have plenty," Kim assured her as they began unpacking the groceries: dried pasta and fresh fruits and vegetables, hunks of sharp cheeses, and some fish caught from the lake earlier in the day.

"I wonder if Andrea's back yet." Heather listened for any sound of life outside of the kitchen. She smiled at Gemma. "She'll be happy to see you."

"I just wish my sisters were here. Ellie will be especially sorry she missed you," Gemma said to Kim.

Kim shrugged and then slid a sly look in Heather's direction. "Well, some people are still on the island. Heather's been spending some time with Billy."

Gemma's gaze flicked to her with interest mixed with confusion. For a moment, Heather wasn't sure what to make of her reaction, until she realized, of course...Gemma thought she was still happily married. Her parents hadn't been able to make the funeral, and Heather hadn't responded to Gemma's condolence letter—it had been all too much at the time, but now she wished that she'd made a better effort to keep in touch.

She wished for many things.

"Daniel and I aren't together anymore," she explained. She released a shaky breath as she began loading the milk and yogurt into the refrigerator. It still felt strange to say it aloud even though they'd parted ways well over a year ago and had merely coexisted for months before that. Now she had to brace herself for the inevitable reaction that usually followed: more looks of confusion, an apology, sometimes even looks of disappointment.

But Gemma just gave her an encouraging smile and said, "It's not easy, I know. I ended an engagement a while back."

"Really?" Kim's cheeks flushed as she blinked quickly. She slowly unpacked the last grocery bag, not looking at either Heather or Gemma. "What happened? If you don't mind me asking," she added quickly.

"Not at all," Gemma said good-naturedly. "He called it off. Left me reeling, honestly. I was upset at the time. My whole life felt turned upside down. My future plans were gone. I had a book due to my editor and I couldn't think straight. I was a mess." She laughed. "But then I came here for a bit and I met Leo, and well, I couldn't be happier."

Heather and Kim both seemed to stare at Gemma for an extended period, soaking this in. Heather couldn't help but relate this to her own life, how Gemma had come out of a major setback brighter and better, and she wondered idly if Kim was too. But that was nonsense. Kim was happily engaged. Gemma's story probably only served to scare her a bit, not that a dose of reality wouldn't be good for her younger sister.

"Living on the island full-time suits you then?" Heather had entertained it before, as a child, when she hated the thought of leaving at summer's end, but as an adult, it hadn't felt practical, or even worth thinking about. But now...

Well, now she was confused, not thinking clearly. She was, to use Gemma's words, a mess.

"That and being with the right person." Gemma grinned.

Kim's brow pinched as she set to work uncorking a bottle of wine and pouring it into three glasses.

Heather raised hers. "Here's to being together again on Evening Island."

"Here's to just us girls again!" Kim said—with quite a bit more enthusiasm than Heather was expecting.

Heather sipped her wine and realized that she hadn't heard her sister mention Bran or the wedding very much since she'd gotten here, and she'd been noticeably dispassionate about setting up the registry at the shop, too.

But her sister was smiling and laughing now at some memory that Gemma was sharing, and Heather shrugged off her concern. Maybe the excitement of the wedding was simply fading—she had certainly exhausted the topic enough.

Heather tuned in to hear what she had missed.

"Do you remember the time that Billy challenged all of us to race our bikes down Cliffside Road?"

Did she! Heather rolled her eyes, even though her heart swelled at the thought of that day. She'd never been one to turn down anything Billy suggested—even some of his crazier ideas like who could hold their breath under water the longest, or who could swim out farthest from shore.

"It's a wonder none of us ended up in the hospital that day!" Heather laughed.

"I'm sure he feels bad, now that he's a doctor and all," Kim said. "I had two skinned knees, and I still have the scars to prove it."

Gemma swatted Kim's arm. "Please! He doesn't feel bad! No one broke anything. Besides, we were just kids then."

Just kids. Something about the way Gemma said it made Heather wonder just how many of her fond memories with Billy could be lumped together with "kid stuff."

Most of it, she knew. But it connected them all the same. They'd grown up together, year after year, they were bonded by their relationships and this love for the island, spending the sweetest and longest days of their youth running free, without a care in the world. These were the people who knew her hopes and wishes. Who knew her heart.

"Should we go outside?" Heather asked. It was stuffy in

the house even with the windows cracked and the ceiling fans going strong. She longed for the evening breeze that would soon come. Knowing there would be a consensus, she didn't wait to lead the way. Andrea was coming down the stairs when they reached the front hall. "Were you upstairs all this time?" Heather looked at her in surprise.

"I was in the attic," Andrea explained. "Just rummaging through some old stuff. If I'd known we had company I would have come down sooner."

Heather felt her feelings toward her older sister shift. Andrea used to love exploring this old house as a kid. Even on the sunny days where Kim would bolt to the beach before ten in the morning, Andrea sometimes preferred to hang back. When they'd return at the end of the day, tired and hungry, Andrea would show them things she discovered: an old album with photos of the island from a time gone by, a ferry ticket stub that had a little love note scrawled on the back from their grandfather to their grandmother, fabric from the original curtains that Heather had happily transformed to fit the windows in their playhouse in the yard.

Gemma held her arms wide, and Andrea—usually a cold fish, that one—reached in. Heather couldn't help but feel slighted, and noting the frown that pulled at Kim's brow, she could only assume that her other sister felt the same way.

It perhaps wasn't fair of them. Andrea was the oldest, but that didn't automatically mean she would fill their mother's shoes. She wasn't maternal like that.

No, that was Heather's territory.

She swallowed back her wine, even though it didn't go down easily, and forced a bright smile that she no longer felt.

"Gemma's staying for dinner. I thought we'd have fish tonight with a side of roasted vegetables."

"Oh, Heather." Andrea chuckled. "You're such a homemaker."

She didn't say it like an insult, and Heather didn't take it as one, but she also knew that she couldn't accept it as a compliment either, because it was no longer true. She had a house, but it wasn't a home.

"Not everyone can survive on energy bars and take-out," Kim said, giving Heather a little wink.

Heather grinned, but her smile felt secret. She was one step away from doing just that, only unlike with Andrea, the thought depressed her. She missed having someone to cook for, someone to think about and care about throughout her day. And other than the holidays, she hadn't sat down to a meal with her family—or anyone—in so long that she now couldn't bear the thought of more lonely nights in front of the television with a bowl of pasta for one.

"Not everyone has time to sit down and eat a meal, much less cook," Andrea replied.

This time, Kim and Heather exchanged a subtle eye roll as they all sat down on the porch.

"Heather manages to do both," Kim said, again rising to her defense.

Heather said nothing. Revealing now that she'd lost her job would only ruin their time with Gemma.

"Well, Heather enjoys domestic responsibilities more than I do," Andrea said. She shrugged. "Not that I'm complaining. You're an excellent cook. I've always enjoyed your food."

"You guys must get together a lot, all being in Chicago," Gemma remarked.

There was an awkward silence that Heather felt obligated to fill. "Oh, well, Andrea's busy with client dinners a lot, and I'm not sure if you've heard, but Kim is getting married next month!"

Kim's cheeks flushed. "I should have invited you. My future mother-in-law took over that task, and it's hosted at her house, and... You should come. I want you there. I want everyone from the island there."

Heather wondered just how Lynette would feel about a sudden change in the guest list, but she had the sense that this wasn't the only thing that Kim was nervous about right now. Her face was pink and she was twisting her engagement ring. Maybe it was guilt that she hadn't invited Gemma. Sure, it was a little awkward, but Gemma would understand.

Across the coffee table, Andrea lifted an eyebrow in question at Heather. Heather dismissed the concern with a wave of the hand. Kim had never been a very organized person and all the little details of a wedding were difficult for anyone— though probably not Andrea. If she ever got married, she'd probably have a binder with color-coordinated tabs for everything.

But then, Heather highly doubted that Andrea would ever make time for romance. She didn't even make time for her own sisters more and more.

"We'll make a trip of it," Gemma nodded. "Stay with Hope. Spend some time with the girls. They're a handful, but I miss those little twins."

"Oh. Good. Good." Kim was nodding, but she didn't

look relieved as she sipped her wine. "Being back here... I just hate the thought of leaving again."

Heather fell silent. Kim was voicing her own emotions, and Gemma gave her hand a little squeeze.

"Then while you're here, we should celebrate! Maybe we could gather up a few locals, get some cocktails? Wednesday night?"

At the mention of the other locals, Heather's heart sped up a bit. Surely Billy wouldn't pass up the chance to celebrate with them, and she wouldn't pass up the opportunity to spend a little more time with him.

Kim's smile looked tense, but she agreed. "That's...really nice of you, Gemma."

It was. And with shame, Heather realized it was more than she had done. Why hadn't she planned it? It was something she would have done—before, when she was still the homemaker and mother hen that Andrea portrayed her to still be. She would have had a complete theme and chronicled every detail in one of her monthly columns.

"Cocktails it is then," Heather agreed. She gave Andrea a sharp look, just in case she tried to make up an excuse about work.

"Just us girls," Gemma said.

And that answered that. And for reasons she couldn't explain to herself, Heather felt distinctly disappointed.

12

ANDREA

Heather and Kim were settled on the front porch when Andrea came down the stairs the next morning, showered and dressed, her daily jog already finished. She walked to the kitchen and started a fresh pot of coffee, wandering the downstairs rooms of the house while it brewed.

It was a formal house, built in the late 1800s and too large to be called a cottage even though that's what it was. Like many of these homes on the island, it was passed down through the generations—something to be cherished as well as enjoyed. Now, as Andrea stood in the living room, admiring the collection of framed photos on the shelving that flanked one of several fireplaces in the home, she felt a strange sense of failure on her part. She'd loved this house, but she hadn't made it a priority in recent years. With her mother now gone, that responsibility would fall on her, and her sisters.

Her father... Well, the man liked to work even more than

she did. And given how alike they were, it was no surprise that he'd been busier than ever this past year.

When the coffee could be smelled from rooms away, she went back to the kitchen and poured herself a mug, wondering if it would be odd to sit out back with her drink rather than join her sisters on the front porch.

Yes, it would be odd, and it wouldn't be nice either. It wasn't that she wanted to avoid them, it was that the strain between them was obvious. Coming here together had once felt so natural, and now... Now, as much as things were still the same, everything felt different.

Her heartstrings pulled when she spotted her mother's favorite mug in the cabinet before closing the door. Andrea had hand-painted it when she was just a toddler and one of the many local artists was offering a children's pottery class one summer. It seemed both wonderful and wrong that the mug had managed to last this long when her mother was no longer here to hold it.

Andrea carefully moved it to the top shelf, where it couldn't be disrupted. Or used.

Yes, this was a house to be cherished. And everything in it, too.

With that, she walked down the hallway and pushed through the screen door. Her sisters were reading in companionable silence. The day stretched ahead as wide and open as the lake that surrounded them.

"How was your run?" Kim asked, setting her paperback down on the chair beside her.

"Great. You can join me tomorrow if you want," Andrea

offered, and Kim and Heather started laughing at the same time. "What's so funny?"

Kim gave her a pointed look. "This is vacation, and running has never been my idea of fun."

"I never said it was fun," Andrea started to say.

"Then why do it?" Kim asked.

Andrea thought about that as she settled into a chair. "I guess it's just part of my routine. I'm not used to having this much time on my hands." For a moment she wondered if Kim would whip out her schedule again, but she just looked at her thoughtfully.

"I'm surprised that you were willing to take so much time away from work. I mean, I'm grateful," Kim added quickly. "But... What made you decide to come?"

"Well, running by all the old historic homes is sort of like work, or at least research." Now, her designs erred in the direction of modern, and just talking about work made the panic rise in Andrea's chest. She swallowed back some coffee, hoping to calm herself. "But you made a good point. About things changing once you're married. And about Mom."

They all fell silent at that.

Andrea looked over at the bicycle that was still propped against the porch. She hadn't ridden a bike in years—maybe not since the last time she'd been here. She would mix it up, change her routine. Tomorrow. But not today. Today she would go back into town, see if she had any responses to her emails from yesterday. See if she had missed out on anything while she was here.

"Did you see my old bike in the shed?" she asked Kim.

Kim nodded. "It might need some air in the tires. And

it's tucked behind some lawn furniture. Want me to help you pull it out?"

She said it so eagerly, that for a moment, Andrea had a flash of the little girl who was five years to her ten, wanting to see what Andrea was up to, wanting to be part of anything that Andrea was interested in at the time. She'd adored her. And the feeling was mutual.

"Sure," she said, setting down her coffee.

Heather stayed behind while Andrea and Kim went to the back of the house, walking past the playhouse to the shed, which was really a large carriage house, from the time in their family's past when they'd owned their own buggy. Now, it was full of wicker lawn furniture, croquet mallets, tennis gear, and of course, the bicycles. There were at least seven of various sizes and ages, but her bike was beside Heather's— one mint green and the other blue—and both covered in cobwebs and dust.

Andrea sneezed and considered she might need to change her clothes after this. Kim, who was wearing cut-off jean shorts and a tee shirt, didn't seem bothered.

"I suppose Leo didn't get around to this spot," she said, but then, the renters weren't given access to the padlock key. Maybe Leo hadn't been either.

"Maybe Dad didn't ask him to," Kim offered. She began moving a wicker chair with Andrea's help. "He's nice. He seems to make Gemma happy too."

"She did seem happy," Andrea mused. "I suppose love has a way of doing that to people."

Not that she would know, she thought with a strange heaviness in her heart. Normally, she didn't have time to think about her single status—she was too busy for a relationship anyway—but hearing Gemma talk last night, she couldn't help but wonder if she was missing something.

She thought back on Pamela's words, on what the clients had said about her design. That she didn't have heart. Was it true?

"I suppose it does." Kim shrugged.

Andrea looked at her ruefully. "You suppose? Says the girl who is madly in love and can talk of nothing other than her bliss?"

Kim frowned and brushed a strand of hair from her forehead with the back of her hand. "That's not all I talk about."

Andrea begged to differ, but she wasn't about to have another argument with her sister who clearly wasn't in a joking mood. "I just meant you didn't sound too convinced just now when I made that comment." She picked up a tennis racquet and ran her fingers over the broken strings. "Is everything okay with Bran?"

Kim looked at her sharply. "Of course everything is okay with Bran! We're getting married next month!" She pushed a wicker side table out of the way with more force than seemed necessary, freeing first Heather's cruiser and then Andrea's. Sure enough, the tires on both were flat.

"Your bridesmaid dresses should be ready for their final fitting in three weeks, in case I forgot to mention it," Kim added as she rummaged around, finally retrieving an air pump.

"You did forget, but Lynette didn't," Andrea said tightly. Lynette was a sore spot. A pleasant enough woman—highly organized, which Andrea appreciated—but slightly cold.

Still, that wasn't the real issue that Andrea had with Kim's future mother-in-law. No, the real problem was that more and more, it seemed like Kim had found a new mother altogether, while Andrea was still finding a way to accept the thought that theirs was never coming back. Or maybe, to forget.

Kim nodded. "Lynette's got it all covered. I suppose I should be grateful. It's the only way I was able to come up here for two weeks."

Suppose? There was that word again. Andrea gave her sister a gentle smile, wondering if there was something she wasn't telling her, but then she thought back on Heather's opinion. It was probably just stress. Kim wasn't used to stress or planning things. Kim was used to relying on their mother for that.

And now, she was relying on Lynette!

They pumped the tires and each wheeled a bike to the front of the house where Heather was still sitting on the porch.

"I'll hose them down," Heather said.

"Thanks," Andrea said. "But no rush. I think I'll walk into town and get some more work done today."

She saw a glance pass between her two sisters. Not wanting any flack for her choices, she said brightly, "Maybe we can do something fun tonight, just us sisters?" When even Kim didn't jump at that, she said, "What time are we meeting Gemma and the girls tomorrow night?"

"Around seven," Kim said.

Andrea nodded. "Good. That will be fun."

Or at least she hoped it would be, because she wasn't sure

what constituted as fun anymore, and from the look her sisters exchanged, she had a feeling that neither of them considered her to be any fun at all.

* * *

A short while later, she loaded her notebook and laptop into the bicycle basket and took off down the road to town, knowing that at least at the Lakeside Inn, she could park herself on the patio without much distraction, enjoy a beverage, and find solid Wi-Fi access, along with much-needed cell coverage.

It didn't take long to be settled at the same table as yesterday, and even less time to connect to civilization, since she'd stored the passcodes into her devices. With a lemonade ordered, she quickly began scrolling through her emails to see what she had missed. News about the Christmas party, which always came out too early, and an event she usually only stopped by for appearances, because most people at the firm had a date or a spouse at their side, and contrary to office gossip, she did not feel any self-pity over her single status. It was a choice. And she had chosen to focus on her career.

Still, she couldn't help her eyes from darting every time a person walked by her table, and more than once she felt a strange sense of disappointment to see the empty table across from her, where that rather opinionated man had been yesterday.

He was probably golfing or sleeping late. The man didn't seem to have a care in the world, after all.

While she... She leaned in closer as her heart picked up

speed. The minutes for the September meeting had landed in her inbox. And unlike most monthly meetings, this was *the* meeting. The opportunity might not come around again for years if she missed it. And there, right there as the last point on the bulleted list was her fate in bold letters: Partner Vote.

It was happening. Now just a few short weeks away. Everything she had always wanted could finally be hers or slip through her grasp.

And she was sitting here with lemonade on a remote island rather than using this time to pad her advantage.

Forgetting her surroundings, and that rather obnoxious man, she dove full force into the final tweaks on the Morrison project. This one was a clear winner.

It had to be.

13

KIM

Hackney's was a local hotspot—and the reason was obvious. Not only did it offer great drinks with a view of the harbor, but the man behind the bar could have wooed every female in the pub just with a flash of his grin.

Their friend Mandy waved from a table across the room, clearly proud at having secured one large enough to fit them all. For a Wednesday night, the room was crowded, but then, such was summertime on the island. The days blurred together, the weekends being no different than the weekdays.

"Is Lena going to join us?" Another year-round resident, Lena worked at her family's coffee shop, meaning her days started early.

"She's going to try, but she said something about taking the ferry to Blue Harbor for some supplies," Gemma said regretfully. "Well, there's always next time!"

Next time. Kim's heart sank a little as they made their way to the table. Would there be a next time? And if so, when? If Bran's family had anything to do with it, there wouldn't be time in her calendar for something more than a weekend getaway, and given the distance, it wouldn't be easy to convince Bran to make the trip. He knew about the lake house, of course. And she'd shown him the painting in her room. He'd said nothing when she mentioned where it might look in his apartment—soon to be their apartment.

If he couldn't even fit a painting of this island into his life, how could he fit a trip into it?

Mandy glanced over at the bar with blatant longing as Kim slid onto her chair. "I once again dared to think this might be the summer that Mack finally looked my way. Now all I can hope for is a little attention once all the tourists go home. It could be a very lonely winter," she said hopefully.

The rest of the women laughed. Mandy's crush wasn't news to any of them—well, other than to Andrea, who hadn't made frequent trips to the island. Since taking over the pub over four years ago, Mack had the object of Mandy's attention, and she was often known to gaze out the window of Main Street Sweets that was conveniently located just across the road from Hackney's.

"You'd have better luck pinning your sites on a tourist," Gemma said. She reached for the basket of popcorn that was handed out to each table and popped a few kernels into her mouth. "But then, I know you don't want to move off the island."

Mandy shook her head. Her family's ice cream parlor had been an institution on the island for generations, and she was carrying the legacy. Kim, however, knew that her business heavily catered to tourists, as did most of the businesses here on the island.

"Have you ever thought of wintering somewhere else?" Kim inquired.

"Maybe, but there's something magical about seeing the island covered in snow. It's so quiet and peaceful. It's special."

Heather looked pensive. "It's hard to believe that for as long as we've been coming here none of us have ever seen the island in the winter."

"Well, it's not exactly easy to access," Andrea pointed out, which was true when the frozen water caused the ferry to stop running in the harsh winter months. "And I know you've always been wary of small aircraft."

Heather laughed. "I'm cautious by nature."

And the island airport only catered to small planes looking for a quick option to cross the water.

"And what about you, Andrea? Anyone special in your life?" Mandy wanted to know between little sighs and glances over to the bar, where Mack was flirting with some tourists who found him just as appealing as every other woman on the island.

"Oh, no." Andrea shook her head. "I'm too caught up with work."

Mandy didn't look convinced. "You mean to tell me in the entire city of Chicago you haven't found true love?"

"Nope, and I'm not looking for it, either," Andrea replied, a little tensely, Kim noted.

"Maybe you've passed right by him on the street and just didn't know it." Mandy sighed again, but her brow pinched into a frown when Mack laughed loudly at something one of the girls up at the bar said. "Although sometimes I'm not sure I'd know love if it was looking me in the face."

Kim wanted to gently tell her that Mack probably wasn't the answer, but what did she know? She had thought that Bran was the one—her perfect match—and now she wasn't so sure about that.

"Oh, I think you know," Gemma said. "There's that little flutter, that feeling that you can't deny. Even if it doesn't make any sense, it makes all the sense in the world. Do you know what I mean?"

Gemma looked around the table for confirmation, but no one seemed to be able to give it to her.

"Love is very complicated," Heather finally said. Kim wondered if she was referring to Daniel or Billy, but of course, she must be thinking of her husband. Or rather, ex-husband.

Kim's stomach rolled over. She could still remember how in sync Heather and Daniel had always been—never arguing, often laughing, building a dream house together, and loving every part of it. Or so it had seemed. If Heather and Daniel couldn't make it, what hope was there for her and Bran?

"Not when it's the right one," Gemma said. And she would know, wouldn't she? Kim couldn't shake the thought that Gemma had been engaged before Leo, and now she was completely content.

"So what would you do, Andrea? If the right guy came along?" Kim asked, because she was curious, and because she hadn't had a conversation like this with her sisters in years, and because she needed more insight, more wisdom. She needed an answer.

"I'm not opposed to finding love," Andrea finally said, a little vaguely. "I just haven't made time for it."

Kim wanted to tell her that she hadn't made time for a lot of things, but that would just lead to an argument that she didn't want to have.

A waitress—college-aged, clearly seasonal staff, and a great disappointment to Mandy who was hoping for Mack himself—appeared at the table to take their drink orders.

"Your pinkest cocktail," Gemma said happily. "We're celebrating a blushing bride-to-be tonight."

Kim swallowed hard. She had hoped this impromptu gathering would fade more into usual chatter and catch-up, not focus on a wedding that might not even take place.

"So, tell us all about the man who stole your heart," Mandy said eagerly. "It's been a long time since I heard a good love story."

"Hey!" Gemma gave a fake injured look. "My books aren't enough of an escape for you?"

Mandy set a hand on her shoulder. "You're going to have to come out with a few more at the rate my love life is going."

Join the club, Kim thought, but she forced a smile she didn't feel. "His name is Bran, short for Branson. Brown hair, brown eyes. He's a corporate attorney. He's good at tennis..." *He's not speaking to me at the moment*. Or if he was, she wouldn't know, because she couldn't bring herself to turn on her phone and attempt to find reception on the island. She didn't want this time to be tainted—not by another argument, not by a reminder of all her problems. Because that's what they were, weren't they?

"He's very nice," Andrea said, sliding Kim a warm smile.

Yes, Bran was very nice. And funny too. He'd lifted her spirits in her darkest days.

"And he makes Kim happy. That's all that matters, right?" Andrea continued, clearly trying to make an effort that Kim wanted to appreciate.

Bran had made her happy. Once. The question was, could he still? And could he make her happy forever?

"And tell us all about the wedding. I assume you two are bridesmaids?" Gemma would of course expect nothing less. But then, she didn't know that the Taylors weren't exactly as close as they'd once been on those carefree summer days. "And is there a big bachelorette party planned?"

Heather and Andrea exchanged glances. It was clear to Kim that neither of them had planned anything—yet—and she wasn't going to hold her breath. She couldn't deny that it stung, but not just because her sisters weren't taking an active part in her wedding planning and celebrations. It hurt because all those little rites of passage that she had once looked so forward to were now passing through her fingers, and they didn't feel very special at all.

"Oh, this is my bachelorette party," Kim said, and it was true. "This trip means a lot to me." She felt her eyes well up when she glanced at her sisters. She quickly blinked them away—it was silly, getting all choked up like this. But the sudden wave of emotions wasn't because of tonight, or even this trip, it was because of everything they'd been through—this past year, and all the years before it, and all the magical summers here on Evening Island. Last night as promised, they'd played cards, had a simple dinner, and gone to bed early. It was not overthought, but it was everything she needed right now and had for some time.

"What I want to hear about is the dress," Gemma said.

"Oh, she's wearing our mother's dress," Heather said before Kim could even think of something to say.

"Oh, and the honeymoon! Where are you going?" Mandy asked eagerly. "As you can see, I am living vicariously through your fairy-tale life."

Fairy-tale life. It was so far from the truth that Kim wanted to burst into tears. Instead, she was grateful to see the waitress bringing a pitcher of strawberry margarita to the table.

"That's still up in the air," she said honestly. Everything was now up in the air, everything other than the fact that she wasn't going to give up her new job, now or down the road, and she wasn't going to give up this island either. Coming back here had reminded her what she was missing—in a bittersweet way—and she wasn't going to let it go just because it didn't fit into the Croft family's packed social schedule.

"I thought Lynette said you were going to Europe?" Andrea looked confused, and Kim felt the blood drain from her face. She scooted back in her chair as the waitress set the salt-rimmed glasses in front of each of them.

"When did she tell you that?" Her sisters had only met Lynette twice: once at the shower and another time at the dress shop.

"At your shower," Andrea said. "I was a little surprised you hadn't mentioned it. You've been so excited about everything."

The shower had been last month. Lynette had already been planning this, weeks ago?

Kim shook her head, fighting back a wave of frustration. "I think Bran is planning something..." But that wasn't true. Bran didn't plan anything when it came to the wedding. Bran let his mother do it instead. And that was just the problem.

She gave Gemma and Mandy a tight smile. "I start a new job two weeks after the wedding. It's only temporary, but it's a teaching position. I went back for my certificate last year."

"Congratulations!" Mandy beamed, and Kim couldn't help but skirt a glance at Andrea, knowing she hadn't garnered the same approval from her sister.

She sipped her drink. Andrea would only take a full-time position seriously, and then it would have to be one where Kim didn't use any vacation or sick days and stuck with for the rest of her life.

Now, she wondered if Andrea was on to something. If Kim did have a problem following a chosen path.

"Well, I say we raise a toast," Gemma said. She topped off Kim's glass from the pitcher and raised her margarita. "To the happy bride!"

"And the wedding of her dreams!" Mandy added.

"And to everything after that," Heather said with a small smile.

Andrea was the only one who didn't say anything, just clinked her glasses with the others, but it was Kim who fell silent as they all took their first sips.

She wasn't a happy bride. And this wasn't the wedding of her dreams. And she didn't know what came after this. She didn't know anything anymore.

14

HEATHER

By Thursday, all Heather could think about was that Billy had mentioned he'd be back on the island today. She tried to keep busy by making breakfast for her sisters—a lavish spread of pancakes with berries and a fruit salad that they took to the porch to eat, even though both of her sisters only poked at the food. Andrea was too regimented to break her diet and kept to the fruit, and Kim fretted that she was worried about fitting into her wedding dress even though she was smaller than Heather had been on her wedding day, meaning that if anything their mother's gown would have to be taken in for her.

Heather tried to focus on their conversations, tried to remind herself that there was no point in getting swept up by Billy's charms. She'd resisted those sparkling eyes and that warm smile once before, letting it fade into a part of her past rather than her real life. Besides, she was leaving the island in ten days.

Not to mention the other matter.

"Don't forget that Gemma invited us to dinner tomorrow night!" Kim told them as they carried their plates back into the kitchen. "It will give us a chance to know Leo better."

"She is certainly in love," Heather remarked. She barely remembered those days when she and Daniel used to enjoy each other's company and not be defined by the absence of something more.

But the feeling of falling in love wasn't completely forgotten. That rush and dizziness, the excitement of seeing a flash of a smile, the graze of a hand. She'd felt it, more than once. With Billy. With Daniel.

And maybe, she'd even found it again.

"Oh now, you didn't seem too closed off to the idea of love last night," Kim said to Andrea. She fought back a smile and slid a knowing glance in Heather's direction.

Heather didn't mind. It was nice to see someone else squirm for once.

Andrea shrugged and turned on the tap. "I told you. I don't have time for that type of thing."

"You could make time for it," Kim continued. Clearly not willing to let their oldest sister off the hook, Kim positioned herself beside Andrea at the sink. "You could make time for a lot of things."

This was a loaded start to the day, and Heather wondered if Andrea wanted to get into it or spend the day checking her email in town again.

Andrea pulled in a breath and scrubbed at the dishes with what Heather could only describe as determination.

"Believe it or not, I don't need a man to complete my life. I'm perfectly happy focusing on my career at the moment."

Kim backed up, looking affronted. Heather felt her shoulders tense as she opened the fridge and slid the bowl of berries onto the top shelf. She hated this sort of conflict, always had. Growing up her older and younger sister never fought—their age differences contributed to a more doting type of relationship. But something had shifted once they'd all become adults, and there was no denying that Kim and Andrea led very different lives, with Kim favoring their mother's path and Andrea, always a Daddy's girl, asserting herself in the workforce.

"You know that I'm starting my new job in October, right after the wedding."

They both knew that it was a temporary position and that Kim had switched jobs many times over the years. And then of course came the fact that Lynette had made it very clear at the shower that Kim was eager to settle down and have children.

Heather's heart felt heavy just thinking of that bold statement—as if there were no question, as if there were no chance of things not working out as perfectly as the oversized flower arrangements that had anchored every table of the posh event.

Andrea didn't look convinced and Heather was silently pleading with her to let it go, but this was Andrea she was talking about, and when Andrea set her mind to something, she didn't stop, and today it seemed she had set her mind to prove a point with Kim.

"What's that look for?" Kim asked.

"You did leave your last job after only a couple of years."

"To go back to school!"

"Because you changed your mind about what you wanted to do." Andrea set down the sponge and sighed. "I'm just saying, we all know that commitment has never been your strong suit."

Ouch. Andrea had touched on a nerve, and the look on Kim's face showed it. There was truth in it, of course. Kim had switched colleges, dropped out of a sorority, and changed majors three times before deciding on a career switch in her late twenties.

"Well, she's committed to Bran," Heather pointed out in her defense, but still, a small part of her could only think: *For now*. Not because she didn't believe that Kim loved Bran, or that he loved her, but because she knew the reality of marriage, that unknown struggles could destroy even the happiest of relationships.

Andrea looked nonplussed but said nothing as she finished washing the dishes. Kim blinked rapidly as she finished drying the plates and then set her towel down on the counter.

"I'm going for a bike ride," Kim said, stepping back. Her ponytail swung at her shoulders as she pushed out the back door to the shed where they were kept. "Alone!"

Heather's shoulders sagged. It was only late morning, but the day already felt soured. She needed to escape this kitchen, too, in case Andrea decided to probe into her personal life next. She should probably start working on that article anyway, even if she still didn't have an idea for it.

"Do you think I was too hard on her?" Andrea asked.

"But if I don't tell her, who will? You know Dad always indulged her because he had me and you as his success stories."

Heather almost choked on the last dregs of her now cold coffee. She was hardly the picture of success. Quite the opposite. But she stayed quiet. Opening up would only bring the hurt to the surface, and it was so much easier to tuck it away and try to forget about it, for a little while at least.

"She was so close to Mom," Heather commented. "I think she's trying to connect with her by becoming a teacher, so maybe she has found her calling now."

Andrea nodded. "She needed Mom in a way you and I didn't. We were always more sure of ourselves. More independent. We figured things out on our own."

That statement couldn't have been further from the truth. The last two years of Heather's marriage had been the most painful, confusing time of her life. She'd wanted to tell her mother, countless times, but her mother had her own problems; it was Heather's turn to be the supportive one, not the other way around. Her mother knew about all the false hopes and the endless disappointments, but she never knew how having a baby had become a fixation, or that it had defined her marriage, and, eventually, ruined it.

"I don't think she meant any harm," Heather said, trying to smooth things over, and partly because if she was going to be sleeping under the same roof as her sisters on a remote island without much room for an easy escape, she selfishly wanted everyone to get along.

"Maybe not." Andrea sighed. "But my job is high pressure, especially…" She hesitated, "Especially with the partner-ship at stake."

"Oh, but you've had that in the bag for years!" Heather couldn't help but feel the sting at how easily her sister climbed the corporate ranks when she couldn't even get an interview. Of course, she hadn't checked her email since she'd left Chicago, but she suspected that she didn't need to hurry if recent history proved anything.

Andrea's mouth thinned. "Nothing is set in stone yet."

Heather began opening cupboards, returning the plates to their proper places. This was what she was good at doing. Keeping house. Keeping her family together was a different story.

"So you never date then?" She'd never heard her sister complain of being lonely, and Heather realized with a strange sense of shame that she was lonely. Not lonely enough to try to go back to the pain of her relationship with Daniel, but lonely enough to wonder if she really could make it on her own. Even if that was probably what she should do.

"I wouldn't say never, but…it's hard to find the time. You know the kind of hours I work."

Yes, Heather did. Andrea made that very clear to every-one, should she ever be asked to meet for coffee or dinner. But then, eventually Heather had stopped asking, not just because it was a moot point but because she had lost interest in those sorts of activities that had once brought her joy. It was Kim who still tried, and Kim who still took it personally when Andrea turned down her offers.

"Kim just wants to connect with you. You were so close growing up."

"But then we grew up, and I have a lot of people counting on me," Andrea said. "She knows I still love her."

Heather raised an eyebrow. "You're only in your early thirties. It wouldn't kill you to carve out a little time for fun, especially while you're here."

"Now you sound like this guy..." Andrea shook her head.

Her sister had her full attention. "What guy?"

Andrea swiped a hand through the air. "Never mind. Maybe you're right. I'll make a better effort with Kim before it's too late."

"Too late?" Heather frowned.

Andrea leaned against the counter and lowered her voice, even though they had both witnessed Kim's dramatic departure. "You know how engrossed Kim is with the Crofts. Once she's married, we'll never see her."

Heather knew deep down this was true, and a part of her was relieved that Andrea shared her concern. But did Andrea share her regret? Heather kicked herself for not reaching out to Kim more this past year. For letting her issues override the bond they'd once shared. Maybe, if she'd called Kim more, gotten together more, met up for dinner more, then...

No. It was wrong to even think that maybe then Kim wouldn't being marrying Branson Croft. Her sister was in love. And Heather wanted her to be happy.

She was just being cynical.

"All the more reason to make the most of this trip then," Heather said firmly. She felt better. Crisis solved. Or at least averted for now. "I think I'll go for a bike ride, too." The fresh air would do her good. Catching Andrea's raised eyebrow, she managed a small laugh. "I'll be sure to take the opposite route."

One that might just pass by Billy's house.

* * *

Heather couldn't remember the last time she'd ridden a bike—scratch that. She could.

It had been her last trip to the island, two years back. Andrea hadn't joined them, of course, and only Ellie Morgan was next door, Billy wasn't there, and she and Daniel were already deep into their problems by then. She'd come up with Kim and her mother—a short trip but a much-needed break from her strained marriage. The three women had taken a lap around the island each morning, then stopped in town for sandwiches at the Island Bakery that they took to the North Shore Beach to eat. Their evenings were spent on the porch, enjoying the sunset and reliving old times, sipping iced tea and playing endless rounds of cards while the carriages and bicycles passed by on their way to the turn into the woods near the Andersons'. It had been a quiet trip, but a good one. Heather had left feeling refreshed and positive and even happy.

It was the last happy memory she could remember having.

Now she took the hill down toward town, turning right just before the street became filled with shops and tourists, and the roads were crowded with horse-drawn carriages. The Davidson cottage was on the western edge of the island, like their own house. As a teenager, Heather could remember sitting on the porch after a long day and admiring the sunset, feeling connected to Billy after he'd gone home, knowing that they were still sharing the same view. It was silly, puppy love, but somehow, much of it hadn't left her completely.

This time Billy was already on the porch when she slowed her bike to a stop outside his house, reading the paper and sipping a glass of juice.

"This is a nice surprise!"

She'd already formulated an excuse, but from the gleam in his eye as she approached the table where he sat, she no longer felt she needed one.

"I've come to reciprocate your hospitality from the other night and see if you're free for dinner tomorrow night."

"You cooking?"

She shook her head. "No, but Gemma Morgan invited us over."

He leaned back in his chair and set down the paper. "The old gang back together. Count me in."

Well, that was easy, and she wasn't sure why she had been expecting the opposite. Maybe because it had been a long time since anything had gone her way, and even then, no amount of effort or trying or tears had helped her out much.

"Great. Stop by at six then. And bring your appetite. I'm making your favorite."

His eyes lit up. "Summer pie?"

Heather laughed. She hadn't thought of that term for it in years, even though she'd rolled out plenty of dough since then. But summer pie was different, special. It was made from the local berries, enjoyed outside, on the porch, not warm, but cool. And it was best shared with her favorite people, here in her favorite place.

Back in Chicago, it was just berry pie. Or fruit pie. But here, it would always be summer pie.

"That reminds me that I should stop by the market for supplies," she said.

"If I was willing to go off-island today, I'd say we could pick some berries from Conway Orchard in Blue Harbor."

"I'm not ready to leave this island just yet," Heather said, her heart sinking at the mere thought of it.

"You could always shop tomorrow, though?" Billy was quick to ask. "I was thinking of taking a walk. Care to join me?"

And how could she say no to that smile or the pleading look in those eyes?

They crossed the road to the waterfront, navigating the large rocks and overgrown shrubs with bright pink flowers. Heather toed off her sandals and hooked them over her finger; Billy did the same. The lake stretched far in every direction, calm and quiet. She almost didn't dare dip a toe in it.

"I remember thinking the water looked clear enough to drink," Heather said, laughing.

"As a doctor, I can advise you that it is not." Billy grinned.

"Look at you." Heather elbowed him playfully as they headed along the coastline, away from town. "A doctor. Your parents are so proud, I know." His mother couldn't hide it last August at the funeral.

"Oh, they'll be prouder when I settle down and give them some grandkids." He gave her a wry look.

Heather felt her smile slip and had to look away.

"Is that what you want?" she finally asked.

"I'd like to get married someday. Have a couple of kids. Throw the ball around. Teach them how to fish. Bring them here."

He shrugged it away as if it were nothing but a given, that in due time all that would happen for him, and it probably would. That marriage and children went hand in hand, even if sometimes, they didn't.

"That's what I love about coming back here," he said. "You must feel it too. These homes aren't really ours, they're just borrowed from our ancestors, and eventually, we'll pass them down to our kids, and them to theirs. They'll be the ones coming up here each summer, looking forward to sunsets on the porch and morning bike rides, and a place to get away from all that technology and noise."

He shook his head and waggled his eyebrows at her in a playful way, but it didn't feel playful, and this conversation had stopped being fun. "It's crazy to think about, isn't it? That these houses will outlive us?"

It was crazy. Crazy to think that she ever stood a chance with Billy. Crazy to think that she might even try.

She could never be the woman in that picture he'd painted so clearly and surely. She was silly to even dare to think she ever could.

Old hurts pushed to the surface, and she wasn't sure how much longer she could keep them from showing. She was relieved when they turned around and Billy's house came into view again.

"Well, I should probably get going. My sisters will be wondering where I am if I'm gone too long. I just wanted to ask you about tomorrow night..." She couldn't look him in the eye when she said it, and even though she was sure Gemma might have invited him if she hadn't, she still wished she hadn't come. Hadn't tried. Because sometimes trying and failing were worse than not trying at all.

That's what Daniel had said, at least. It was their last big fight, the moment when she knew that her marriage was over, long over, and that she had been holding on to the scraps of it, unable to accept what was so clear. She couldn't have a child. Not with Daniel. Not with anyone.

"See you tomorrow," Billy said, as she hurried away.

She managed a weak smile and hurried to her bike, pedaling fast and hard like the young girl he'd just described, back when this was her happy place, her summer place, the place where everything was right and nothing was wrong. But she wasn't that young girl anymore. And try as she might, she couldn't go back and do it all over again, or do it better.

The tears flowed fast and hard as she peddled against the lake breeze, but she didn't stop until she'd rounded the bend, out of sight. Tourists passed by on rented bikes, laughing and smiling, but she parked hers off the path, walked onto the shore, and dropped onto a large rock, keeping her back to the island and her eyes to the water. She'd go to the store later. Tomorrow, so the berries were fresh. And tomorrow night she'd smile and socialize and pretend that everything was fine.

That her heart didn't break every time she thought of her future. That she wasn't just lonely, but she was alone, and she might always be alone, and that she didn't know how to accept that.

But for now, she would sit here, and she'd cry good and hard until she couldn't cry anymore, and only then would she know there was nothing left for tonight. That she could get through it. That for tonight at least, she'd be okay.

15

ANDREA

Dinner at Sunset Cottage, as the Morgans had named their lake house, was exactly what the Taylor sisters needed, or at least what Andrea needed. A night of shared memories, easy conversation, and best of all, some much-needed distraction from the nagging thought that somehow Andrea had survived an entire week away from the office, even if she wasn't sure her career plan had.

Andrea walked into the kitchen to see Heather pulling a lattice-crust pie from the oven. The entire room smelled sweet and fruity, and Andrea almost didn't mind the additional heat it created in the house. Heather's pie was always an exception to the rule their mother had put in place all those years ago when the lack of air-conditioning left the house warm on the days that the lake breeze didn't flow easily through the open windows. Now, Andrea wondered fondly if that had been an easy excuse to get out of cooking.

"You look cheerful," Heather commented.

Andrea noted the surprise in her voice. "I was just

remembering how Mom never let us use the oven on the hotter days because it would heat the house."

Heather smiled. "I loved her cold pasta salads. They were never the same because she would toss whatever was on hand into the bowl. Do you remember that?"

Andrea did, but only because Heather had stirred the memory. "I miss her," she said softly, hating the emotion that had crept into her voice.

Heather set the pie down on the counter and nodded slowly. "Me too. I feel bad that I didn't go see Dad with Kim. He must be so lonely."

Andrea wondered if Heather was speaking from experience, tapping into her own situation, but didn't press. It was clear that Heather didn't like talking about Daniel, and she was much better off discussing Billy instead.

"Well, you certainly have a lot of Mom in you," Andrea said. Everyone knew that she was the most like their father—driven, busy, satisfied with a hard day's work. It hadn't ever bothered her until now when she was left wondering just what part of her mother she did inherit, other than the hair color she and her sisters all shared. "Both you and Kim."

"Oh, Kim for sure, but I don't know about me..."

"Are you kidding? Mom was...well, she was a master of running a house, you know? All those homemade Halloween costumes, all the special birthday parties, and no one did a holiday like Mom. You're the same way. I can already picture you knitting baby blankets someday."

Heather's cheeks flushed as her smile faded. "You're forgetting that I'm no longer married."

Andrea looked at her quizzically. "I know, but I also know that you're still really young. Once you get over this—"

"Who said I'm not over it?" Heather snapped back. She walked to the cabinet and pulled out some tea towels, the kind their mother used to buy in the shops in town. She spread one out and transferred the pie onto it.

She looked pretty tonight, Andrea noticed, in a light blue cotton sundress and her chestnut hair flowing freely at her shoulders. She looked like she had lost a bit of weight, now that Andrea looked at her properly, but then, they hadn't spent much time together since Christmas, and the past year had been hard on all of them. Heather had always been the most sensitive of the group. Maybe she was depressed.

Or maybe, she was considering dipping her toe into the dating scene again despite all her protests to the contrary.

"Is Kim ready?" Andrea asked, pulling a bottle of wine from the fridge. Clearly, they could use a buffer right about now.

"Right here!" Kim looked flushed as she entered the kitchen. It was a warm night and Heather had pushed up the temperature more than a few degrees. Andrea could only hope for a strong lake breeze and a cool drink.

Kim was wearing white shorts and a simple pink tee shirt. Both of her sisters managed to make Andrea conscious of her attire of white capris and a linen blouse and heels, even if they were of the strappy variety. She looked like she was ready for dinner at her father's club, or perhaps a summer office party, rather than a casual dinner with old friends.

Maybe they were right. Maybe she did need to learn to loosen up a little. Truth was, she wasn't even sure she knew how. She'd lost the ability to slow down, lost the rhythm of this island somewhere along the way too.

"Am I underdressed?" Kim asked when they reached the door, but then her expression turned to one of knowing as they stepped out onto the porch and saw Billy Davidson coming up the road. "Well, Billy! I heard you were back on the island!" She flung a devilish glance in Heather's direction and ran down the creaking stairs to greet him with a hug.

"And I hear little Kimberly Taylor is about to become a married woman! Hey, Andrea!" He gave her a quick embrace, even if it seemed as though his gaze never left Heather.

Well, that explained the dress.

"I didn't know you were joining us tonight!" Kim continued, which was only slightly odd, because usually her upcoming wedding was the only thing she could speak of these days, and before that, it was Bran, Bran, Bran. Where he took her, what they ate, what she wore, what he said. There was only so much of it that Andrea could take, and from the shadow in Heather's eyes at Christmas, she could assume the same went for her other sister.

"Heather stopped by yesterday and invited me. Wouldn't miss it."

Oh, did she now? Andrea slid her sister a knowing look. Heather's cheeks flushed subtly.

"If the whole gang is getting together, we can't have Billy miss out!" her sister insisted.

Kim pinched her mouth and gave Andrea a conspiratorial smile. Andrea felt something in her soften toward her younger sister. Kim was many things, and one of her best qualities had always been her ability to look at the bright side, even when others couldn't.

"Oh, look, there's Gemma now!" Heather waved with both hands as they cut across the lawn to the large Victorian where they had spent so many summer days, coming up and down the stairs, sitting on the porch, letting their towels dry over the railing. They were in and out of each other's homes so much, it was hard to know where the properties even divided.

Gemma hurried down the stairs and greeted each of them, but she didn't seem surprised to see Billy. "Hey you," she said. To the rest of them, she said, "Who would have thought that Billy and I would be the ones to end up here year-round?"

"In fairness, my primary residence is Pine Falls," Billy corrected, but he looked pleased. He jutted his chin at the porch. "Is that John Bowden talking with Leo?"

Gemma nodded. "I invited him tonight, seeing as he's sort of becoming an extended member of the gang. The new gang." She laughed, but Andrea was too startled to feign amusement.

There, sitting on the porch, talking with Leo, was none other than the man from the Lakeside Inn. The two men turned as the group came up the steps, and there was no denying the flash of recognition in the man's face when he saw her.

"We meet again," he said, giving her an appraising look.

Andrea could feel both of her sisters' and Gemma's eyes on her, but she refused to look at any of them. There was nothing to explain other than a passing interaction at a hotel restaurant. Certainly nothing more to that gleam in the man's admittedly beautiful hazel eyes.

She smiled, even if she wasn't completely thrilled to see him. The man had been judgmental and outspoken, and with her stress these days, she didn't appreciate either, especially from someone who didn't have a clue what her life was like. But this was a party, and she was a guest, and Gemma and Billy and Leo seemed to have found something redeeming in the man.

"We meet officially," she said, extending her hand. "I'm Andrea Taylor."

"John Bowden," he said, giving her a firm but slow shake, one that signaled to her that he wasn't going to be quick in releasing her palm.

A strange emotion rolled through her stomach. If she didn't know better, she might call it attraction. *If* she didn't know better, which she did. After all, the man was attractive, but he was also checked out from her world, opinionated, and... Well, it didn't matter. She didn't have time for romance, suitable or not. She had a partnership at stake, one that she had been invested in for a very long time.

"I brought wine," she said, using it as an excuse to snatch her hand back, so she could hold out the bottle with both hands.

"And I brought a pie," Heather said, giving a humble smile. "As if that isn't obvious."

"And Leo's grilling," Gemma said with a laugh. "I wish Hope was here. Not only would she love to see you all, but she's also a much better cook than I am."

"Hey, speak for yourself," Leo chided, sliding an affectionate hand around Gemma's waist.

"Considering that most of my meals are from a restaurant, anything homemade sounds wonderful," John said.

So the man ate out every night while living here, on this idyllic island. He probably didn't have a care in the world. While Andrea...she had a lot of cares. A lot of worries, too. For a moment, she couldn't help but feel a flash of envy at the way everyone else around her seemed so capable of shedding their troubles and enjoying a warm evening with friends.

"How is Hope?" Andrea asked, realizing that they hadn't talked about her much yet. She thought she saw a strange shadow come over John's face but didn't read into it. Likely, the man had opinions on Hope and Ellie, too. She doubted that she alone had been singled out by his attention because she rarely was. In Chicago, she occasionally caught the eye of a man in a bar after work, sometimes even chatted through one drink, but she didn't give off the impression that she was interested in more than that, and it would seem from the company tonight that she didn't dress as if she were, either.

She was all business. That was the message. Even if it hadn't always been intentional.

Gemma skirted her gaze to John and back to Andrea. "Hope is good. Busy. She has a side business now while the girls are in school or camp. I know they were going to try to get up here this summer, but it might not be until Labor Day weekend."

"By then we'll be gone," Heather said, and this time it was Billy's expression that Andrea noticed. He looked more than a little disappointed. Andrea wondered if Heather had picked up on it, but she was already walking across the porch to set the pie down where it wouldn't be disturbed.

"I was hoping Ellie would be here," Kim said, accepting a glass of wine from Leo.

"Oh, she'll be back by next spring," Gemma said knowingly. "She loves this place. But it's been nice for her to travel knowing that we're looking after the place. It's been nice all around."

She shared a little smile with Leo and now it was Kim's turn to frown, and something told Andrea that it had nothing to do with her favorite summer friend not being part of the group tonight.

Or maybe it was because Bran wasn't here.

"Wine, Andrea?" It was John who spoke, and reluctantly, Andrea nodded. She needed something to take the edge off, because as much as she'd hoped this would be an evening where she'd be distracted from her troubles for a bit, it wasn't turning out that way so far.

Tonight, her life back in Chicago felt forefront on her mind, and not because it was Friday evening and she'd missed a solid five days while her competition had gained an advantage. No, tonight she was starting to wonder if her choices and sacrifices had all been worth it, or if next month she'd be toasting to the newest partner named Jace, rather than celebrating for herself.

Celebrating *by* herself, she realized, even though she hadn't given that much thought before. She'd slowly made her personal life smaller, even though it hadn't been intentional.

"Why not?" She was off the clock. The office was closed. She'd put in some work on the Morrison project and she'd do more over the weekend. She'd been working off her original idea, one that wasn't much different than another design she'd done last year—one that had been well received. There would be no more urgent emails to Nicole tonight, or even tomorrow. Until Monday morning, she should focus on her sisters and friends. And maybe, she thought, slightly reluctantly, on this man who was determined to befriend her.

John poured her a glass of white wine from an already open bottle and handed it to her. "When Gemma told me that the family from next door was coming over tonight, I didn't realize that you were an islander."

"Summer people," Andrea corrected. "We've known the Morgans since we were just little girls."

"I've heard all the stories over time. I didn't connect you when we met the other day."

"Well, I live in Chicago now," she said, realizing she had already told him that. "And I haven't been back to the island in a while."

"Shame. It's a wonderful escape." His stare was so intense, that Andrea shifted the weight on her feet.

"For those who have the luxury," she said briskly, and she didn't just mean financially, she meant time—away from work, away from responsibility, away from all the little things that filled her days.

"Maybe you can convince her to have a little fun," Kim said, coming to join them. Her eyes shone with mischief, and her lips curled into a little smile when Andrea flashed her a look of warning. "We've been trying to get her to put her work aside for years. I'm almost ready to give up!"

It was said with a laugh, but Andrea felt the sting of the truth in her sister's words. How many years had she passed up the opportunity to come here with her mother or sisters? How many years had she let slide by, thinking there'd always be another time, a better time, until time had run out?

Luckily, John kept things light, with a broad smile and a lingering gaze in her direction. "Oh, I don't back down that easily."

Andrea's stomach rolled over. God help her. He was singling her out, and she...she was out of her element.

She took a steadying sip of her wine, noting the wide-eyed and less than subtle look that Kim gave her as she moved over to the table and helped herself to some chips and dip.

Andrea wondered how she could follow her. In business, she never struggled like this. But then, in business, there was commonality, a point to the conversation. And now... Now there were just John's eyes. He had very nice eyes.

She was relieved when Heather popped up next to them to pour a glass of wine.

"So, John, what is it that you do?" Heather asked.

"I own the Lakeside Inn," John said, mildly.

Andrea nearly coughed on her drink, and clearly, her surprise wasn't lost on him. He lifted an eyebrow playfully.

"I thought the Kesslers owned it," she said, tipping her head.

"They retired," Gemma contributed. "Thank goodness for John or who knows what might have become of it."

"Oh, I love that hotel!" Kim chimed in. "We used to go

there for lemonade with our mother. We'd sit on the deck and admire the view and feel like we were back in time, because they always brought the drinks in those funny-shaped glasses. And those cinnamon rolls... Tell me you still have them."

John chuckled. "Of course. And the glasses too. When I bought the hotel, I knew that there was a lot of renovation work to be done, but I also wanted to keep the place true to its roots, to preserve what people love about it most. I want it to be a place that people return to, year after year, a place where they feel nostalgic, not just a place where they drop into bed at the end of a long day."

Andrea stared at him pensively, letting his words sink in. That was how she felt about their lake house—about the island in general—even if she hadn't stopped to think about it in too long. She'd always counted on it being the exact same when she returned. Now, she realized just how much she'd depended on it.

"Where were you before this?" Heather asked.

John looked at Andrea and grinned. "Chicago."

Andrea pursed her lips. He had her. And he knew it. And she couldn't say that she was annoyed by it, either. If anything she'd say that she was surprised. Pleasantly so, in fact.

16

KIM

Kim was being sensitive, she knew. But sitting at this table, she couldn't help but feel like an outsider at what was becoming a very intimate dinner, and not because there were only seven of them present. No, Gemma and Leo were enamored, partners in the truest sense of the word, and not just in starting up a horse riding business as Sally Hayworth had already told them. They knew each other's patterns, they got each other's jokes, and the way they looked at each other... Kim could now be certain that Gemma had probably never looked at any other man like that before, not even her ex-fiancé.

And then there was Heather and Billy; the fondness between them was obvious to everyone, possibly even Heather, try as she might to deny it. When someone shared a memory, they were quick to exchange a small smile. They had a history, but more than that, they had a connection, and from the looks of it, so did John and Andrea. Why, the only time that Heather even took her eyes off Billy was to shoot wide-eyed suggestive glances at Kim every time Andrea laughed at something this inn owner said.

"Your laugh is exactly like your mother's," Gemma said to Andrea, her tone a little wistful.

"It's probably the only thing I inherited from her," Andrea said as she reached for her wineglass. "Well, other than my hair of course, and we all got that."

"What more could you possibly ask for?" John grinned at her, and Andrea, Kim, saw, struggled to hide her smile.

"Don't forget the house," Billy said. "Your mother left that to you girls. She loved that house."

Kim nodded, wondering if it could possibly mean as much to Andrea or even Heather as it meant to her, and then thought that was unfair of her. They'd come to the island, hadn't they? Even Andrea, now, after all this time.

"If it hadn't been for Leo I'm not sure what would have become of our house by now," Gemma set down her fork and sighed.

Kim and her sisters looked at her in surprise. "You mean if you hadn't moved back to the island?"

Gemma nodded. "That, mostly. There was a time last summer when I thought the best thing to do would be to sell this old place."

Heather gasped. "Well, I'm happy to hear you came to your senses!"

"In a way, without someone living here full time, it didn't make sense to keep it, especially since we all stopped visiting regularly. It was fine when my grandmother was still with us, but after she was gone, the upkeep became too much for Ellie."

This was starting to sound familiar, and not in a good way. It was what Kim's father had said, in so many words.

"What do you think would have come of it if you'd sold?" Andrea asked, leaning in.

Kim looked at her sharply. Surely she couldn't be gathering information, thinking that they might do just this? Kim was very aware that Andrea was keen to keep up with the latest design trends so that she could stay relevant in a competitive industry.

But Andrea said, "That's the thing about these homes, just like the inn." She gave John a small smile. "Not everyone will appreciate the history. These are old properties. They require a special level of care."

"And love," Kim added. "Our mother loved the house here so much, and I think that's why she kept coming back each year. It takes that kind of emotional investment to hold on to a property through the generations."

"They're also expensive, and a lot of work," Gemma pointed out.

"But they're special. A throwback to another time. A better time, in many ways," Andrea said. She gave a little smile. "These homes were the reason that I became an architect."

John looked at her with interest. "Is that so?"

"You sound surprised," she replied.

Kim looked at Heather, who hid her smile behind her wineglass. Yep, Andrea was flirting, even if she might not yet know it.

"Not surprised, but rather impressed." John jutted his lip. "This is a historic island, in many ways you could even argue that it's been frozen in time. For me, that's the appeal, and it's why I'm so careful with every change I make at the inn. Even so, it's been a little challenging to get some bigger projects approved by the historical society."

"Hey, that's a topic idea for your article, Heather," Kim said. When she saw the look of confusion fall over most of the table, she said, "Sally asked her to write a feature column."

"Well, that's exciting!" Gemma leaned forward. "Remember that summer we made our own newspaper? We must have been about nine or ten."

Heather laughed. It was a sound that Kim hadn't heard in a long time, she realized.

"*West End Happenings,*" she cried. "I recall we even mentioned how Mrs. Anderson had changed her hair color since the previous season."

Gemma's shoulders shook. "Look how far we've come. What are you planning to write about?"

"I was hoping to pick your brain, Gemma," Heather said, standing up to retrieve her pie from where it sat cooling on the porch rail. She brought it to the center of the table. The men all leaned in excitedly. "I'm a little out of my element writing something about the island."

"Nonsense!" It was Billy who looked at her crossly. "You are every bit as much an islander as everyone else at the table."

Heather flushed at that, and Kim looked over at Andrea, who seemed to feel just as uncomfortable by that as Kim did. Sure, they'd come every year as kids, and the house had been passed down through the generations, but Kim's father's words loomed loud in her ears. What if they stopped coming back to the island? What then?

***

By the time Kim made it downstairs the next morning, the kitchen was quiet, and only the sound of Andrea tapping on her laptop through the screen door gave any indication that she wasn't alone in the house.

The breakfast dishes were still in the sink, and when Kim filled her mug with coffee she realized that it had gone cold. There was no microwave in the house, meaning she could start a fresh pot or drink it as it was. She poured the liquid into a juice glass and added a few ice cubes and a splash of milk, deciding to make the best of the situation. Like she always did.

She took a sip of the iced coffee, but it did nothing to clear her head or undo the knots in her stomach when she thought about the fact that it was Saturday. A week had passed, and even though she was here in this house on Evening Island, her mind was back in Chicago. Specifically, it was on the event tonight that she wouldn't be attending, much to Bran and Lynette's disappointment.

She opened the fridge, looking for something to eat, and then closed it again. A week had gone by since her last conversation with Bran, and they hadn't exactly left things off on good terms. Would he be going tonight? Would they talk about her? Would he have the same second thoughts she was having?

She could check. Go upstairs and turn on her phone and

see if he had tried to reach her. But she didn't know what would be worse right now. Seeing that he had left a message or realizing that he hadn't. Besides, she couldn't get a signal in this house if she tried. She'd have to walk around, searching for a connection to the outside world. She'd have to make an effort. And truth be told, she was tired of making an effort for Bran's family when her own family had so many problems.

Instead, she plucked an apple from the fruit bowl and walked down the hall to the front door, where her sisters were both occupying most of the wicker furniture—Heather reading a book and Andrea, of course, working.

"You slept in," Heather observed, looking up.

Kim pushed aside a pillow and wedged herself onto the other side of the small wicker sofa. "I guess it was all the wine."

In truth, she'd had more than usual. She hadn't intended it, but it was soon becoming obvious that there were three pairs at the table and she was the odd one out. It was silly to feel like this, she knew. She technically had a fiancé waiting for her back home. She was in a deeper relationship than anyone else at the table, but it didn't feel that way sitting alone, knowing how she and Bran had left things. And when she saw the way Gemma and Leo had such an easy way about them, talking and laughing, both so relaxed and carefree, well, then she really started to drown her sorrows.

"Leo's taking me riding tomorrow if you want to come," Kim said, but as she suspected, Heather shook her head. She'd been wary of horses ever since they'd rented a carriage one time as teenagers and taken a turn a little too hard and a little too fast, causing them to nearly crash into a lakefront boulder.

"Gemma and Leo make a cute couple," Heather observed. They hadn't had a chance to talk much the night before. Kim had gone straight to bed, and Heather and Billy had remained out on the porch, their murmured conversation filtering through Kim's open bedroom window, interrupted with bursts of laughter.

"I could say the same about you and Billy," Kim said, raising an eyebrow.

Heather set down her book with a long sigh. "Billy and I are just friends."

"Not from what I heard last night," Kim said. "You forget that we keep the windows open here."

But there was no amusement in Heather's face. "And what did you hear last night? Two friends talking over one last glass of wine?"

She supposed that was all she'd heard, or at least Heather wasn't willing to say anymore, and decided to let it drop. Besides, Andrea wasn't off the hook just yet.

"Maybe it was Andrea and John," she said, not bothering to hide her smile.

Andrea rolled her eyes. "Please."

"What? He's a good-looking guy," Kim remarked.

"And you did seem to light up around him," Heather added, sparking a flush from Andrea's cheeks. "You seemed to really relax and have a nice time."

"I did," Andrea said, and Kim and Heather exchanged a brief glance. "This break has been good for me. I'll be refreshed and ready to hit the ground running by a week from Monday."

This time it was Kim who rolled her eyes.

"It's a warm day. I think I'll put on my suit and go to the beach for a while. Anyone care to join me?" Kim didn't hold her breath, but she was relieved when Heather pushed up from her chair and nodded.

Daring to test her luck, she looked at Andrea, who was staring intently at her screen. "Did you manage to get internet access?"

Andrea didn't look up. "It's just an idea I had for a project I'm working on. But...maybe I will go to the beach for a bit."

Kim knew that her expression probably matched the surprise shown in Heather's face, but she wasn't about to question Andrea's sudden change of heart any more than she would find a reason to delay. Her sisters wanted to spend some time together at the lakefront, just like old times.

Surely this was worth ruffling the Croft feathers a bit. It certainly beat another stuffy dinner, making polite conversation with people she'd never see again, that was for sure.

They all changed quickly, eager to make the most of the day, and with a canvas beach tote filled with books, magazines, towels, and provisions for lunch, compliments of Heather, trekked across the road to their favorite sandy spot.

"Do you remember how we used to see who could swim out farther in under a minute?" Kim laughed at the memory. Andrea always won, of course, and not just because she was the eldest. It was because she was the most determined.

"I should have let you win a few times, Kimmy." Andrea's smile was apologetic. "I'm sorry."

Kim blinked at her, sensing that her words were referring to more than some summer swim race when they were just kids.

"I didn't mind," she said honestly. "I just liked spending time with you."

And she still did. It just didn't happen often enough. And more and more, it felt like that wasn't entirely Andrea's or Heather's fault. With the Crofts consuming her social circle more and more, she was going to be the one making all the excuses before long.

Unless...

She pulled in a breath, not wanting to ruin this day worrying about what would happen when she returned, but it was there, and she couldn't completely ignore it.

"It's hard to believe we've been here a week already. And in a week we'll be leaving again."

The women all fell silent as they adjusted themselves on their towels. Kim was expecting Andrea to make an impatient remark, underscoring how much she had to get back to, but instead, she looked oddly pensive.

"I'd like to think that Mom would be happy to know we all came here," Kim said. She couldn't deny the ache in her chest when she thought of how much more she still wanted to ask her mother, how much advice she needed, especially now.

"Oh, she would be. For sure." Heather gave her a sad smile. "She loved coming every year with us, even when the trips became shorter. It meant a lot to her that you were planning to join us last year, Andrea."

Andrea vigorously applied some sunblock to her shoulders. "It's difficult to get away from work."

Kim wondered if they'd been too harsh on her. "She understood that."

Andrea just shrugged. "Dad does, but did Mom? I'm not so sure she understood that side of me. You and Mom were closer," Andrea said, and even though it hurt Kim to think that her sisters might feel this way, she also knew that it was probably true.

"Well, you had her for the longest," Kim pointed out. At first, this had upset her; it had even felt cruel and unfair because Andrea had her job, and Heather had her husband, and Kim hadn't settled into life, hadn't figured anything out yet.

"I know what Sally said hurt the other day." Heather readjusted her towel. "About how much Mom would have liked to see your wedding. But at least you'll be wearing her dress. She would have loved that."

Kim swallowed hard and stood to dip her toe in the water, until she was wading up to her knees, not wanting to answer that question much less even think about it. She could still remember trying it on, standing in front of the full-length mirror in her mother's closet, knowing that a piece of her family's history would be passed down, that maybe, just maybe, she'd be lucky enough to find the kind of love her mother had found.

Kim's lips thinned when she thought of how special and rare that marriage had seemed. She'd seen her other friends' parents—they fought and argued, some had affairs, many divorced. But not the Taylors. And every weekend in the summer when their father would arrive on the island, their mother would flush in the cheeks like a young girl still in the first rush of love.

She'd thought that kind of bond was special. Now, considering how quickly her father had moved on, she wasn't sure what it had been. And if she couldn't believe that her parents had a magical kind of love, how could she ever think that her own relationship would be a happy one?

HEATHER

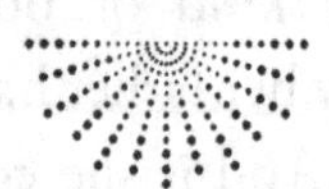

After a warm shower and a change of clothes, Heather was in her room reading one of Gemma's books when there was a knock at the door. She dog-eared her paperback and set it down, not exactly minding the interruption. She'd lived alone for so many months now but she hadn't grown used to the quiet, and she feared she never would. She hadn't even realized how much she missed the comforting sounds of someone else coexisting under the same roof until she'd come here to this house. A part of her feared just how lonely she'd be come next weekend when she went back.

To what? To a home that only housed memories and the aching reminder of a lost dream? To the halfhearted job searches, because more and more, her heart wasn't in anything?

But that wasn't exactly true, was it? Her heart was in this place—on the island, in this house full of happy memories and none of the sad ones.

"Come in!" She watched as the aged brass door handle

turned and Andrea poked her head around the door. She had a mischievous gleam in her eye that was typically reserved for Kim. Heather felt her heart skip a beat. She didn't like surprises. She'd had too many of them in the past couple of years and so far, none of them had been good ones.

"Billy is downstairs on the porch," Andrea whispered.

Heather's heart began to pound, and her eyes darted to the window, even though her room faced the rear of the house, and even though she'd closed it when she woke up because the morning breeze was making her chilly.

She and Billy had talked for a good hour after leaving Gemma's, mostly reminiscing, laughing about fond memories that only seemed to surface in the company of those who had been there and shared the experience. She'd gone back inside with that ache in her chest that she'd always felt after leaving him for the day, or the summer, but this time it was something deeper than lust or longing. This time it was the knowledge that she cared for him, still, and that just like so many other things in life, love wasn't always enough.

"Can you tell him I'm in the shower? Or that I must have gone out the back door while you were busy?"

Andrea frowned and stepped deeper into the room. The bed was made, of course. Heather always kept a tidy house, a proud home, one that she liked to think would have an open door, where her future children could come and go as they pleased, bringing friends over without a prearranged invitation. Now, as Andrea sat on the bed, where Heather slept alone, it seemed silly to even think that she'd have to smooth over that faded blue quilt after Andrea left the room, because what did it matter?

"Why don't you want to see Billy? I thought you were friends." It was clear that Andrea had made a point of using Heather's description of their relationship.

There was no irony in her statement, or jest either. She was speaking frankly, and the look in her eyes was one of concern.

"I can't explain it," Heather sighed. In all honesty, she wouldn't know where to begin. She'd kept so much to herself for so long, hiding each disappointment in the hopes that soon she'd have better news to share and she didn't want to cloud it, telling herself that she'd get through this rough patch until somehow, she'd ended up here. Hiding from her first love, a man she might even still love. Or could love. In another life.

"I don't want to jump back into a relationship," she finally said. "And spending time with Billy like this, it's just confusing."

Andrea hesitated. "If that's what you want, I'll tell him."

What Heather wanted was the impossible. To fall in love, get married, stay married, to have the family she'd always thought she'd have. To bring her children back to the island each summer, just like Billy dreamed about doing, too.

"It's what I want," she said firmly. It had to be.

Andrea nodded, saying nothing more as she stood and walked out of the room, closing the door behind her. Heather sat in the quiet room, not moving and almost not even breathing as she strained to catch any murmur of their conversation. There was no way she could hear from this part of the house, though, and it was for the best.

Just like not spending another day with Billy was for the best.

She waited until she heard the sounds of Andrea's footsteps coming up the stairs, and knew that Billy was gone, that she'd sent him away. That she had made a choice and now she would have to live with it. She opened her book and closed it again, finding it impossible to focus on anything right now, other than the image of Billy walking down West End Road, fading from view.

She fought the urge to stand up, run down the stairs, run after him. He'd smile. She'd smile. She'd feel it all the way to her heart. That rush of hope that she hadn't dared to think she'd ever feel again. But just like the last time, reality would settle in, and she'd be left hurt and alone.

No, it was better this way.

Even if it was disappointing.

The pull in her chest had returned and Heather knew that sitting around by herself would only make it more glaring. She set Gemma's book in her tote and headed downstairs. Her sisters were nowhere to be seen, which was probably for the best, because even though Andrea hadn't pressed, Kim probably would.

She'd go into town. Check out the galleries, maybe buy herself a pick-me-up, even if it was just ice cream. Maybe she'd be struck by a wave of sudden inspiration and she could get this article written—she was running out of time at this rate. If she ran into Billy, that would be fine. She'd keep it casual, and cut it short. The walk would be good for her, get her out of her thoughts.

The walk to town was short, and Heather stopped in a

gift shop off the main street first, pleased when she saw her dear friend Ellie Morgan's painting in the window display. She pushed through the door, where a bird was sitting on its perch in a large cage, staring at her with beady eyes.

"He—"

A woman about her same age came rushing out from behind the counter, waving both hands, her eyes wide. "Sorry, did you see the sign?"

Confused, and slightly alarmed, Heather turned from the left to the right. Was this not a shop? Had she barged into a place where she wasn't welcome? But then she saw it, the laminated sign with big bold letters next to the birdcage.

"What happens if I say...you know?" she asked, glancing back at the sign, explicitly telling her not to greet the bird as she had intended.

"Do you really want to know?" The woman's eyes hooded, and Heather started to laugh. "Is this your first time in here?"

"I guess so," Heather said, looking around and trying to find something familiar about the quaint space and the last time she'd been shopping here, with her mother. But that now felt like a very long time ago and so much had changed since then. "But it's been a while. I saw you have a painting in the window from my friend Ellie."

The woman smiled. "You know Ellie? She's one of my closest friends."

No wonder she felt such a kinship to this woman. "I'm Heather Mit—," she began, and then shook her head, catching her error. She didn't go by that name anymore, not since the divorce. "Sorry, force of habit. I just...divorced." She saw the woman's head tilt with sympathy. "I'm Heather Taylor. Our family has the house next to the Morgans. We grew up playing together every summer."

"Heather Taylor!" The girl nodded. "I'm Naomi—Ellie told me all about the Taylors!"

"Naomi! I remember Ellie mentioning you. My visits in recent years have been so brief."

"You have that fantastic playhouse in your backyard. Whenever I stopped by Ellie's I would admire that thing. It even had curtains on the windows!"

Heather laughed, but there was no denying the tug in her chest. She'd always loved that playhouse, and been foolish enough to think that someday her kids would too.

Heather laughed again. "That part might have been my doing. I always liked pretty things."

"Then you've come to the right place! I'm always finding new things for the shop, not just for the locals but for those of us who live here year-round too."

"You live here year-round?"

Heather was still amazed by the people who braved the cold and isolation during the winter months when the only exit off the island was by a small aircraft. But now, the more she heard that others did it, the more she almost envied that ability to spend her days in her favorite place, where she was always at her best.

"People always seem fascinated by it, but I have a group of friends here, and my family lives close by, in Blue Harbor, so I'm never lonely. Except when it comes to love." Naomi sighed.

A common theme, Heather noticed, thinking of

Mandy's woes the other night, but then not common enough to bother being the focus of her article. Gemma had found love. And Mandy had found someone—even if the feelings weren't reciprocated. No, it would seem that even here on an island this small, happiness could be found, if you looked hard enough.

Or maybe, if you were lucky.

"Not many options on the island other than the seasonal workers," Naomi continued. Then, she paused and waggled her eyebrows. "However...there is one guy I have my eye on. Well, me and probably half the other year-round single women, and that's not a lot of us."

"The guy from Hackney's?" There was no denying that Mandy had set her sights on an eligible bachelor and that she wasn't alone.

"Oh, no. He's all Mandy's," Naomi said with a brush of her hand. "You must know Mandy?"

Heather nodded. "Nearly all my life." She thought about that for a moment. How many people could she say that about? Certainly not about anyone in Chicago, and she'd lost touch with most of her old friends from Grosse Pointe by now.

But if Naomi wasn't talking about Mack, then who was she talking about? It could be John, from the inn, but he seemed a little too old for Naomi's tastes. And that left....

Heather was aware that her heart was beating quickly, even though Naomi hadn't even spoken yet. She knew what was coming because that's how this trip was going. All roads were leading back to Billy. Billy with the gleam in his eye and the friendly smile. Who for years wasn't even on her mind and now couldn't seem to get off it again.

"You might know him," Naomi said, looking excited. "He was friends with the Morgans. Billy Davidson? He's a doctor now on the mainland, but he's here every chance he has. Well, other than the winter, of course. And he works at the Island Hospital sometimes too."

Heather tried to keep her expression neutral. "Billy and I go way back."

"Isn't he handsome?" Naomi gave her a long look.

"Always was," Heather said with a smile. She picked up an object that didn't look too expensive but was pretty just the same—a small jewelry box that was carved with images from the island. It was probably only big enough to hold a few earrings or rings, but it was special, sentimental, and it would make a nice gift for Kim. After all, if it hadn't been for her baby sister's invitation, she probably wouldn't have even thought to come back this summer. Never would have seen Billy again. Never would have had this unnerving sensation as this Naomi woman continued to talk about how friendly he was, always popping in with a smile, or sometimes buying a round for everyone down at Hackney's.

She could picture it all. His inviting eyes, his infectious grin. And she wanted to be the girl he was buying drinks for. She wanted to be the one who got all star-eyed and excited just talking about him.

But she wasn't that girl anymore.

"I think I'll take this." She set the jewelry box down on the counter, eager to get out of the shop even though Naomi was perfectly sweet and meant no harm. She had no idea that

Billy had been Heather's childhood crush, her close friend, and now, as adults, her glimpse of a second chance, or maybe...what might have been.

"Gift wrapped?"

Normally Heather would have said yes, but today, she needed air. She needed to walk and to think, but she also didn't want to be alone. She was so tired of being alone, holding everything in, and pretending that everything was okay or would be okay even when it was becoming abundantly clear that it wasn't and might never be.

She felt dangerously close to crying and hurried to slide her sunglasses down her forehead, shielding her eyes. "No, but thanks. I'm fine."

She was very far from fine, but it was easier to say that than to admit why she wasn't. To anyone, including her sisters.

18

ANDREA

Later in the day, Andrea decided to take her laptop down to the Cottage Coffeehouse to work, only today she didn't intend to check email or fret over what she was missing back in the office. Today she was bursting with ideas for the Morrison campaign, something that she'd been thinking about all morning on her daily run through Forest Bluff and then later, as she walked through the old house, refamiliarizing herself with the small details, taking in a newfound appreciation for the original builders and her ancestors who had preserved the structure ever since.

She thought about what Billy had said at the party, about her inheriting more than just her mother's hair. Her mother had left the girls that house and Andrea intended to appreciate it, not take it for granted.

Lena was the first person Andrea saw when she pushed open the door and let herself into the small and cozy establishment just off the main street of town. She smiled at her friend as she came around the counter to hug her.

"I heard you were back!" Lena's cheeks flushed as her eyes turned tender. "Oh, I'm so sorry about your mom. I know how much everyone was hoping to see her last summer."

Last summer felt like a lifetime ago. Andrea had filled the time somehow, pushed the days together until they blurred, each one repeating the last. Until she stopped to think that she'd managed to get through more than three hundred fifty days without her mother, it didn't seem possible. It was easier to not think about it at all.

Andrea managed a smile, but her voice was locked in her throat. She wasn't used to talking about her mother—not her life, not the end of it. At work she could get away with this, focusing on business, keeping her personal life tucked away in a neat little box that she didn't ever have to open if she was careful. But here, there was no escaping it. These people knew her. The real her. Not just the person in the expensive A-line skirt and silk blouse and heels. No, they knew the girl who had ridden her first horse at the stable near the woods, the girl who had fallen off her bike after attempting to ride it with no hands, only to end up with severely scraped knees and stitches compliments of the local hospital, which was smaller than her doctor's office back in Chicago. They knew the girl who ate watermelon slices with a sloppy grin, who swam in the water despite the lake's cool temperature, and who swore that she would always come back here, that nothing could stop her.

Even when it did.

"You know what I always say…" Lena winked as she went back around the counter. "Nothing cures a broken heart better than a piece of chocolate."

Andrea laughed if only to lessen the weight in her chest. If only that were true. Still, she couldn't deny that the large brownie Lena was pulling from one of the baskets behind the display case did look delicious and she had already clocked five miles this morning on her daily run. Maybe after this, she'd take a bike ride out near the North Shore Lighthouse, draw some inspiration from the homes set high on the hill looking down over the water.

"How could I resist?" She couldn't, and she didn't want to either. "I'll have a coffee too."

"On the house," Lena said, holding up a finger when Andrea started to protest. "You're on the island now, not in that big fancy city. We do things a little differently around here."

They did. And they also did it better.

"We missed you for drinks the other night," Andrea said as Lena picked up the coffeepot.

Her friend sighed. "We were completely out of flour, and so was the market, if you can believe it. An emergency run to Blue Harbor was in order, and then I got to talking to some of the girls I know over there. Such a cute town."

Andrea nodded, even though she hadn't explored it much, other than stopping for a quick bite a few times while she and her family waited for the ferry. She supposed it was a good thing that the idea of crossing the water for a visit hadn't been broached a few days ago; it might have tempted her to get in Heather's car and not look back.

Funny how now all she wanted to do was look back, and not just at the memories, but at history, at these homes, not only in how they were laid out or how they captured the light and the views, but who they were built for, and what they achieved.

She took her coffee and plate with a promise of seeing Lena again before she left, which she probably would, now that she knew that the Lakeside Inn was off-limits unless she wanted to look like she was seeking John out, which she didn't plan on doing. Sure, he was nice enough, surprisingly appealing, and clearly one of the gang, even if she was starting to feel like the outsider.

But he also lived here. Year-round. And she wasn't even sure if she'd make it back here next year. Or if any of them would, she realized a little sadly, thinking of how much their lives had changed and continued to do so.

Carefully, she set her coffee mug on the table beside her brownie and then unloaded her laptop from her bag. A glance around showed that other people were talking with friends or family, some reading a book, others looking out the window, where hydrangea bushes bloomed big and high.

She smiled at that as she waited for her laptop to power up, happy that she'd had the sense to charge her battery before coming here today.

Who was she kidding? She always charged her battery. Always did everything right. This was partly why it was so distressing that so much still went so wrong.

"Well, we meet again."

Andrea looked up to see John grinning back at her, and despite her earlier reservation, she felt her stomach roll over. "It's a small island," she replied, giving a little smile.

"Not that small," he said, and she knew it was true. Evening Island catered to tourists and was therefore full of restaurants and dining options, some independent, other extensions of inns but welcome to the public.

She realized that he was stalling, as if waiting for something. Her eyes flicked to her empty chair. "Would you like to sit for a minute?"

It was out of character to even ask. Back in Chicago, nothing could have pulled her attention from her work, but here on the island, it would be rude to dismiss someone, even someone she barely knew. But what she knew of him she had started to like. He was a surprise. Like a house that looked one way from the outside and another on the inside, or like the big mansions framed as summer "cottages" here on the island, that were full of stories and mysteries, and fine-crafted details that made each one unique. She didn't know what she would discover as she explored things further, but now she was curious.

She held her breath, not sure what he would say or even what she wanted him to say. His eyes glimmered for one telling second, and she tipped her head, riding out the wait. It was so much easier when it was a business meeting. With those, she immediately fell into the role, knowing her place. But here, she was on unsure footing.

"I don't want to interrupt your work," John said, but he was already pulling out the chair.

Andrea closed her laptop. "It's not exactly work today. Well, technically it is. I was feeling inspired. I haven't felt that way in a while."

He looked interested as he sipped his coffee. "The island has a way of doing that to people. I'm living proof."

She couldn't disagree with him. "I was a little surprised to hear that you used to live in Chicago."

"Don't judge a book by its cover." He looked sheepish. "Though I suppose I could be accused of the same."

She mulled this over for a moment and then said, "No. I think you had a good read on me. Well, other than the part about me not appreciating the island. It's probably my favorite place in the entire world, and I've traveled a lot." At least, she did before she got on the track for partner at the firm.

"What makes it so special?"

She was a little taken aback and took a long drink of coffee while she considered her answer. "I suppose it's the house. It was full of happy memories. The happiest really," she added softly. "It's not just a house, but it's a home, even though it's not lived in for most of the year."

She smiled at that thought. It was probably the closest thing to a real home that she had, even if she didn't visit often. Her apartment in the city had architectural appeal but it was functional; the most personal item in the entire eleven-hundred-square-foot space was probably the single family photo she had resting on her mantle. The artwork was meant to impress, same with the furniture. In some ways that was how their house in Grosse Pointe was, too, but the lake house...it was impressive, with its Victorian size and structure and waterfront location, but it was old and weathered and designed for comfort. For life.

She frowned on that for a moment.

"And you're feeling inspired enough to spend this beautiful day sitting here instead of being outside enjoying the island?"

She couldn't deny the irony in that. "Just while I have a coffee. I didn't want to lose any of the ideas I had in my head. And my sisters and I could probably use a break from each other."

He arched a brow. "You all seemed to get along just fine last night."

"We're not used to spending this much time together," she said with a laugh. "This is more time than we've spent together since we were all still living at home."

And it could be the last time, considering Kim was getting married.

"But you're right. I think I'll take my laptop over to the harbor in a bit. All that talk about preserving the architecture on the island got me thinking about how rare it is to see such care taken for more modern designs. It would be wonderful to create something classic enough and special enough to withstand the span of time."

He gave her a funny look. "You love what you do."

She thought about that for a moment. "I do. But I lost it for a while."

He grinned and set down his coffee. "I can relate. Sometimes, it takes stepping away from something to appreciate it a little." He checked his watch. "I should probably head back. I have a guy coming over from the mainland to give me a quote on some new patio furniture."

"I like that furniture," she said with a fond smile. It was old and weathered, but it was comfortable and familiar. New wasn't always better.

Something she hadn't thought about in a long time, or considered at all lately.

"Good to know," he said, sliding back his chair. "I do value your opinion, you know."

She gave a little laugh. "But you don't even know me."

Only that wasn't completely true, not after the dinner. He'd spent most of the night talking to her, and she hadn't complained or used one of her sisters as an excuse to get away. He was an interesting man. And she'd be lying to herself if she said she was interested in just his conversation.

"Then maybe I should get to know you," he said. "You know, so I can be sure I'm not sending this guy from Blue Harbor back on the next ferry for nothing."

She felt her cheeks flush at the compliment. "You wouldn't really…"

He grinned. "I was thinking of changing all the outdoor furniture, but maybe instead I'll just ask for a quote on the pool deck. You've given me something to think about. A lot to think about it, actually."

That made two of them.

John stood. "Why don't we try this again? Maybe without the laptop next time?"

She tried to suppress her smile, but her nerves got the better of her. "What did you have in mind?"

"Oh, I'll think of something to make it worth your while. What do you say I swing by your place after lunch tomorrow?"

Andrea couldn't think of a polite excuse, and she wasn't sure that he'd accept one either. Besides, she was rather looking forward to spending a little time with this man. He was a friend of Gemma's, after all, a part of their island world. Once, he would have been a part of hers.

"Okay then. Tomorrow it is."

Her smile lingered for a while after he'd walked out the door. Suddenly tomorrow wasn't just another day closer to getting back to the office. Now it was something to look forward to.

19

KIM

Kim set out her clothes on the bed, knowing that if she was going riding today, she should probably wear pants rather than the cut-off shorts she'd been living in since arriving here. Fortunately, it was a cooler day with a strong lake breeze. She found the small canvas backpack she'd kept over the years resting on the top shelf of her closet, happy to see that renters hadn't tampered with it. She and decided to fill it with a water bottle, some snacks, and her wallet, in case she went into town after her ride with Leo.

Her cell phone caught her eye as she tugged on the jeans. She eyed it with trepidation, hating the funny roll of her stomach when she considered all the information it might hold. News. Updates. No doubt email about the wedding plans—final menu options and confirmation of the center-pieces. An entire reminder of a life that felt so far away and one that she wasn't so sure she was ready to return to just yet. If ever.

She hesitated as she reached for the doorknob and then,

just in case, she snatched the phone and tossed it into the bag, telling herself that she might need to check the time or something. She wasn't wearing the watch that the Crofts had given her. It was nearly as difficult to look at as her engagement ring, not that she'd removed that yet, and not that she was sure she ever wanted to, either.

There had been a time when she and Bran had fun—when he'd made her laugh on days she'd never thought she'd smile again. He'd given her something to look forward to in life, something to enjoy. Sometimes it was a movie or a play or a walk through a part of town she hadn't explored much before—but always it was just his company that perked her up and made her forget her troubles.

She didn't know when things had taken a turn. It had been gradual, but there was no denying that everything had changed for the worse when Bran popped the question and slipped this ring onto her finger. That was when the demands started: the endless family obligations and expectations of her now that she was about to become a Croft.

By the time Kim reached the bottom of the stairs, she was already in a sour mood and regretting bringing the phone with her at all.

"You going riding with Leo?" Heather asked when she came into the kitchen. She was seated at the old table, nicked and scratched from years of use that gave a view of the backyard and its lush landscaping through the French doors.

Kim pulled a bottle of water from the fridge and tucked it into her bag. "As I said, you're welcome to come along if you'd like."

Heather shook her head. "You know me and horses don't

mix well unless I want to end up falling off a bluff into the lake. Besides, I should probably work on this article. I'm running out of time."

Kim fell silent for a moment.

"Have you figured out what you're going to write about yet?" She scrutinized the fruit basket, which was picked over enough to warrant another trip to the market.

Heather sighed. "No. Any other ideas?"

Kim thought about it for a moment and then scrunched up her nose. "If it's supposed to be a lifestyle piece, then maybe you can write about something in your life. Reuniting with old friends. Summer people. That sort of thing." She checked the clock above the wall and realized she would be late if she didn't hurry. Giving her sister one last smile for encouragement, she patted her arm and said, "You'll figure this out. This is what you do for a living, after all!"

Heather's smile seemed weak in return. "Have fun!"

Kim grinned. She intended to, for a little while at least. Just the thought of riding perked her up and brought out a side of herself that had been hidden away for too long.

Leo was already outside waiting for her when she pushed through the screen door, but she was startled to see that he was holding the reins of two horses.

"I thought we were going to walk over to your stables!" Not that she wasn't pleased. She'd been looking forward to riding again ever since he'd mentioned it at the party. But she was also interested in seeing what he was doing with the stable. He'd described it as a carriage house tucked in the woods. A little off the beaten path for tourists, but with

Birchwood Stables' steady demand, she doubted that would pose an issue.

"I got an early start. Thought I'd give these boys a little walk before their run. Gemma told me you're pretty experienced."

"Well, it's been a while," Kim said, setting his expectations. She was fully aware that he'd been raised on a ranch out west and was more experienced than she'd ever been or would be.

Still, she slipped her sneaker into the stirrup and hoisted herself up onto the saddle without too much effort. Leo let out a low whistle. "Could have fooled me."

She gave him a slow grin as she patted the horse's mane. "Let's walk for a bit first, if that's okay."

"Fine by me," he said, saddling up beside her.

They trotted along the dirt road, past the Morgan and Anderson family cottages, which were both so large they were hardly cottages at all, and eventually turning onto a wooded path where other homes were tucked into the forest. The shade felt good after so many warm and sunny days, and Kim sighed as they moved along, taking in the scenery.

"This is my place here," Leo said when they rounded a bend in the path. There, just as he and Gemma had described it, was an old carriage house tucked beside a fenced pen where a few other chestnut-colored horses trotted happily.

"What a sight," she breathed, taking it in. Only here, on an island without cars, did you round a bend in the woods to see horses running free.

"I'm lucky that my grandfather introduced me to this

island," Leo said. His grin turned bashful. "And Gemma, of course."

"I think…" Kim swallowed hard. "I think that Gemma is very lucky to have found you."

The path ahead was clear, and now that she was feeling more sure of herself, Kim gave her horse a little kick until they were moving at a steady trot. Her ponytail flew behind her, and for a while, she was able to enjoy the feel of the wind in her face, the clean air in her lungs, and the thrill of the speed as they moved through the trees.

It wasn't until they'd reached a clearing and stopped to decide their next direction that Leo looked at her with concern. "You okay?"

She was so used to saying that she was fine, wonderful really, that she answered automatically, with a nod and smile. "Of course. Why?"

"For a minute there it looked like you had been crying."

She hesitated. She had been crying. Once the thrill of the ride had faded, she was overwhelmed with mixed emotions. Loss of time, and opportunity, and fear of missing this place even more than she already did, even though she was right here, now at this moment. Fear of none of them returning, never being together like this again, fear of her father selling the house and never seeing it again. The mere thought of that made her miss her mother so much she didn't think she could bear it.

And then there was the other thing that she missed, the part she hadn't dared to miss all week. Bran. Leo was great, and this was fun, but it would be so much more special to share it with Bran.

"Hair flew in my eye," she explained, brushing away some strands with her hand. She grabbed the reins and turned the horse toward the East Bluff with a big smile. "Shall we?"

She didn't need to ask twice. Leo grinned and took off at a faster clip, and with a laugh that momentarily made her forget all her problems, Kim raced after him.

* * *

Leo told her to keep the horse for the afternoon, considering it was a common form of transportation on the island and he did live right next door. With a promise to return sooner than later, Kim spent another hour exploring the backland of the island on her own before heading into town, enjoying the shaded paths and the natural beauty that wasn't always discovered by tourists willing to part from Main Street.

When she came to the base of the path, she pulled on the reins, bringing the horse to a stop. She was close enough to town now that she might be able to pick up a signal. Up until now, she'd refrained, left her phone at home, told herself that it was better not to look. But this time next week she'd be back in Chicago. And she didn't know what would be waiting for her.

She could find out, or she could continue to worry about the worst—even though she was no longer sure what that was. Once, she would have thought it was not having a big wedding, and now she no longer looked forward to the one that was only weeks away. Once she might have thought it meant losing Bran, but Bran came with an entire life that she wasn't so sure she wanted.

She pulled her phone from her pocket and turned it on. Maybe it wouldn't even get a signal, and this impulsive urge would—Well, never mind that. There was a signal, and now Kim waited with bated breath for the alerts to start popping up on her screen.

There were two. One from the bridal salon confirming the next fitting and another from her friend Kate, telling her that she was back from her trip, that she'd just gotten Kim's message, that she hoped that she was enjoying her time away and that she couldn't wait to catch up when Kim got back into town.

There was nothing from Bran.

Her heart was beating so fast now that she felt like she might actually be sick to her stomach. She stared at the screen, wondering if she'd missed something, if she'd lost reception again, but no. Her worst fears were coming true. Bran wasn't speaking to her. He hadn't tried to get in touch. And there really might not be a wedding in a few weeks after all.

And for reasons that Kim couldn't explain, even to herself, through the strange mix of feelings that washed over her as she turned off her phone again, wedged it into her pocket, and saddled the horse, the one that stuck out most was relief.

* * *

Andrea and Heather were in the front room of the house when Kim returned, dusty and tired and in serious need of a shower. Leo was already home when she'd brought back the horse, and he'd wasted no time in jumping on the saddle and riding off into the woods at the top of the road, making Kim almost wish that she'd prolonged her ride a bit, even though her legs were sore from lack of practice, and she longed for a nap. Her sisters were huddled around something, and both stopped talking when Kim came in, brushing the sweat from her brow with the back of her hand.

"What are you guys up to?"

"Look what Andrea found in the attic," Heather said, stepping back.

Andrea reached into a box and pulled out an ivory lace dress. A wedding dress, to be exact. It was discolored from age and a little old fashioned in style with its long sleeves and high neckline, but there was no denying the fact that it was beautiful.

"It must have belonged to our grandmother," Andrea said. They had never known her, at least Kim hadn't. She'd passed away when Andrea was still just a baby. It saddened their mother to talk about her and so the only details of her life were the ones in this old house. "I wonder if she got married on the island."

"She must have if you found the dress in the attic!" Kim looked at the lace more carefully without touching it. "Did you find any wedding photos?"

Andrea shook her head. "No, but I'll look again."

Kim thought about what Heather had said, about how their mother would have loved to see one of her daughters have an Evening Island wedding, and she wondered if this was the reason.

"Maybe she got married here in the house?"

"Grandpa did give her this house as a wedding gift," Andrea reminded them. She held the dress out to Kim. "Here. Try it on."

Kim felt herself blanch. "Me? No."

Andrea just smiled at her. "Why not? You're the bride-to-be!"

"Because it would be...bad luck. Besides, I'm all dirty." She glanced at Heather. "Heather can try it."

But Heather looked pained at that idea and Kim immediately realized her error. "Or you, Andrea. Maybe you'll wear it someday."

Andrea rolled her eyes. "Please."

"Then try it on anyway. It might be your only chance to wear a wedding gown given your decision to marry your career." She gave her a rueful grin and Andrea just shook her head, unable to hide her smile.

"Okay. Fine." She laughed and ran with it into the adjoining library, closing the pocket doors behind her.

Kim raised an eyebrow at Heather. "I didn't think she'd really do it."

Heather gave a little smile. "What can I say? The island brings out the best in all of us."

"It does," Kim agreed. "But I'm wondering if there's more to it."

"You think something has put Andrea in a better mood?" Heather didn't look completely convinced. After all, Andrea had complained about her work for nearly the whole of last week.

Kim gave a little shrug as her attention was snagged by something in her periphery. "Maybe. Or maybe, someone."

She turned to get a better view out the front window. "Is that the man from the party coming up onto the porch?"

Heather stared in wonder as the new owner of the Lakeside Inn started climbing the steps. "What's he doing here?"

Kim grinned. "May as well find out." She was closest to the door, and she walked back into the hall and opened the screen. "Hello. John, was it?"

He grinned. Ah yes, she now recalled he had a very nice grin. Nice eyes, too. "Kim. Nice to see you. I had told Andrea I'd stop by."

Kim's eyes went wide when they met Heather's who had now come to join her in the hall.

"I see. Well, come into the living room. Andrea will be right back. You remember Heather, of course."

"Of course." He shook her hand. "A pleasure."

Just then, the doors to the library flung open and Andrea emerged, looking like she had just come off the cover of a bridal magazine or emerged from a black and white Hollywood film. Her auburn hair was pulled up in a messy bun, and the dress swished as she walked. And her cheeks...well, they were positively blushing.

"John!" She blinked in surprise, but there was no denying the panic in her eyes.

John gave a low chuckle, but it was clear to Kim that he admired what he saw. "Is there something you haven't told me?" he teased, but Andrea just pinched her lips, clearly unable to find a witty retort.

Kim decided to throw her a bone. Andrea might have more experience when it came to her professional life, but when it came to men she was utterly hopeless.

"We were just playing dress-up." Kim grinned wickedly at her sister. "It was Andrea's turn to be the bride."

"And a beautiful one at that," John said, drawing a deeper flush to Andreas's cheeks.

"I'll change," she said. "It won't take long."

"I don't mind waiting," John said good-naturedly. There was still a gleam of amusement in his eyes as he watched her disappear behind the doors. A moment later, Andrea was back again, in her regular clothes of white linen pants and a classic navy tee shirt which was cute but hardly date-worthy, if that's what was happening here, and Kim suspected that it was.

"Shall we?" she said a little breathlessly, not meeting Kim's or Heather's eyes as she led John swiftly back into the hall.

A moment later, they were gone, with John giving a friendly wave, and Andrea all but dashing down the steps like she used to do as a child.

Heather and Kim stood in the hallway, staring out the screen door, completely gobsmacked.

"What was that all about?" Heather finally whispered, looking at Kim with obvious interest, and all Kim could do was shrug in response.

It would seem that both of her sisters were finding love no matter how much they tried to deny it. How ironic then that she was the one getting married.

OLIVIA MILLER

20

HEATHER

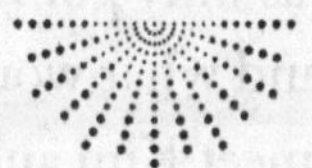

Heather had every intention of spending Monday afternoon by herself. Andrea was out—possibly with John again, not that she'd revealed as much—and Kim had gone down to the beach with Gemma. After lunch, she took her notebook and a glass of lemonade out to the porch, and nearly spilled it all over the front of her sundress when she saw Billy sitting on one of the wicker armchairs, admiring the view as if he owned the place.

"You scared me!" Heather set a hand to her racing heart, but she couldn't fight off her grin. It was just the thrill of the scare, she told herself firmly. It had absolutely nothing to do with the way that Billy was smiling at her, his eyes so bright even from a few feet away, his smile one that she could never resist.

Even when she really should.

"Scared you or surprised you?" He cocked an eyebrow.

She set down her glass with a shaking hand. "Both?"

"A good surprise, I hope," he said, looking at her expectantly.

He was probably waiting for her to sit down and join him, but she couldn't, at least not yet. Her heart was still pounding even though the shock had worn off and she had a bad feeling that today was only going to make her fall a little more in love with Billy, and what would be the good in that?

"I was just about to meet Kim and Gemma at the beach," she explained, though it felt like a random comment, and certainly not an answer to his question.

"With a glass of lemonade, ice and all?"

She laughed a little nervously. She'd always been honest, never good at hiding her feelings, much less telling even the smallest of white lies. It was part of the reason why she didn't mention even the vaguest details of her divorce with her sisters—it would open the floodgates, and that was just too painful. Now, her eyes darted to the beachfront across the road, searching for her sister or friend. There was safety in numbers.

"We could join them?" she offered.

"I'd rather be with you," he said, giving her a slow grin that made her knees more than a little weak.

So he wasn't going to leave then, or make this easy. But then nothing in her life felt easy. Nothing other than talking to Billy, spending time with him, falling right into step, like they always did.

"Can I get you a glass of lemonade?"

"How about you let me buy you one in town? It's a weekday so there won't be as many tourists."

She had already tried to make an excuse and failed,

besides, seeing him now, she knew she couldn't resist. And maybe, he wouldn't let her. They were friends after all, and she didn't have many of them left, let alone ones who knew her as long as Billy had. There was no reason to hide from Billy. Well, except for the fact that she felt like she was fifteen all over again when she was around him.

"Okay, then." She set the notebook and lemonade on the table as he stood, and together they walked down the steps onto the gravel path that led to the road, pausing only to let a family on horseback trot by.

He waited until they were alone again to say, "I stopped by to see you on Saturday but your sister said you had gone out for the day and she wasn't sure where."

Heather wished she had grabbed her sunglasses from inside so she could hide her shifting eyes. What was she supposed to say? That Andrea had never given her the message?

"It was late when I came back to the house. I figured you'd left for the mainland yesterday." She felt her cheeks warm.

"I'm working at the Island Hospital all this week," he said. "My shift's over for the day."

He gave her a sidelong glance, as if trying to figure out what exactly was going on between them. She'd like to have someone explain it because she wasn't so sure herself. She lived in Chicago, he lived here. Nothing could realistically evolve between them based on that fact alone, so why was she wasting this time fretting about a future that could never happen?

She should do exactly what Kim had told her to do. She

should live in the moment and enjoy this day, because come this weekend, she'd be back in her quiet house, eating cereal for dinner, waiting for a job opportunity to present itself so that at least one part of her life could get back on track.

"Oh? Any exciting cases?" She'd always wondered what went on behind the doors of the Victorian home in the center of town that was the island's only medical office. Andrea had gone once, but in her haste and worry, their mother had insisted that Heather stay behind and keep an eye on Kim.

"Two bike injuries and an inebriated tourist."

"Inebriated?" Heather laughed. "But it's only afternoon."

"And a Monday." Billy grinned.

"So what's the plan for the rest of the day?" she asked. She stopped herself, shaking her head. "Actually, I don't do plans anymore. It's much better to see where the day takes you." And it was already taking her off course. She'd planned to draft her article, just to have something down on paper, or pick Gemma's brain a bit when she and Kim returned from the beach.

He grinned. "I couldn't agree more."

They stopped at the Lighthouse Bistro, deciding to have a drink while looking out at the ferries crossing back and forth to Blue Harbor. Pine Falls, Heather knew, was within sight from this view.

"Can you see your house from here?" Heather asked once the waitress had brought a bottle of white wine to the table and poured them each a glass.

"You can." Billy leaned forward in his chair and pointed at the mainland, and she tried to follow his direction, but couldn't make sense of what he was indicating. "I'll show you."

He pushed out of his chair and came to step behind hers, leaning down until his chin was near her shoulder, his breath in her ear, his cheek so close to hers that she felt her entire body stiffen. He reached down and took her hand softly in his, lifting it as he dragged it ever so slightly to the right and then stopped.

"Do you see that white spot, between the two pines?"

She swallowed hard, feeling the scratch of his stubble on her skin. She wasn't sure what she was looking at, and she no longer cared so much about seeing the house, not with the heat of Billy's body so close to hers, making her barely even trust herself to speak. "Yes."

"That's my house." He could have dropped her hand then, stood, and took a few steps over to his chair, but instead, he stayed that way for what felt like an immeasurable about of time. She wondered if he was thinking what she was, that they were so close, all she had to do was turn her head ever so slightly and...

Their eyes locked, briefly, but long enough for her to know that she wasn't imagining any of this. His mouth found hers before she could come up with a good excuse, and she didn't resist. Instead, she kissed him back, savoring the sensation of his lips on hers, the excitement of being this close to the one person who had made every trip to the island so worthwhile.

"I was wondering if we would ever get a chance to do that," Billy said, giving her a lazy grin.

She was too, not that she'd be saying so directly. "Well, up until recently I was married."

"You know that was the biggest regret of my life," Billy admitted, forcing Heather to look at him in surprise. "I mean, I wanted you to be happy, if you were happy, but I couldn't help but kick myself for not taking a chance, seeing if there might have been more between us than just friends."

Her heart was beating fast when she considered what might have been if she and Billy had kissed all those years ago and made her girlish dreams come true. She'd never have gotten together with Daniel. Never would have known the pain of their arguments, the depth of their mutual loss, and eventually the sadness of watching him walk out of the home they'd built together, leaving nothing but bare walls.

She'd loved Daniel, but in the end, that hadn't been enough for her. Would it have been different with Billy?

"So what do you think?" He looked at her. "Is there a chance for us to be more than just friends?"

She swallowed hard, unable to answer his question even though she knew the answer in her heart of hearts. There wasn't a chance, not for happiness, not with what he wanted and what she could give. But she wasn't ready to tell him that just yet. She wasn't ready to lose the magic of this one perfect moment.

"Oh now, you're asking for a lot from just one kiss," she said nervously, but that didn't seem to deter Billy. His eyes sparkled with the challenge and he leaned down and kissed her again, softer this time, and deeper.

She finally pulled back when she knew that it was the last thing she wanted to do, but that it was best that she did. She needed to get home, clear her head, think things through. Because the only person she didn't want to hurt any more than herself was Billy.

21

ANDREA

Since they had run into each other at the coffeehouse, Andrea had spent the last two days with John, riding bikes, tasting fudge at his insistence, and doing all the things usually reserved for tourists, even though she was starting to feel like one herself. Today she was meeting him at his inn to hear some ideas he had for the next phase of redevelopment. She could see the suspicion in her youngest sister's eyes when she stepped outside dressed and ready.

Kim arched an eyebrow from her perch on the patio chair. "No laptop again today?"

Andrea gave a little smile. "Nope. It feels sort of nice to be free of it." She looked at the notebook and pen that Kim held in her hands, something she seemed to be frowning over. "Wedding details?"

"Seating plans," Kim said. "I'm sure that Lynette already has it figured out, but there might be some additional guests."

"Oh?" Andrea flushed, wondering for a moment if Kim

was going to tease her about John, but both of her sisters had been strangely quiet about his arrival at the house on the weekend, instead choosing to exchange small smiles and knowing glances, which was preferable to a full interrogation. There was nothing to hide, but she wasn't exactly sure that there was anything to share, either. And as for bringing him as a date to her sister's wedding, well, for once, she couldn't think that far out. By then she would be back in Chicago, the partnership would be determined. Life would be back to normal.

For some reason, this depressed her.

Kim, however, licked her lower lip: a sure sign that she was holding something back. "Well, you've seen how much time Heather and Billy have spent together on this trip. And I didn't have Gemma and Leo or Hope and her husband on the list. That was a huge oversight. It's a shame we haven't made more of an effort with them while they were living in Chicago."

Andrea nodded her agreement. It was difficult for her to make time for anyone in the city, including herself. Other than the gym, which was to burn off stress more than anything, and monthly highlights and trims at the salon, which was to maintain her appearance for client meetings, she couldn't remember the last time she'd made time for fun, much less a social life.

"I could always add someone for you..." Kim's smile was suggestive, but Andrea wasn't going to take the bait. "You know, there's something different about you. Something lighter. You laugh more now, ever since the party. It suits you."

Andrea pulled in a breath. There was something lighter. Her shoulders felt less heavy. Her mind wasn't so busy. She felt like she was able to think clearly for the first time in months, maybe years. Able to see for the first time in longer than that.

Still, she couldn't pin it all on John. No, it was more than that. It was this house. The island. And the company.

"I'm not so sure that anything is going on with Heather and Billy," she warned her sister. She was still perplexed by Heather's refusal to see him on Saturday. They'd gotten along so well the night before at the party. There was a spark there—always had been. But Heather had been closed off and distant for a while now. "She's just coming off a divorce. I wouldn't press it."

Kim seemed to consider this. "I'd just like to see her happy."

"I think every bride says that." Andrea laughed. She'd heard it said around the office enough times. Any time one of the women finally had that ring on her finger, she was suddenly eager to see everyone else matched up and as content as she was. Andrea had been on the receiving end of suggestions of setups one too many times, until she'd finally earned the reputation of being "married to her work."

But it wasn't true, not according to Pamela, and not in her own opinion, either. She *had* lost her passion along the way. Had stopped remembering why she loved it, why she cared, and why she was even doing it.

"Where is Heather, by the way?" she asked.

"Don't know. Maybe she went to the market. You know how much she loves to cook, not that I'm complaining."

"Me either," Andrea grinned. She didn't miss her take-out sandwiches or energy bars or soggy bowls of cereal before climbing into bed any more than she missed her empty apartment.

Kim closed the notebook firmly. "I think I'll take a bike ride if you care to join me."

"I'm meeting John," Andrea said after a hesitation.

"Again?" Kim gave her a coy look that Andrea brushed away.

"We have a lot in common," she insisted, even though she couldn't convince herself that was all that it was. Like her, John was hard working and, contrary to her initial opinion of him, he understood the pressure of corporate life, and city life, too. And like her, he loved this island. "We're friends. It's nothing more than that."

She could tell by her sister's expression that she didn't believe that any more than Andrea did, and she began walking down the porch steps before she protested or explained further.

"Seeing as you're meeting a *friend*," Kim called out, "why don't you at least let me lend you one of my outfits? For your date with your *friend*."

Andrea rolled her eyes but then, looking down at her linen pants, wondered if her sister was right. She was still young, John was handsome...and she was dressed for a summer business lunch.

"You don't expect me to wear those cut-off shorts, do you?"

Kim just smirked.

Three minutes later, they were standing in Kim's bedroom

at the back of the house, her belongings spread out before her on the four-poster bed covered in the same blue quilt that had been there long before Kim had even been born, back when this was just a spare room. Most of the clothes were too youthful or casual for Andrea's comfort, but she couldn't find an excuse for the cotton sundress Kim held out to her in a light shade of blue that she knew would look just as nice with her shade of auburn hair as it did with Kim's slightly darker waves.

"You always did have a knack for dress-up," she recalled fondly as she slipped into the dress and admired herself in the mirror, catching her sister's wide smile over her shoulder.

It was strange to see an older image of that little girl staring back at her in the reflection. It had been so long since she and Kim had spent time like this, long enough for her to forget that Kim wasn't a kid anymore. She was a grown woman, soon to be married, and maybe, in some areas, she even knew more than Andrea did.

"Now, let's do something with this hair," Kim said, pulling out a brush.

* * *

Andrea hurried up the path to the Lakeside Inn, the borrowed sundress swishing at her knees, her hair pulled back in a ponytail that Kim said showed off her "swanlike neck" and gave her a "playful appearance." Andrea laughed now just thinking about it, but still, a part of her almost hoped that Kim was right. And she suspected that she was.

Today, she'd offered to look over some of John's ideas for

a new pool house at the inn. As arranged, John was waiting for her on the back porch, with the long, uninhibited view of the lake. He rose when she appeared in the doorway, pulling out a chair for her.

She couldn't hide her smile as she sat down and scooted into the table, where he leaned in across from her, his eyes gleaming and unwavering. She wasn't used to being under the focus like this.

"My sister did my hair, in case you're wondering," she said.

"It looks nice." He grinned. "This is the second time I get to see you in a dress. Although, I'm not sure anything tops that wedding gown."

She felt her cheeks flame. He had kindly not teased her about that embarrassing moment yet, but it would seem that the time had come.

"Just sisters being sisters," she said, thinking of how much it was true.

He tipped his head. "Have you ever been married?"

She sipped the glass of lemonade that had already been set in front of her place. "No." Pausing, she wondered if the same could be said for him. "You?"

He nodded. "I was married once before."

Andrea knew she did a poor job of hiding her surprise. "Is that what brought you here?"

He shrugged. "In a way. I'm afraid I wasn't a very good husband, at least according to my ex-wife. I worked too much. I was married to the job. Eventually, I realized that she was right, but by then our relationship was long over." He dragged out a sigh. "We never had kids. I would have liked to have kids, but...again, I just never made the time."

Andrea understood. She could be accused of the same herself, never making time for anything that she couldn't pull up on a computer screen or deposit into her bank account. She didn't even take vacations, other than this, didn't enjoy the city restaurants or theatre scene or even take in a movie. She did well, she worked hard, but now she had started to question what it was all for if she didn't get that partnership. Or even...if she did.

"And you never met anyone after that?" She found that hard to believe, with his looks and charm.

"I dated, but to answer your question, no. I did meet a special woman, last summer, actually, but it wasn't meant to be, and that was okay. She went back to her home and I stayed here. This is where I belong, but I'd be lying if I said something wasn't still missing."

He'd tapped into something she couldn't bring herself to admit—that something was missing from her life, too. That she'd managed to fill her time with work to stop from even thinking about anything else, but here, now, with this beautiful view all around her and this handsome man at her side, she dared to imagine how things might have been, if she'd taken a different path.

She'd thought her life was full. But now she realized, it wasn't.

"I don't remember seeing you on the island last summer," John said, grinning at her.

Andrea pulled in a sigh. "I haven't been back in a few years. My sisters have, but it's been too difficult with my workload." She gave him a knowing smile. "We'd planned to come back last summer with my mother, but we weren't able to make that happen."

Her heart felt heavy when she looked down at her hands, hating the tears that burned the back of her eyes and threatened to spill.

"All the more reason it's good that you and your sisters are here now," John said gently. "Were you close with your mother?"

Andrea nodded, managing to look up. "I've always been closer to my father, but yes, my mother was wonderful. I haven't thought about her much. I've tried to think of anything but it, really. But now that I'm here... Well, it's like you said. Sometimes you don't realize what matters in life until it's too late."

Her phone buzzed, and she blinked in surprise, because it had been days since she'd checked for cell reception or searched for Wi-Fi.

"Work?" John just gave her a knowing look.

She looked down at her screen, seeing the text from Nicole, asking if everything was okay, expressing concern that she hadn't heard from her all week, even though it was only Tuesday.

She smiled at John and turned off the phone before slipping it into her bag. "The office checking in."

"I don't miss those days," he said.

No, she didn't get the impression that he did. Still, the transition couldn't have been without a few internal struggles or at least some doubt. "You don't get lonely here then? Or..."

He cocked an eyebrow. "Bored?"

Her grin was rueful. "It's hardly the pace of city life."

"And that's why I prefer it. All that business in the city…" He shook his head and looked out over the water. "It didn't mean anything at the end of the day. It was empty, and this is so much more satisfying. Here, I feel like I'm able to do what I love, watch people enjoy it, and carry down some traditions that I'm only just now lucky enough to be a part of every day. But as for being lonely." He gave her a long look. "I'm fine on my own, I'm used to being on my own, but I welcome the opportunity to share all this with someone special."

Andrea's heart began to pound as he continued to look at her across the table and she broke his gaze, looking instead at the blueprints he had, eager to steer this back to territory that was in her comfort zone, even if right now she wouldn't mind another bike ride like yesterday.

She gave her thoughts on the plans, and he nodded at her suggestions, jotting down notes as she pointed out how he might change the windows to match the large, arched one near the grand staircase in the main building, and a portico to give guests some shade.

"I wasn't going to mention this," John said when they'd set aside the papers and he'd ordered a bottle of wine for them to share. "But when I was over at the mayor's office this morning, I mentioned that I had a brilliant architect with connections to the island looking over my plans."

She shook her head ruefully. "Flattery will get you anywhere, huh?"

"I'm only telling you what I see," he said, sliding her a glass of wine before pouring his own. "Anyway, they mentioned that they'd be open to talking to you if you were ever looking to take on some projects on the island."

She blinked, unsure of how to even respond. "I'm always happy to lend a helping hand," she said slowly.

He nodded and leaned back in his chair, letting the sun hit his face. "I know. But if you were ever looking for a bigger stake in things, they could use someone like you, from what I understand."

Her mind was racing when she considered what he was implying. A job, even a career, here on the island, overseeing and approving renovation and design permits, preserving the history of the architecture which was slowly being phased out by everyone else in the world, it seemed.

They shifted topics, thankfully, and John pressed her for more stories about her childhood days on the island until she was feeling downright nostalgic and the afternoon had started to wane.

"Maybe tomorrow we could head down to the harbor," he said as he walked her around to the front of the inn. "I'm thinking of investing in a boat, and I wouldn't mind the company or your opinion."

She hesitated only long enough to consider that he was either making an excuse to see her again or that he did value her opinion. Either way, she was flattered, and interested.

"Okay, then." She smiled, feeling suddenly shy at the growing fact that she too, was showing that she wanted to spend more time with him.

"Meet here? On the pool deck? And about the thing I mentioned earlier," he said before should go. "Consider it,

Andrea. You have a real appreciation for these old buildings that not everyone else does. You have a legacy here."

A legacy. He was referring to the house, she knew. The house that her mother had passed down to them. And the memories that she had, too.

"Well, you've certainly given me a lot to think about," she said as she stepped away. She glanced over her shoulder to see him still watching her, his hands thrust in his pockets, his gaze steady.

And he had. About a lot more than just a job.

Kim decided it was probably her turn to cook dinner—but there was no denying that her motive was slightly ulterior. She'd been restless all day, feeling just as anxious about going back to Chicago as she was about the guestlist for a wedding that might never happen.

The Main Street Market was, like many establishments on Evening Island, family-owned and operated and passed down through generations. It was small but cozy with warm woods and a deli counter at the back that served Kim's favorite potato salad. Kim loaded her basket with all that it would fill before piling the bags into her bicycle basket and pedaling home, resisting the urge to check her phone again while she was in town and more likely to get a signal.

Heather was working on her article on the front porch when Kim arrived out of breath a few minutes later.

"Do you want some help?" her sister asked, setting her notebook to the side.

Kim waved off her concerns. "I do know how to cook, you know. But maybe just not as good as you."

"Oh, I rarely cook anymore," Heather said a little sadly. She gathered the second bag from Kim's hand and followed her into the kitchen. "Being back here has given me an excuse to do it again. I...didn't know how much I missed it."

Kim couldn't imagine missing cooking—the clean-up alone was so unappealing—but she sensed something in her sister, a need, perhaps, that went above her own.

"Well, if you don't mind..." She began unpacking the dried pasta and fresh tomatoes.

Heather perked up when she pulled three ears of corn from the bag. "Oh, I know exactly what to make with this. You'll love it!"

Kim smiled as Heather eagerly rinsed the vegetables, feeling better, even if it was only because she liked seeing her sister this way. Excited, happy, not frowning or hiding away from the world like she'd been doing all these months. For the first time in a long while, Heather seemed almost hopeful.

Funny how the tables had turned.

"Andrea home?" she asked as she opened the cabinet to retrieve some plates. The least she could do was put together a nice table setting. She'd pick some flowers from the yard like their mother used to do.

"She came back while you were out," Heather said. She pulled a cutting board from a drawer and set to work chopping the produce with the proficiency of an expert.

Kim slid her a sly look. "She was out with John again, you know."

"Oh, I know!" Heather's lips pinched around a smile. "It seems that our sister isn't so cut off from the idea of love after all."

"It's funny how life can take such a sudden turn. Things happen, people surprise you. One day you're on a path and then the next day you realize you might want to switch directions." Kim sighed as she pulled three glasses from the cabinet and closed it again.

Sensing that Heather was now giving her a strange look, she said brightly, "I'll get things set up outside!"

She stayed busy, creating a floral arrangement with happy-colored blooms, setting out candles and her mother's favorite linen napkins, half wondering if she should run next door and invite Gemma and Leo to join them, but then she remembered that Heather was cooking for three based on limited ingredients, and besides, it would be nice to spend this time alone with her sisters. It was already Tuesday, the days were winding down, and this time next week, they'd be right back to where they were two weeks ago.

Or would they? Her entire future had never felt more unknown; she was almost as lost as she'd been last August, unsure of how to move forward.

Kim's anxiety was only stronger by the time Andrea and Heather came onto the porch, Andrea carrying a bottle of wine and a salad, and Heather a giant bowl of pasta that smelled good enough to pull a smile from Kim's face.

"Mom used to make this every time we came up here!" She spooned some onto her plate, and then, because she probably didn't need to worry about that ugly wedding dress fitting, added more.

"Only on weekends. It was Dad's favorite," Andrea said fondly. She was still wearing Kim's sundress, and her eyes had a light to them that hadn't been there just a week ago.

"It's too bad Dad couldn't have joined us for a few days," Heather said.

Kim stopped chewing and reached for the wine bottle instead. It had already been corked and she filled her glass liberally. Just thinking about her father made her tense.

"Oh, you know Dad," Andrea said lightly. "He's always traveling for work, especially lately."

Heather gave a conciliatory nod. "True. I just thought, with Mom's anniversary coming up, and with everything... Well, it might have been nice."

"I understand," Andrea interjected. "Work has been an escape for him. His way of dealing with things. In a way, it's been mine too."

Kim felt a softening toward her oldest sister, and she saw Heather stop eating for a moment. It wasn't often that Andrea bared her feelings. She was tough that way. Like their father.

Which made all of this more difficult. They were finally taking a turn, coming together as the sisters they'd once been, and the last thing Kim wanted to do was ruin things.

"Dad hasn't been traveling for work," Kim said, knowing as soon as she said it that she couldn't take the words back, couldn't undo the events she'd set in motion. Even though the truth had to come out eventually, she resented having to be the one sharing it nearly as much as it relieved her to finally talk about it.

"What do you mean?" Andrea didn't look convinced. "He's on the road more than ever."

Kim swallowed hard. "He travels, but not for work."

Heather looked at her in confusion. "But if he's not traveling for work, why is he always away from home?" Then, as if it had only now occurred to her, her shoulders slumped and she looked at both of them. "That's a big house. An empty house, now. It must be so hard for him to be there without Mom."

Kim took a long sip from her glass. The truth was about to come out, and there was no sense in delaying things further.

"Dad has..." She didn't even know what to say. Found a replacement for Mom? Moved on without a glance back? She knew that wasn't fair, but that's how it felt. She could feel the heat of her sister's eyes on her, sense the tension. They were expecting the worst. "Dad has...met someone."

The porch fell completely silent, and Kim's heart was beating so loudly that she half wondered if her sisters could hear it. It was still light outside, and a passing carriage passed by on the road, kicking up dust, no doubt transporting its occupants to one of the island's best restaurants tucked deep into the woods. Kim listened to the sound of the horses' hooves until they completely faded.

"What? When did you find out?" Heather finally said.

"Last week when I visited him." Kim looked at Andrea, whose expression was impossible to read. "That's why I got so edgy when you asked about him our first night here. I wanted us to have a nice time. I didn't want to think about all the things that were bothering me."

"What other things?" Heather asked.

Kim shook her head. "Just...you know. Life. Stress. This was supposed to be our chance to get away from everything. Then Dad dropped that in my lap, right in the middle of dinner at the club."

Heather gave her a look of sympathy. "I don't know what's more upsetting. That you didn't tell us sooner or that Dad has..."

"Replaced Mom?" Kim looked at her miserably. "He said they've been dating since January."

"January!" Andrea stood to reach for the bottle of the wine, but she didn't sit back down again after refilling her glass. Kim watched her pace along the porch as if she were trying to work something out. "But he never told me, and I speak to him regularly, at least a couple of times a month."

That was more than Kim could say, and from the shrug Heather gave, the same could be said for her.

"And he never hinted at anything?" Kim sighed. "I suppose he was waiting until it was serious."

Andrea stopped walking. "You think it's serious?"

Kim nodded. "He told me that she's going to be staying with him at the house."

"She's moving in? How old is this woman?" Andrea wanted to know.

"I asked the same thing. He told me they were roughly the same age. I think...I think he loves her."

Andrea made a dismissive sound. "Nonsense. The man's lonely, that's all it is. People do crazy things when they're lonely and grieving."

Heather shifted in her seat and then stood. "I think I need some more wine too. I'll get us another bottle."

Andrea watched her disappear into the house and turned to Kim defiantly. "Well, I don't care if he's lonely, or if she's his age. It's too soon. Mom has only been gone for a year, and they were married for decades."

Kim had had over a week to process this, but she understood Andrea's denial. She'd felt it herself when she'd first heard the news. With a sigh, she looked up to see Heather emerge through the screen door. She'd grabbed a cardigan along with the bottle of wine, and Kim longed for the same sense of comfort, even though it was a warm night.

"He told me that he's happy," she said softly. "And...isn't that what Mom would want? For him to be happy? For all of us to be happy?"

Heather topped off Kim's glass and her own and then sat down again. "But happiness is fleeting, not permanent. Nothing lasts forever."

Kim studied her sister, wondering if she was still talking about their father or if she was thinking about her marriage.

"Dad's clearly lost it. All his life, he was focused on his career and his family. If he was lonely, why didn't he visit us more often?" Andrea looked at them for an answer that neither of them could give.

"He probably didn't want to be a burden," Kim said, thinking it through. "We all live in Chicago. I was dating Bran and then busy planning a wedding. You were going through a divorce, Heather, and Andrea, Dad knows that you're just like him. That you threw yourself into your work even more when Mom died."

"Only Dad didn't throw himself into his work, did he?" Andrea raised an eyebrow. She sipped her wine, shaking her head. "I've been too focused on work. And look what's happened. It's all a giant mess. And for what?"

Kim glanced at Heather. This wasn't the type of talk they were used to hearing from their oldest sister, and certainly not in such broad terms. Andrea could never be "too focused" on work in the past. Work had been everything to her. Until, perhaps, now.

"Is everything okay with your job?" Kim couldn't even imagine that anything could be wrong in Andrea's life; she gave the impression of always being in control, always on track.

If Andrea didn't have it all figured out, then what hope was there for her?

"It's fine, just…" Andrea shook her head. "Just stressful. But what else is new? Besides, we're talking about Dad now."

"Maybe he's lonely," Heather said softly. She poked at her food, shaking her head. "I should have gone to visit him."

"We *all* should have gone to visit him," Kim stressed. "But we didn't even make time for each other."

Heather's frown was deep when she dropped her fork. "I feel bad about that. It wasn't intentional. Time just slips away and before you know it…it's too late."

"It's not too late," Kim insisted. "We're here now. And you guys have your jobs and I…." She didn't quite know how to finish that sentence. She was still figuring things out. "And Dad kept saying he was fine, that he was busy, traveling. I wanted to believe that."

"Well, he's certainly been busy!" Andrea narrowed her eyes.

"Maybe he's just having a little fun. A little company." Heather looked at them for affirmation.

"True. She'll probably be gone by the holidays. We won't have to meet her." Andrea looked certain of this as she dropped back into her seat as if the problem had been solved.

Kim finished her last swallow of wine and passed the bottle to Andrea. She was going to need it. "He invited her to the wedding."

Both sisters stared at her with such wide eyes that Kim felt almost sick just thinking of how it would all play out. She was already stressed just thinking of having to explain the change in seating arrangements to Lynette, and now she would have two angry sisters to deal with, too. This wasn't the way the wedding was supposed to play out. She was supposed to be wearing her mother's dress and veil. She was supposed to go shopping for all the details with her mother, or at least her sisters. Her family was not supposed to show up like strangers to her wedding.

Her father was not supposed to bring a surprise guest.

And her mother...her mother was supposed to be there.

She stood up. "There's no use in getting all worked up about it because right now, I'm not even sure there will be a wedding at all!"

And then, because she couldn't hold it in any longer, she burst into tears.

HEATHER

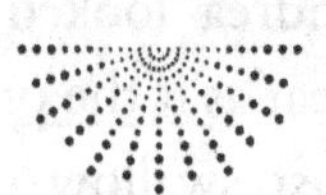

Heather watched Kim flee from the table. Seconds later, she heard the screen door bang shut.

"What was that all about?" She turned to Andrea, who was unable to hide her shock. It wasn't like Kim to be so moody, even if their discussion about their father had been upsetting, to say the least. But to threaten to call off her wedding? All because of this woman?

Andrea could only shake her head. "She's done nothing but talk about that wedding for months. I assumed she was excited."

"Me too," Heather said, chewing her nail. She replayed their conversations since the time of the engagement, realizing with some shame that there hadn't been many and that she hadn't been able to match Kim's enthusiasm, only listen and find a polite way to cut the conversation short.

Sometimes she didn't know what part was more difficult: hearing about how wonderful life with Bran was or about how close she had become with his mother.

"Maybe she has jitters," Andrea said, draining what remained in her glass. "The wedding is next month and Dad did just throw a wrench in everything."

Heather nodded miserably. Their father had found someone. Moved on. With his life, with his heart, and as much as it upset her to think of him already setting their mother in the past, it also rattled her to think that others could find love again so easily. But it wasn't that easy, not for her. Even if it might look that way, or could be that way, if situations were different.

But then, if the situation was different—if she had been able to have a child or any future children—then she and Daniel might still be married. Billy would still fall into the friend basket.

Maybe, it wasn't meant to be.

"Do you want to talk about Dad?" she asked wearily. It was getting late, but the days were long here on the island, and nightfall wouldn't come for at least another hour or more.

She was relieved when Andrea shook her head and began clearing the table. "Not really. I think...I think I'll go for a walk and clear my head."

Heather decided to do the same, but not together. She needed some time to think, and she suspected that each of her sisters felt the same. Instead, she carried the dishes into the kitchen, went upstairs, changed into more comfortable shoes, and waited a few minutes after Andrea had left to pull her bike out from the shed. If she knew Kim, then she'd be at North Shore Beach, staring out onto the water, or maybe even taking a swim. The cool temperature of the lake didn't bother her, and by this time of summer, it was the warmest it would ever be.

Andrea was probably going for a jog, a long one, circling the island, or maybe she was in town, doing work, or looking for John. Something was going on between the two of them—much as Andrea might try to deny it. Her sisters had more going on under the surface than either of them was willing to share, it was starting to seem. And maybe, the same could be said for herself.

She knew without thinking about it that she would go to Billy's house. The memory of their kiss was still fresh on her mind, and that troubled her. She didn't want to think about it, she didn't want to hope that it might happen again. Instead, she wanted to focus on the reality of her circumstances. She and Billy had no chance for a future. They never did.

Sure enough, Billy was on his front porch nursing a beer when she came to stop on the stone path. He perked up when he saw her, his eyes crinkling into a smile that lingered as she walked up the path to join him.

Heather felt suddenly like the shy young teenager on her first day of summer break all over again. Just like back then, her heart was beating with expectation and hope for something she couldn't have, but wanted, oh so badly. She set a hand to her stomach to settle her nerves.

He stood, leaning down to kiss her on the cheek. "This is a nice surprise. Can I get you a glass of wine? Beer?" His grin flashed on that. He knew she'd never liked the taste of it, even when they were eighteen and a group of them had snuck off to the North Shore Lighthouse with a picnic basket full of beer and chips.

"Wine would be great," she said. She settled onto a chair while he disappeared inside, giving herself a silent lecture while she heard the sounds of a fridge door closing and a cabinet opening.

This was not a date. Or a breakup. It was just two old friends enjoying what remained of the warm nights until they went back to the real world. It was the same as it had been every summer. The only difference now was that Billy was staying.

For some reason, she couldn't shake the way that made her feel as if this time she had a choice, that this time she was leaving him behind. That this time, she had nothing to go back to and everything to part with instead.

He came back onto the porch with a bottle of white wine and two glasses. A floorboard creaked under his steps as he set everything down on a round side table. "I figured it was a better night for wine anyway."

Heather's smile felt tight when she accepted her glass. She could have guzzled the whole thing back, so great were her nerves and her dread and all those other emotions that she'd tried to push away, but Billy was raising his glass in a toast now, looking at her in expectation.

"To summer," she said, thinking that was quite appropriate. This was her summer place. Her happy place. Her favorite place. And Billy had always been one of her favorite people.

"To old times," he said, his gaze lingering on hers. "And to first loves."

She could feel her cheeks burn and she looked away. She'd always thought Billy never knew about her truest feelings, but maybe she'd been fooling herself. He knew her better than most people. In some ways, he knew her best.

He frowned a little, perhaps noticing her silence, but then lifted his eyebrows playfully. "Unless... Don't tell me I wasn't your first love?"

He'd managed to pull a smile from her. A real one. Like always. "Well, not unless you count Rusty McCalister in the first grade. He might have taken me into the clubhouse on the school playground and taught me what a French kiss was."

Billy laughed. "He didn't."

"If a peck on the hand is a French kiss, then he did." Heather chuckled and sipped her wine. "This feels nice," she said, then, catching herself, she added, "I mean, relaxing like this. I had quite a night."

"Oh?" Billy raised an eyebrow.

"Apparently, my father has a new girlfriend." She pulled in a sigh. "Just saying that feels wrong and depressing."

"If it makes you feel better, I've heard it said that those who loved the most find love again the quickest." He hesitated. "Or something like that."

Heather swallowed back a sip of wine, wondering if that was true and wishing that it was as easy as that. But love was complicated.

"Yeah, well, try telling that to either of my sisters. Kim seems to want to cancel her wedding over it and Andrea... Well, you know that Andrea has always been a Daddy's girl. She feels like he broke her trust by not telling her sooner."

"Your father is still a relatively young man, though." Billy's expression was compassionate when he said this. "You wouldn't want him to be alone for the rest of his life?"

Alone for the rest of his life. She wouldn't wish that on her father any more than she could bear it for herself. She pulled her eyes from him, wondering if he saw in her expression that he'd hit a nerve, and took another sip of wine, trying to pace herself, because she needed to keep her head clear tonight, not get mixed up with all her feelings and wants, which would only lead to more heartache.

"Of course we want him to be happy. I just don't think we realized it would be so soon. I mean, I've been on my own for longer than my mother's been gone, and it's not like I've moved on yet."

Billy gave her a funny look, and the silence told her that she'd misspoke. Maybe, that she'd hurt his feelings.

"I didn't mean that," she said, extending a hand, and then, catching herself, pulling it back safely into her lap. "I meant...he's serious about this woman. I think that she's moving in with him."

His eyebrows shot up. "That is serious. But he's a grown man. You have to trust that he knows what he's doing."

Heather sipped her drink. She supposed Billy was right, even if it hurt to admit it.

"And you?" he asked. "Are you open to something more serious again?"

Heather pulled in a breath. This was it. The confrontation. The ultimatum. Or maybe just the cold harsh truth. It would be so easy to give in, to fall, to believe that this feeling could last—but this island and all that came with it was an escape from the real world. It wasn't her reality.

"I don't plan on ever getting remarried if that's what you're asking." She couldn't look at him; she focused instead on the porch rail, the fresh white paint that Billy had probably applied himself one spring weekend.

"Never?" His tone told her that he didn't believe her any more than her sisters did. "But you're only thirty—"

She shook her head. Her heart was pounding, aching really, and she wanted to scream, and cry, and say that he didn't need to tell her what she knew. That she was only thirty-one, that she did have her entire life in front of her, that she didn't want to be alone, but that she also couldn't imagine being disappointed again. Hurt again. And she didn't want to do the hurting or disappointing either.

"It's not about age," she said quietly. She met his eye, hating the sadness she saw there. "I was married, and it didn't work out, and now I've gotten used to being on my own again. It...it suits me. It's better for me." She lifted her chin, forcing herself to remain strong.

But Billy wasn't buying it. He pursed his lips, giving a wry smile as he shook his head and sipped his wine. "Ah, no. You say that now because you got burned, but once things cool off, you'll feel differently. I guess...I was just hoping that I would be the one to make you feel that way."

The pain in his eyes was back, and Heather could feel a lump rising in her own throat. She leaned in to him, hoping that he would hear her words, understand what she was saying. "If there was ever anyone who could make me believe in a better future, then you would be it, Billy."

Because he had. These last few days, he really had.

He gave a sad smile. "I sense a but..."

There were many buts. But none of them would stick. In the end, her circumstances hadn't changed—and couldn't be changed.

"But marriage isn't for me after all," Heather finally said.

Billy nodded and turned to look out at the water. "I see."

Heather set down her glass. She realized that she was shaking a little. Her stomach felt sick, and alcohol was the last thing she needed. She'd said what she needed to say, but somehow, she didn't feel any better, only worse. Like she'd lost something precious all over again, only this time, not just a part of her past but the final part of her dream for the future. "I should go."

He didn't argue with her or try to convince her otherwise. It was dark and the streetlamps gave little light on the ride home, but she pedaled with confidence, on the path that she knew by heart, one she had taken so many times over the years, knowing every twist and turn and tree branch to dodge.

But once she knew what she would find there. Her mother on the porch, drinking gin cocktails and laughing with Mrs. Morgan and Mrs. Anderson. Her sisters in their rooms in fresh pajamas and hair still damp from the shower, the windows opened, reading or drawing, or spreading out the treasures they'd collected in town.

Now, as she approached the house and saw the darkened interior and the empty porch, she thought of how much had changed, and how much had been lost. And she didn't know where she could turn for that one safe place, anymore. That one sure thing. Because right now, it didn't feel like it had ever existed.

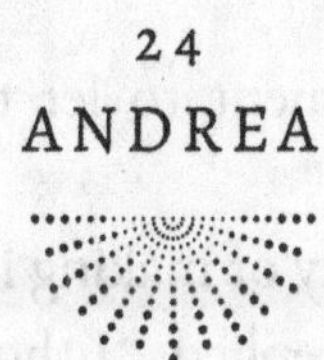

Andrea's phone pinged the moment she stepped inside the lobby of the Lakeside Inn. Knowing that John would be waiting for her on the pool deck, she checked the time and, deciding she had a few minutes, dropped onto a striped chair in the lobby.

She'd assumed it would be another text from Nicole, seeing as she hadn't yet replied to the last one. Instead, she was surprised to see that Pamela was reaching out with two ominous words: Call me.

Now worried, Andrea quickly connected the call and held the device to her ear. Pamela answered on the second ring.

"I wasn't sure you'd call back," she said. "Nicole said she hasn't heard from you all week."

Andrea felt a wry grin creep into her tone when she said, "Just following orders." But it was more than that—she hadn't cared to know what was going on back in the office, not when she had so much going on right here around her.

Pamela sighed, "Well, I'm going to have to break those orders, or at least cut them short. There's no easy way to say this so I'll get right to the point. Jace is having dinner tonight with the Morrisons."

Andrea took a moment to let that sink in fully. "He wasn't on their shortlist."

"He has a strange way of making it onto everyone's shortlist eventually," Pamela replied. "I thought you should know what you're up against. You might want to have something ready to pitch first thing Monday. And I think this goes without saying, but it's going to have to be your best work."

Or the partnership would go to Jace, were the unspoken words.

Andrea's heart began to race when she considered what her boss was telling her, not as a boss, but as a friend. "I've been working on it while I've been here," she said, thinking of the shift in direction she'd taken, even some of the liberties with the design. She felt confident, more sure of herself than she had in a long time, but this time because she was trying something new, even if in many ways, it had been a part of her all along.

"Good. Send me what you have and I'll give you my feedback. Monday will be a big day."

Monday. It was only five days from now, barely a blink of Pamela's eye, but it felt like another lifetime to Andrea, another way of life completely. And now, with her palms sweaty from the reminder of the daily stress, she felt more detached from it than ever.

"I'll send you what I have," she agreed before ending the call.

Andrea stared at the files in her lap. They were ideas for John's expansion, mostly, but tucked underneath were the sketches for the Morrisons'. The original concept, and the new one. She knew the first design was a slam dunk, her best work, only in that it was a nod to her recent work.

But the other design... It was a gamble.

Without giving it any more thought, she snapped a few photos of the design she'd put together over the past few days and sent it to Pamela. Then she turned off her phone again before she could give any more thought or worry to the outcome.

John was sitting at a poolside table when she joined him, wearing another of Kim's sundresses, grateful that he had a bottle of wine chilling in an ice bucket.

"Normally I don't drink during business meetings," she said only half-apologetically when he held a glass out to her.

"Who said this was a business meeting?" he countered, flashing her a grin.

She took the bait. "Then what would you call it?"

He mulled it for a moment. "A meeting of the minds?"

She smiled and held out her glass for a toast. She liked that. She liked a lot about John.

"Here are some of my other thoughts on your expansion," she said, sliding him the files. The rest she tucked into her handbag, but he stopped her.

"What are these?"

She brushed away his curiosity. "A design for a project I'm pitching. It's a family house."

"Can I see?"

She saw no reason not to share and slid the papers across

the table. He studied them with a furrowed brow and then grinned up at her. "I can see why you're in such demand."

She held her breath, flattered, but something else too. Scared, perhaps. Scared of finally having everything she always wanted just when she wasn't so sure that she wanted it at all.

"Let's look at what I have for you now," she said, firmly putting the Morrison plans back in her bag. She couldn't help but wonder what he would have said about her original idea, the soulless but extremely functional concept that was meant to be on the cutting edge of design rather than a warm nod to the past. "Much more interesting," she said, giving him a little smile.

And she wasn't just saying that.

John flipped through them, looking impressed, and it wasn't until he said as much that she exhaled a long breath. Once there had been a time where she was sure of her work, but that had disappeared somewhere, along with her inspiration. The setback at the office was only part of it, and maybe, it was more of a symptom. Here, she was in her element, doing what she did best. Doing what she loved.

"Can I keep these?"

"Of course!" She sipped her wine and watched as he handed over the files to one of his staff, asking for them to be brought to his office.

"Now, with that out of the way, how about we walk down to the harbor soon?"

"You weren't joking about that boat," she teased.

"Oh, when I want something, it's no joking matter," he said with an easy grin that made her stomach roll over.

They finished their wine and stood. The harbor was a short walk and the weather was pleasant. Midweek, the tourists had slowed down, and Andrea took in the view of the shimmering water as they walked along the lakefront path.

"Was it difficult for you to give up the corporate life and slow down?" she asked.

"Who said I've slowed down?" He laughed. "But I have, considerably. I love to work, I thrive on it, but it no longer consumes my life, you know?"

She didn't know, but she was starting to wish that she did.

"Here my work feels like it has a purpose. It's not about getting the biggest deal or bringing home the most money. Here I see a daily impact of my work. It's very rewarding."

"Sometimes I feel like I'm on a hamster wheel," she admitted. They'd come to the harbor now, and she leaned against a weathered post, wondering which of the boats John had chosen. "At first it was about making my father proud, then it became something else. I'm up for partnership, next month."

His eyebrows shot up at this. "Congratulations."

"Oh." She shook her head. "It's not a done deal. And...to be honest, I'm not so sure how I feel about that. For the longest time, it was all I wanted. All I worked for. All I lived for really. Now, I feel like I lost sight of what it was all for in the first place."

"I imagine a partnership comes with more than just a title and a bigger paycheck."

"If you mean even longer hours and pressure, you'd be correct." And the thought of it made her feel tense.

"Is it still what you want?" he asked.

She looked at him thoughtfully, surprised by her hesitation to such a direct question. "I can't be sure anymore. I... gave up a lot for this partnership. It seems just as upsetting to give it up or lose it as it would be to give up everything else I've just recently found."

Their eyes met for a moment until she looked away.

"I learned a long time ago that you can't change a person unless the person wants to be changed." John gave her a little smile. "Only you can decide what you want, Andrea."

Maybe, but it was so much easier when there were fewer options on the table.

"You said yourself that the island had inspired you," John said.

She looked at him. He seemed to remember everything she said. She couldn't remember the last person who did that, other than her parents, maybe, but her mother was gone now, and her father... Well. Her father hadn't made his professional life as much a priority all this time as she'd thought. No, she alone was guilty of that. And she wasn't exactly happier, was she?

"Enough about my work. Let me see this boat."

He grinned like a kid on Christmas morning and led her over to the farthest dock, where a white sailboat was tethered by a rope, bobbing in the soft waves.

She let out a low whistle. "It sure is pretty. You have a name for it yet?"

He gave a little shrug. "I suppose I'm just waiting for

inspiration to hit me."

"Touché," she said, grinning. She was aware that he was watching her, and her stomach fluttered with nerves when she glanced his way. "And do you think you've found it?"

Her mouth felt dry as he stepped closer to her, closing the distance between them. She could feel the rocking of the dock, the movement of the water below them, the sensation that she could fall over at any moment, lose her footing, end up in the water.

But there was no fear of that. John's arms were tight around her waist now, and his eyes lingered on her mouth before he tipped his head to kiss her, pulling her against his chest, making her forgot all about Pamela and Jace and even that partnership.

Making her instead think of all that she'd been missing.

"I'm working on it," he said, when he pulled back, before leaning in to kiss her again.

* * *

Heather was writing on the porch when Andrea pulled up on her bike later that afternoon, happy for the company so that she could stop thinking about that kiss, what it meant, and how it would feel to never have it again come next week. The Morrison project was her last hope for partnership. That should excite her, give her hope even, but instead it left her strangely numb.

"Kim home?" She hadn't seen her baby sister since the big announcement last night, and she wanted to see how she was doing.

"Inside," Heather replied.

Andrea climbed the steps to the porch. A pitcher of lemonade was resting on the coffee table, along with two glasses, indicating that the women had been talking recently.

"Has she said any more?"

Heather shook her head. "No. We just read, looked at the view. She's getting a pack of cards. You in?"

The look her sister was giving her made Andrea feel ashamed. It was one she'd seen before, one that was resigned, already anticipating a rejection before the words were spoken. Work was always her excuse—irrefutable, inarguable, a priority greater than anything, or anyone, else. But not today. And maybe, not anymore.

"Sure," she said, dropping onto a chair.

Heather looked startled but pleased, and grinned at Kim when she came back outside, waving a deck in her hand triumphantly. "Andrea's joining us!"

Kim gave Andrea a funny look but went about shuffling the cards just the same. Andrea didn't need to ask which game they'd be playing; it was always Rummy in their household, always on this porch.

Heather stood. "I'll grab another glass for you, Andrea. Maybe some snacks, too."

It was always pretzels, and Andrea wasn't surprised when Heather returned with a bowl of them a brief moment later. Kim, meanwhile, was busy dealing.

They played one round—Kim won, which seemed to perk her up a bit—and then another, which also went to Kim.

Hating the lingering tension and feeling like their conversation last night was still unfinished, Andrea tried to lighten the situation. "Clearly, you played more hands with Mom than I did."

It was meant to be a joke, something to lighten the mood, but Kim's eyes flashed as she shuffled the deck again. "Of course. I still came back here every summer while you were working."

Andrea knew that her sister was just stating facts, but it hurt all the same. "And that's something I envy you for, Kim."

Kim frowned, looking suitably surprised. "I don't understand. I always thought you looked down on my decision not to prioritize my career the way you and Dad did."

Andrea set down her cards and reached for her lemonade. She was going to need something stronger soon if this conversation continued to shift in this direction.

"I'm sorry if it came across that way." She offered her sister an apologetic smile. "I guess I always felt judged and blamed for not having the time to give to family." Or anyone else for that matter.

Kim sighed. "I guess I did blame you. It's been hard not to take it personally when you chose work over us every time."

"It didn't feel like a choice," Andrea explained. "But now...well, now I'm starting to wonder if it was, especially this past year. I distracted myself with my work. I should have been there more for you. For both of you."

Heather's face was redder than usual, and Andrea realized with a jolt that her sister had started to cry.

"I'm sorry, I'm sorry," she said, fanning away their

concern. "It's just...been a long year. A bad year. But...it was bad for a long time before that."

Andrea frowned, catching Kim's eye. "You mean, with Daniel?"

Heather swallowed hard. "We'd been separated for a while. Before Mom died. I didn't want to worry her."

"But...but you could have told me!" Andrea insisted, but she knew that wasn't true. She hadn't been available. Not for lunch, or sushi dinners, or even coffee. Not even for a talk on the phone.

"But you and Daniel were so in love," Kim said, blinking hard. "I don't understand."

"I'm not able to have children," Heather said flatly. The porch went so quiet that the only sound that could be heard was the rustling of the leaves from the breeze coming off the lake.

Andrea knew that all her life, all Heather wanted was to be a mother, like their mother. This was quite possibly the worst thing that could have happened to her.

"Oh, Heather," she said softly, coming around to sit closer to her. She looked at Kim, who appeared as unaware as she had been. "But there are other options..."

"Daniel didn't want to try any other options. We'd had some hope, treatments, even going through an adoption agency at one point, only to have the mother change her mind at the last moment." Heather's tears ran fast and steady. "Daniel just wanted to move on from it. And I couldn't. All I ever wanted was a family, and now...I have no hope of one."

"Just because Daniel didn't want to try doesn't mean you

have to stop." Kim was pinching her mouth in the way she used to do when she was defending something. "You're only a couple of years older than me. You could meet someone, try again."

"And be hurt again?" Heather looked at her, searching for an answer that she probably knew none of them could give. "There's no guarantee it would work out."

"I hate to say it, Heather, but there's no guarantee about anything in life," Andrea said gently. "And what's the alternative?"

But she knew the alternative. It was to live alone, be alone. Share your life with no one. It was the life she had signed up for, however unintentionally, only now she felt like she had a choice to make, and she didn't know whether to listen to her head or follow her heart.

Heart. She almost smiled at that word.

Heather grew silent. "I just don't know how much more disappointment and heartache I can take. It was...the loneliest experience."

"But it didn't need to be that way," Kim said. "And it still doesn't. You have us. You could have told me."

Heather looked at her frankly. "And ruin your joy? You had just met the love of your life. You've been so excited about your wedding. You have an entire future ahead of you, full of all good things."

"I'm not so sure about that," Kim replied.

Andrea looked at her sharply. "What do you mean?"

"I mean that I'm not so sure that Bran is the guy for me or that I should be marrying him at all," Kim said quietly. She gathered up the cards, pushing the deck away.

Andrea stared at her. "But you've done nothing but talk about this wedding for months!"

"Because I'm trying to get myself excited about it," Kim said, shaking her head. "Bran's a great guy, but I'm not his first priority. And this wedding, it's not my wedding. It's Lynette's wedding."

"I thought you adored Lynette," Heather said.

Kim looked at her with a slacked jaw and then started to laugh, loudly. She laughed so hard that she clutched her ribs, long enough to eventually make Andrea and Heather exchange a nervous glance and join in, tentatively.

"You mean, you don't love Lynette?" Andrea clarified.

"I can't stand her!" Kim cried. "I tried to make myself like her. I tried to see her in a good light. I tried to be positive and tell myself it would all work out…"

"And here I thought that you found a replacement for Mom," Heather said quietly.

Now Kim looked stunned. And, Andrea realized, very hurt. "That could never happen. And certainly not with Lynette. At first, I thought she was trying to fill Mom's shoes, like she felt bad for me that Mom wasn't here to help me plan everything. But this wedding is more about showing off to her friends than helping create something that Bran and I will enjoy." She paused for a moment, and Andrea could tell that there was more she wanted to say. "She doesn't want me to wear Mom's dress."

Heather's brows shot up. This was the first they were both hearing of this!

"She doesn't even want me to take that job I'm supposed to start. I know it's just temporary, but it's important to me." Kim looked at Andrea, her eyes pleading.

Andrea nodded, feeling ashamed. "I know it is. And you should take it. I'm proud of you, Kim. And Mom would be too."

"She wants me to be a society wife. She wants me to be like her. I just...I don't know how much of myself I'm supposed to lose in the name of love."

Heather reached out and squeezed her hand. "That's a question I've asked myself a lot over the years."

"And that's a question I haven't asked myself enough," Andrea said softly. "I've never had to sacrifice anything, but now I realize, I might have sacrificed everything."

"It's not too late," Heather said, looking at her hopefully. "A lot of women balance family and careers. Is that what you want?"

"I didn't think so," Andrea admitted. "But now...now I'm starting to realize that something was missing, and if I go back to the way things were, I wouldn't feel satisfied anymore knowing what's not there."

"Are you talking about John?" Kim gave a little smile.

Andrea reached for her lemonade. "Maybe," she said coyly. But it wasn't just John. It was this island. This feeling. It was something she'd lost along the way, and never found in the city.

"Well, he has my vote," Heather said.

"And mine," Kim agreed. She looked at Heather. "And so does Billy."

Heather pulled in a shaky sigh. "Billy is...well, he's Billy. He's always been Billy."

"And he always will," Kim said gently.

"Look at my baby sister, so wise when it comes to love," Andrea said, putting an arm around her.

Kim grumbled. "For other people. But not myself."

"Have you talked to Bran about your concerns?" Heather asked.

"Yes. And no. I went along with it for a while, because I thought Lynette would lighten up, and because...because I loved him. And I think I still do. But I want to start my job. I don't want to be pressured to live on Lynette's terms. I want to be able to make my own choices about my wedding. And about my life."

"Then you need to say all this," Andrea said.

Kim nodded. "I know. I haven't before because...well, I guess I was afraid of losing him. Only now I think he's lost me."

"Then now is the time. No regrets. That's one thing I want to be sure of going forward, that nothing is left unsaid. That I left nothing behind," Andrea said. And no one, either.

Heather exhaled a sigh. "That leaves us both with a lot to think about," she said, looking at Kim.

"More like that leaves *all* of us with something to think about," Andrea said, managing a smile. Because tonight, for the first time in longer than she could remember, tomorrow didn't feel planned out or scheduled, and next month didn't seem like a repeat of next week, either. Now, everything felt uncertain and even a little exciting. And she wasn't quite ready to let that slip through her fingers just yet.

25

KIM

Since being back on the island, Kim had reverted to her old routine. She woke with the sun, tossed on shorts and a tee shirt, and padded down the curved stairs to the kitchen at the back of the house, where, if she was the first one up, she would brew coffee, or if Andrea had beat her to it, she helped herself to a mug with a splash of cream and a heavy helping of sugar.

Lately, Andrea hadn't been going for her morning runs, meaning that today the kitchen was dark and quiet as Kim started the task of scooping coffee grounds into a fresh filter.

A knock at the door made her jump, but she smiled when she considered the possibility of Gemma or Leo or Billy or John stopping by. Just like in years past, their world was full here, their circle large, even if the island was small.

She set the coffee to brew and walked down the hall, unable to make out the figure behind the frosted glass-paned door. She undid the locks—silly, perhaps, but with so many tourists, it was a habit—and pulled open the door, her hand freezing on the handle when she saw Bran standing on the porch staring back at her.

He looked the same as always, with his brown tousled hair and deep-set eyes that had grown so familiar, but here, out of place from their usual lives, she felt like she was seeing him for the first time all over again. For a moment, she couldn't find any words, even though it felt like a hundred thoughts were running through her mind at once. She started with the most obvious, and perhaps, the easiest.

"Bran? But...how did you know which house to go to?" A strange question, but a neutral one.

He gave her a sheepish grin. "I asked around. You were right. This is a small island, and I didn't have to look too far to get my answer."

She nodded. Of course, all the locals would know their house. The seasonal people too.

"Did you drive all night?" She couldn't help but feel flattered, but she also felt confused. Just when she was starting to adjust to the idea of a future without Bran, he'd popped back up, leaving her feeling guilty and more than a little conflicted. She'd thought she was ready to walk away from the life they'd started to plan together—but now, she knew it wouldn't be that simple. There was still something between them, and not just attraction. There were all those good memories, the knowledge of how he'd lifted her up when she'd needed it the most.

"I took the morning flight and caught the first ferry," he replied.

Ah. That explained why he looked so fresh and rested. She hesitated, unsure of what to say or do next, not when she didn't know why he was here. "Well, I was just making coffee. My sisters are still asleep. Why don't I bring two mugs outside and we can sit on the porch?"

She felt eager for some space, a chance to clear her head and think, because he had sprung this visit on her just like he had sprung everything else—even, she realized, their engagement.

He nodded and walked over to the wicker seating. Kim left the door open, only the screen now separating them, and hurried back to the kitchen where the coffee was still dripping into the pot. She could have invited him in, of course. It wasn't about making sure they didn't wake her sisters. Her sisters were likely awake by now; Andrea for sure never slept this late. But this world was special. This house was sacred. And this island...it was their place. Their family's place.

And Kim didn't know how Bran fit into all that any more than she knew how she fit into his life.

When the coffee had finished percolating, she filled two mugs, preparing each cup the way they preferred, and carried them out to the porch, pushing open the screen door with her hip just as Bran rose to help her.

"I'm fine," she said, even though that was very far from the truth. Her hands started to shake as she locked eyes with Bran and handed him the mug. He had made himself at home in her favorite chair on the porch. She knew this shouldn't bother her, but it did. It felt like one more small, special part of her life that was being taken away.

She sat on the wicker couch instead. "How was the gala?"

It was a sore subject, but she wasn't ready to delve deeper just yet.

"Boring. Those things usually are. But it would have been fun with you there." His mouth pulled into a smile but his gaze was wary. "I meant what I said about wanting you by my side."

She stared at him, her defenses softening again. For Lynette, it was all for status and show. But Bran had heart. The question was, did he still have hers?

"I'm surprised to see you."

"I didn't like how things ended between us," he said. "And you didn't take any more of my calls."

She frowned, thinking of the calls that had stopped shortly after they had started that day in Grosse Pointe.

"I've called every day. Sometimes twice, three times a day." He stared at her, and she believed him. Bran had done many things in recent months, but he'd never lied to her. "I didn't leave any messages."

"I don't exactly have good reception here," she pointed out, but that was only a half-truth. If she'd wanted to make an effort, she could have.

And he had.

"I didn't even think you knew how to find me," she admitted.

"Was that what you wanted?" There was hurt in his eyes that she didn't like to see, enough to make her question herself all over again.

She didn't know what she wanted, but she knew what she didn't want. It was time, she knew, to have her say, to get it all out. Before it was too late, for her, or for them.

"Let's go for a walk," she said, setting down her mug. Her sisters would be interrupting them sooner than later and she needed to move, to clear her head, to get away from this feeling of being locked face to face with Bran and all the decisions that came with him.

He didn't argue but instead set his mug beside hers, just as he had done a hundred times at least. Kim looked at the mugs for a moment, wondering if this was the last time they would share a cup of coffee, if this was the last time they'd talk at all.

She pulled in a breath and led him down the porch steps. She didn't have a plan in place, however loose, and she turned left, toward town, because even though there would be more people there, no one would bother them.

"This is a beautiful place," Bran surprised her by saying as they walked down the hill toward Main Street. The lake stretched far and wide to their right, and Kim kept it in her sights as much as possible, finding it easier to look at than Bran right now.

"It's a special place," she said quietly. "And it was important for me to come back here."

She wondered with a jolt if he had come to try to convince her to return a few days early. If his mother had some new demand.

Or if he'd come to end things altogether.

She wasn't sure which of those three scenarios was the worst at the moment. He'd only had a single bag with him, which he'd left behind on the porch. Anything was possible.

Instead, he said, "When I was coming up the hill, it looked exactly like that painting you have in your bedroom."

She snapped her head to him. "I didn't realize you'd even noticed that."

"Of course I noticed!" He looked injured at her insinuation. "I pay attention to you, Kim. I guess I've just done a poor job of listening lately." They fell silent as they walked more. "I can understand now why you wanted to come back here. I shouldn't have tried to stop you. You were right that now was a good time, before the wedding, when everything gets crazy."

She cleared her throat, remembering what her sisters had said. "To be honest, Bran, I've been a little worried that I won't be able to come back here very often if I marry you."

He stopped walking to stare at her. "*If* you marry me?"

She didn't correct him.

"So there is a problem," he said, shaking his head.

"Of course there's a problem!" She tossed up her hands. "There's been a problem ever since we got engaged, and I just haven't said anything about it until now. Maybe that wasn't fair of me. I was trying so hard to make this work, and I didn't realize how much of myself I was giving up or how unhappy I was."

"What are you telling me?" Bran's eyes were injured when she finally looked at them.

She swallowed hard. "I'm saying that this entire wedding isn't the way I wanted it. I mean, at first, maybe, but now it's all wrong. I'm going to be wearing a dress I don't like, even a veil I don't want, and you seem to care more about taking a honeymoon that your mother chose rather than doing something that works for both of us. You know how much I'm looking forward to starting that job, but do you even know why?"

He blinked, looking downright confused. Kim fought

back tears. Maybe it was her fault for not standing up for herself sooner, or maybe it was his fault for not taking an interest.

"Because you finished your degree?" He ran a hand through his hair. "Heck, I don't know, Kim. And I certainly didn't know it was enough to make you run off or think about canceling our wedding."

They'd approached a bend in the road, near the big old hotel that was a nod to another era, right down to the shady, walled-in pool and cricket sets. She dropped onto a wrought-iron bench, and Bran did the same.

"Did I ever tell you that my mother was a teacher? Before she had all of us." But of course, she hadn't mentioned it. Bran had been an escape from thinking about her mother in many ways at first, but it felt wrong that he would never know her in person or through her stories now. "My mom and I were very close, and when I lost her...I suppose I was just trying to find a piece of her to keep with me. I wanted to feel like she'd given something to me, or like I could keep a part of her going."

He nodded and reached out to squeeze her knee. "I wish you'd told me that sooner, Kim. If I'd known how much it meant, I wouldn't have pushed for that honeymoon. Because it's a temporary position, I guess I figured that you could wait for the next opportunity."

She looked at him skeptically. "Really? Because I made it pretty clear that it was important to me."

He had the decency to look ashamed. "I'm sorry. I should have respected your wishes. A honeymoon should indeed be something we both enjoy. Same with the wedding. I've gotten used to my family's ways."

"But I have a family, too," Kim said. "And that's why coming back here was so important to me. Not just this year, but every year. "

"Who said it has to stop?"

She nailed him with a look. "It's one thing after another with your family, Bran, but if this is going to work, then we have to be our own family. That means you and me. And there are things in my life that are important to me. That job and this place, those are just two of them."

"What are the other things?" He tipped his head, and Kim hesitated, wondering if she could even say it.

"I don't want to get married if this is how the wedding or marriage is going to be." She could feel her heart racing, knowing that she'd spoken the truth, knowing that she had been honest with Bran, and herself.

"Then I don't want to either," he said.

She blinked at him, realizing that her hands were shaking. Was he saying that he didn't want to marry her? Because that's not really what she was saying to him. She loved him. Seeing him here, in her favorite place, with his soft brown eyes that were looking right into her own, she could already feel herself missing him if he were to get up and walk away right now. They'd been so good together, and he'd been so good for her. Until...

"I think you've already established what kind of marriage you want," he said. "One with more balance. One where you feel more comfortable having a voice. Now tell me what kind of wedding you want."

She stared at him as the tears finally filled her eyes. "Bran. Are you serious? But..."

He shook his head. "But nothing. I don't care what kind of wedding we have. I just cared that you were happy. But if what's been planned isn't what you want, then forget it."

"And your mother?" She had to ask.

He gave her a little grin. "My mother will get over it. She'll have to, because I love you, Kim. I want to marry you. I want to share a life with you, and I mean that. Share a life."

She felt his hand slip into hers, warm and familiar, and she held it, not wanting to speak for fear of ruining this moment, and when she looked into his eyes again, she knew she didn't have to say anything. That was one of the things she liked about Bran. They were comfortable together. They could sit in silence as easily as chat and laugh in a restaurant. They'd just gotten away from it for a while. But maybe, just maybe they could have a chance to start again.

26

HEATHER

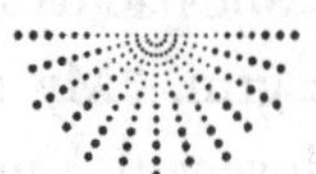

Heather woke on Friday morning with a strange sense of dread, and one that didn't have to do with the fact that she'd promised her article to Sally by the end of the day. Tomorrow she'd be leaving the island, and with it, this house, these memories, and a feeling that she hadn't experienced in more than a year, and never thought she'd feel again. It was the company of her sisters, perhaps. The sounds of other footsteps on the floorboards. The feeling of life within the four walls.

Kim and Bran were downstairs laughing and making coffee by the time Heather finished showering. They'd been in good spirits last night over dinner, and Bran had been very grateful for the meal she'd cooked, even though Kim had reminded him that this talent fell solely with the middle Taylor sister.

Things had worked out for Kim. Heather was happy for her, no longer feeling the need to dodge her sister and all her excitement about this next phase of her life. Everyone had their struggles. And it was better when you had someone to share them with, much like everything else in life.

It was midmorning; she'd dragged out the time, but she couldn't waste the day. It was her last day on the island. It needed to count.

"What do you say we do a big dinner tonight?" she asked Kim, trying to cheer herself up a bit. It was a tradition they always had—a summer's end send-off dinner, complete with all the summer treats that they enjoyed here at the lake house. "We could invite Gemma and Leo."

"Oh, I'd love for you to meet them, Bran," Kim said, smiling at him. She turned back to Heather. "And we can ask Billy?"

Heather swallowed hard. She should invite Billy. It wouldn't be summer's end without him. But somehow, she was no longer so sure that he would agree to come. They'd left things off badly the other day. And that, well, that was almost as upsetting as the thought of packing her bags tomorrow.

"I'm sure that Andrea will want to invite John," she said. "I'll make a list and pick some things up in town." It would give her something to do, even though what she should be doing was finishing that article. She'd have to think of something or use one of the topics Kim had suggested that didn't quite inspire her.

"We'll divide and conquer," Kim said. "Bran and I are spending the day in town so we can help. I promised him all the sights, including some fudge tasting."

With that settled, Heather left them to talk. She sensed that they craved more privacy, and she was yet to get Kim alone for enough time to ask how things were going. She'd learned from personal experience that it was best not to assume what anyone was going through, even her own sister. People shared when they were ready. And she was finally ready to do just that.

The Island Hospital was on her way into town, a short bike ride from the house. She parked her cruiser against the picket fence that was lined with blooming hydrangea and walked up the brick-paved path to the front porch, knowing that the door would be open. A woman she didn't recognize looked up from the front desk, the only indication that this was a place of business and not someone's home.

"Do you have an appointment?" When Heather shook her head, she asked, "Emergency?"

Suddenly, talking to Billy felt like an emergency, like something she had to do right now before she lost her nerve.

"I was just hoping to speak with Dr. Davidson for a few minutes. I can wait." She went to take a seat near the big bay window but the woman waved her over. "It's fine. Things are slow at this hour. It will pick up as the day goes on and people rent bikes or hit the pubs." She grinned. "He's just down the hall and to the right."

Heather pulled in a breath. Down the hall and to the right. It didn't take long to find him. The building was quiet and Billy was sitting at a desk reviewing some charts when she stopped in the open doorway. She reached out to knock anyway, but instead, she lingered for a moment, thinking of the boy she'd known, the one who shared all her happy memories, the one who shared this place, and the man he had become.

What did he really think of the woman she had become? She supposed she'd know soon enough.

"Hey," she said quietly, forcing him to look up at her. His hazel eyes were soft and kind, and her stomach rolled over at how handsome he was. That was a feeling that had never completely faded. Some things in life would always stick with you.

His expression shifted from one of surprise to confusion but still, behind it all, she could see that he wasn't displeased.

"I hope it's okay that I'm stopping by. We're leaving tomorrow, and I couldn't go without saying goodbye."

Now the light went out of his eyes and he nodded. "I see. That's right." He sucked in a breath and leaned back in his chair. "Back to your city life then?"

Back to her empty life. She'd gotten so used to a full house. And a full heart. Two things she hadn't expected to ever find again.

"I'm sorry for how our conversation went the other day," she started, but he held up a hand.

"It's fine, Heather. You were being honest. I respect that."

She could stop now, leave things as a truce, no hard feelings, at least not completely. But she didn't want to leave things like that. She didn't want to leave Billy at all.

"But I wasn't being fully honest," she said. "The reason I don't want to get married again is because of how my marriage ended."

He tipped his head, staring at her intently.

She drew a breath and closed the door behind her, stepping closer into the room. "The reason that Daniel and I broke up is that I can't have children."

His face folded into one of understanding as he shook his head. "I'm sorry. I had no idea."

She shrugged. "No one did. It was easier that way. At least I thought it was. If I didn't talk about it, I didn't have to think about it. I guess I thought that I'd learn to adjust, be content with less." Only now she wanted more, so much more. She wanted Billy. She wanted this island. She wanted to believe it all could last. "Now, after telling my sisters, I realize how much better I feel opening up about it."

He gestured for her to sit. "I can only imagine that it put a lot of stress on the marriage."

"In the end, we wanted different things. Daniel wanted to move on, accept life as it was. But it wasn't enough for me. I wanted to keep trying. I wanted more."

"And what do you want now?"

She swallowed hard, almost afraid to speak the truth as she was to admit it to herself. "I want what I've always wanted. A family of my own. Trips here to the island. I want to show my children the house on West End Road, and I want to hear their laughter from the playhouse."

"But the other night you said that you didn't ever want to be married again," he said.

She nodded. It was true. She had said it, maybe even meant it at the time, or wanted to convince herself of that at least.

"I guess I'm afraid. To try again. But I realized that by doing that, I'm no different than Daniel. And I loved him, but he wasn't willing to keep trying to make that dream come true. And I'm not willing to stop trying either."

Billy lifted an eyebrow. "Does that mean that you're open to a relationship?"

She sighed. Here came the tough part. "You want children, Billy. I heard you the other night, dreaming big, the way I always did. What if..." She shook her head. Her cheeks felt warm. He was just talking about a relationship. Not marriage!

"There are other ways to have a family if two people want it badly enough." He grinned at her, his smile crinkling the corners of his eyes. "I just want to see you happy, Heather. That's all I ever wanted. Well, maybe not all I ever wanted. I'd be pretty bummed if you told me you'd be happier going back to Chicago this weekend."

She shook her head, the image of it filling her mind with such dread that she almost couldn't bear it. "I can't think of anything that would be more unhappy."

He looked at her with fresh excitement. "You mean?"

"I have nothing to go back to but an empty house. And here...I have more than a house. I have good memories, and good friends, and...I have you."

He gave her a slow smile. "Sounds like you've convinced yourself then."

"No. You did that. You made me think that maybe I could be happy again. That maybe my life could be full again. It's been a long time since I've felt like that."

"So you'll stay?"

She nodded before she could change her mind. "I'll stay."

He grinned broadly now, pushing himself out of the

chair. "I think we need to celebrate! What do you say? A big lunch, with champagne—"

She shook her head, laughing as she stood. "We have time for all of that. All the time in the world. But today I have an article to write, and hours to finish it."

And she knew exactly what she was going to write about. She was going to write about home life, as she always did, only this time she was going to write about the things that defined a home. For it wasn't the shiny new appliances or the hand-sewn window treatments, or the imported bathroom tiles. It was people who made a house a home. And simple traditions, like her summer pie recipe. Any other place, it was just pie, but here, it was special. And here she was home.

"I almost forgot. It's still summer's end." She might be staying on the island, but her sisters would be leaving, back to their lives. "We're having our dinner tonight. Per tradition."

Tradition. Oh, how she loved a good tradition.

"Wouldn't miss it." He grinned as he came around the desk. "But you forgot one other thing, too."

She looked at him in surprise. "Oh?"

He wrapped his arms around her waist, pulling her close. "This," he said, before kissing her. And this time, she didn't hurry off.

It was officially summer's end, a day that Andrea hadn't thought about in too many years. It was a day that was meant for celebration, not just goodbyes. A day that was meant for reflection and gratitude, and this year, strangely more than ever, Andrea was able to do just that.

Her design for the Morrison house was complete. It was, in her opinion, her finest work yet. A clear winner, one that would no doubt earn her the business and quite possibly the partnership.

But somehow, that didn't matter anymore.

The sisters were gathering the dishes and linens that were always used for the party, the ones that their mother had collected over the years, held on to, and cherished. Andrea stroked the paisley-printed tablecloth in her hands, knowing that this was one of her mother's personal favorites, because of the bright colors. The food had been purchased by Kim and Bran, and Bran had even been sent back out with another list. Gemma and Leo would arrive shortly, a few others, too. There would be candles and wine and lots of reminiscing.

"I'm glad we're doing this," she said to Heather. "What I should say is that I'm glad we did this. Coming here was long overdue. I haven't felt this good in too long."

Still, she couldn't fight the heaviness in her chest as Kim roped an arm over her shoulder and squeezed it. The last night at the house was always bittersweet, and this year would be no exception.

"I...I wish Mom was here." Andrea pushed back the tears that had threatened to spill. Her work had been her salvation this past year—her purpose, but also her crutch. She could let her guard down here, with her sisters. She could open up, share her sadness, and she could know that she wasn't alone. That they didn't care about whether or not she made partner or got picked from the latest shortlist or if she was ever featured in a trade magazine. Truth was, her father probably didn't care either. All her family wanted was the same that she wanted for them. To find happiness, even if it wasn't the way she might have chosen it.

"She is here," Kim said. "I've felt closer to her since being back than I have since she left us. I think she knew that we needed this time. I think everything is going to be better from now on."

Heather was quiet for a moment, but now she set down a stack of plates and turned to them. "I have an announcement to make. I'm not going back to Chicago. I'm going to stay on the island."

"Billy?" Kim's grin was sly but pleased.

Heather couldn't fight her smile. "Billy, but also, this

island. Coming back here made me realize how little I have back in the city, and how much I have here, and always did. I thought I needed certain things to have a full life, but it's not how much you have, but what you make of it."

Andrea nodded slowly. She'd been thinking about that all morning—all week really, even though it had crept up on her. What did making partner even mean? More prestige? More money? Who was she even trying to impress? The people at work went home to their spouses, children, family, and friends. They didn't care about her, not in the way that her sisters did. Not in the way that John possibly could.

She hadn't seen him since Wednesday, hadn't known what to say. She knew she would see him again, if only to say goodbye, or until next time, and now she saw no reason to delay. John, like Gemma and Billy, was part of the story that made up their time here on the island. It was only right that he should be here tonight.

"I'll go into town for some extra bottles of wine," Andrea said, knowing that they could only manage a couple each trip, given the weight of the grocery bags.

"Hurry back, because I have an announcement too," Kim said, with a devilish waggle of her eyebrows. "Although, I think that Bran and I should share it together. If you see him on the way, don't let him say anything."

Andrea glanced at Heather, who just shrugged. "Good news, I hope?"

Kim nodded firmly. "Very good news. I'll share every-thing over dinner. When we're all together."

All together. Andrea liked the sound of it.

She hurried down the hill to town, but she knew she

wouldn't stop at the Main Street Market just yet. Instead, she went past it, scanning the harbor, recalling the day John had shown her the boat. The kiss they'd shared. It felt like something in her distant past even though it had been only a few days ago. But time was funny here on this island. It made you slow down and catch your breath. It made you think.

She was nervous by the time she got to the Lakeside Inn, not about what she had to say, but about the possibility of not being able to find him before she went back to the city tomorrow. She scanned the lobby and then the dining room, but she suspected that he would be outside on this beautiful afternoon, and she was right. She found him down near the pool, talking with one of the staff, going over some of the paperwork she recognized from their conversations.

He turned when she said his name, looking just as confused at seeing her as he was pleased. He said something to the other man, who nodded and walked away with the folder tucked under his arm.

"Well, this is a surprise." John smiled as he approached.

"I hoped to find you," she said, suddenly unsure of what she wanted to say. "I...I wanted to invite you to a party we're having tonight. Everyone will be there. Gemma. Leo. Mandy. Lena. It's a tradition."

His eyes turned knowing, and a little sad. "A going away party, I take it."

Her shoulders sank, but not for the reasons he might think. She had lost time, or maybe squandered it. But she wasn't the type of person to make the same mistake twice.

"I have to go back to Chicago tomorrow," she said. "I have a big project due on Monday."

He nodded. He knew all about it, of course. He gave her a kind smile. "The one that might seal your fate for partnership. I'm sure it will."

Andrea was nearly certain that it would too, even though Jace had a way of worming his way into Arthur's good graces. The design was original, unique, curious, and inspired. And most of all, it had heart.

And that was why it didn't matter if it landed her the partnership. It wasn't about what the design could do for her. It was about the way it made her feel.

"I promised the client I'd have it to them next week, and I like to think I'm a person of my word," she said. Which was why what she was about to say next meant so much. It was a promise. To herself. To her mother, maybe. And possibly, to John. "But I'm not going to accept the partnership if it's offered. I'm going to be giving my notice instead."

John stared at her, and for a moment, she wasn't sure if he'd even heard her, if she'd even managed to say the words, because she hadn't said it to her sisters, even though it was there, noodling in her mind all week, taking root, building a new plan in better clarity than any blueprint.

"I stopped by the historical society yesterday, just to get a feel for things. It was...well, it was very inspiring. But then, a lot of things are here."

His eyes were wary despite a hint of a smile that curved his mouth. "But that partnership is something you worked hard for, Andrea."

She nodded. "It was, but somewhere along the way, I lost sight of why it mattered. My mother left us that house, but it wasn't just the walls and the banister and the pocket doors and the crown moldings that she passed down or cared about, really. It was what the house held inside it. The memories. The laughter. The people. I've been designing houses all this time but I haven't stopped to think about who they're for, or why they matter. And now that I see it, I can't go back to the way it was. And I don't want to either."

"You won't regret giving it up?"

She had thought about this, a lot, but every time she did, she came to the same conclusion. She had regrets. A lot of them. And now was the time to start fixing them.

"The only regret I'll have is walking away from this island again. And..."

His eyebrow cocked as he stepped toward her, his grin pulling a smile from her face. "And?"

"And...I'd like to see what I could build here. Professionally, and personally."

"I guess that means I don't have to chase you down in Chicago." John's hands found hers as he grinned.

Her heart skipped a beat. "You weren't...?"

He shrugged. "It's like you said, Andrea. No regrets. And I would have regretted not coming after you. Life doesn't always give us a fresh start or a second chance, but that's what I came to the island to find."

She blinked back tears as he leaned down to kiss her, and she wrapped her arms around his neck, pulling him tight, because just like him, she'd followed one path, only to change course and pursue another. And just like him, she'd found her heart. Right where she'd left it.

EPILOGUE

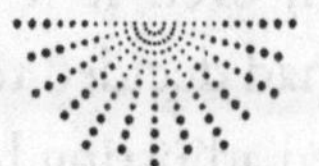

Everyone knew that Kim had always wanted a big wedding, but they weren't surprised to learn that she had changed her mind.

Now, when Kim thought of her dream wedding, she thought of her closest friends and family, the man she loved standing at the end of a petal-strewn path, her father at her arm, her mother's veil atop her head, and her sisters at her side.

And today, all of that was coming true.

Her friend Kate had hand-delivered Kim's mother's wedding gown and veil. There was the small matter of shoes to consider, but this was a simple wedding, one that would be held outside, along the lakefront, just as the sun was starting to set.

Heather had of course volunteered to handle all the food for the reception, as well as most of the decorations, and Kim couldn't help but notice how she came alive at the task. She was in her element, doing what she loved, and with Billy as her right-hand, she was perhaps also with the one she loved.

John had offered up his hotel for the reception, but Kim knew that this house was where everyone was meant to gather. It was large enough to host them all, and it had been empty for long enough, even if it would never be empty again now that Andrea had decided to stay on the island.

Kim had just finished adjusting her veil when there was a knock at her door. She expected it to be one of her sisters, who would wear matching blue cotton sundresses from one of the boutiques in town, but instead, she was surprised to see her father standing in the doorway.

"I wasn't sure you'd be able to come on such short notice," she said when she saw him.

"And miss your wedding day? Impossible."

Kim's pulse quickened when she thought of the impact of her father's arrival. Introducing his girlfriend might be even more awkward than listening to Bran explain to his mother that they'd decided to essentially elope, and that had been a conversation that had not gone well at all.

Still, after a few days of adjusting to the idea, Bran's parents had made the trek to Evening Island and were gathered across the road along with the other small pool of guests. Andrea had already whispered to Kim that she'd heard Lynette admit, however reluctantly, that this was all much nicer than she'd expected it would be.

Nicer. Better. The way it was meant to be.

"Is..."

"Barb is visiting with her sons this weekend," Kim's

father explained. "It's her eldest's birthday, and... This day isn't about me, it's about you. And all of us. I want to introduce you to her, of course, but when the time is right. I'm sorry if I caused any stress for your wedding, honey."

Kim almost laughed out loud. There was so much stress leading up to this day that it almost didn't happen at all. But had it not been for all of that, they wouldn't be standing here right now. She in her mother's gown and veil, her father in a seersucker suit, tears shining in his eyes.

"You look beautiful, Kimmy," he said quietly. "You look happy."

She squeezed his hand. "You too, Daddy."

"Your mother had a better way with words—"

"It's okay," she whispered. And somehow, it was. She pulled in a breath. "Walk me out?"

He held out his elbow and she slipped her arm through it. Carefully they made their way down the stairs, the ones that she and her sisters would sprint down eagerly those glorious summer mornings, eager to start another carefree day on the island. She half expected to see her mother standing at the base of the stairs, shaking her head at her with an amused smile gracing her mouth, but instead, she was met by her sisters, each clutching a bouquet of local flowers. Andrea held the largest one out to her.

"I cleared a space on the wall for you," Andrea said, motioning to the framed photos that she had eventually found in the attic. One of their grandparents on their wedding day, standing on the porch of this very house, and another of their parents, looking young and happy, laughing on the wicker chair. And another of their mother, sitting on the lakefront across the road, her auburn hair blowing in the breeze, her smile one of laughter, as if she'd just heard something wonderful. Kim stared at it, wondering what might have brought such joy to her in that moment.

She'd never know, but she'd always remember her like this. Full of life.

"You're carrying down the tradition," Heather said wistfully.

Kim looked down at her dress, which she'd carefully preserve for Andrea one day, just in case... "We all are."

Heather beamed. She had a glow about her since deciding to move to the island, even though it had only been a week since she and Andrea had made their journey back to the city, and quickly returned. Kim would visit next summer when her work schedule permitted, and Bran would join her too. The island would bring them all together again, like it always had.

"I can't believe I'm doing this," Kim said as the reality of the moment hit her. "I can't believe we're all standing here. In this house. It feels..."

"It feels like yesterday," her father said, pulling Heather in for a squeeze with his free arm.

"It feels like home," Heather said.

It felt complete, Kim thought to herself, as she looked around the room, at the knicks and scrapes on the woodwork that were evidence of years of love and memories.

And as they walked together out onto the porch and then down the creaking steps toward the water, where so many people she loved and cherished were waiting for her on the rocky shore, she closed her eyes and thought of that picture again.

Her mother wasn't here to witness this perfect day, but Kim knew that she was with her, her hair blowing in the breeze, and her smile radiant. That this was what she'd always wanted...for all of them.

ABOUT THE AUTHOR

Olivia Miles is a *USA Today* bestselling author of feel-good women's fiction and small-town romance. She has frequently been ranked as an Amazon Top 100 author, and her books have appeared on several bestseller lists, including Amazon charts, Barnes and Noble, BookScan, and USA Today. Olivia lives on the shore of Lake Michigan with her family and an adorable pair of dogs.

Visit www.OliviaMilesBooks.com for more.